THE HOUSE THEY GREW U

Planting her forearm on the table, Quincy leaned forward. "Remember the picture we found in Susan's bedroom, the one with us in a kiddy pool? We think it came from the same album. You should see all the family pictures in there. Rose and I were so little then. We thought if you looked through it with us, you could help us remember."

"Maybe I don't want to remember." Tears prickled the backs of Margaret's eyes. Irritated with herself and wondering exactly how a person let go of the past and moved on, she blinked hard, set her jaw, and stood to toss her spoon and bowl into the trash.

"Nothing wrong with crying again," Quincy said. "I've been doing a lot of that myself. We're all suffering. At least we're doing it together."

"Thank heaven for that." Rose nodded. "We lived in this house our entire childhoods, so we understand each other in ways no one else can."

"If there's anything you want to say, we're here," Quincy said.

Margaret saw that Rose looked equally sincere and willing to listen. The sisterly love and encouragement shining in their eyes gently prodded Margaret to open up. . . .

Books by Ann Roth

ANOTHER LIFE

MY SISTERS

Published by
Kensington Publishing Corporation

My Sisters

ANN ROTH

ZEBRA BOOKS
Kensington Publishing Corp.
http://www.kensingtonbooks.com

ZEBRA BOOKS are published by

Kensington Publishing Corp.
850 Third Avenue
New York, NY 10022

All Kensington titles, imprints, and distributed lines are
available at special quantity discounts for bulk purchases
for sales promotion, premiums, fund-raising, educational,
or institutional use.

Special book excerpts or customized printings can also
be created to fit specific needs. For details, write or phone
the office of the Kensington Special Sales Manager,
Attn: Special Sales Department, Kensington Publishing
Corp., 850 Third Avenue, New York, NY 10022. Phone:
1-800-221-2647.

ISBN-13: 978-0-8217-8035-0
ISBN-10: 0-8217-8035-2

First Printing: November 2008
10 9 8 7 6 5 4 3 2 1

Printed in the United States of America

To sisters everywhere

Chapter 1

Saturday

Margaret Lansing was carefully dropping lichen extract onto a sterilized chromatography plate when the phone rang. Startled out of a deep concentration, she jerked. The contents of the capillary tube dribbled across the plate, ruining it. "Crud," she muttered. "I'll have to make a new one."

A few feet away, Bruce Cropper, the other PhD working on the project, frowned. "Who in hell would call the lab on Saturday night?"

"Probably a wrong number."

"Let's hope they figure that out and hang up."

They couldn't afford the interruption, not with Hassell Pharmaceuticals pushing them for results. Shutting out the distraction, or trying to—the darned phone rang at least ten times—Margaret returned to her work, which required care and focus. This was why she and Bruce had turned off their cell phones, to avoid unwanted intrusion.

Not that anyone she could think of would call her on a Saturday night. She wasn't dating anyone, and most of her friends were either already out or at home with their families. Whether Bruce had a late date or something else planned, she didn't know. They never discussed those things.

By the time she finished the plate the annoying *Rrring! Rrring!* started again. Bruce shrugged.

Margaret wasn't so unflappable. "All right!" Carefully setting aside the capillary tube, she slid from her stool with her lips compressed.

"Whoever they are, I don't envy them talking to you mad," Bruce said. His grin softened the words.

He was an attractive man, and the smile was contagious. Margaret strode across the white linoleum floor in a better mood.

The phone, a dingy yellow wall model that had seen better days, was at the far end of the lab, and by the time she snatched the receiver from its cradle she was slightly winded. "Margaret Lansing."

"Hello, Maggie," said a kindly, masculine voice she hadn't heard in years.

No one had called her Maggie since she'd turned eighteen and moved to Seattle fifteen years ago. People here called her Margaret or Dr. Lansing. "Dr. McElroy? Is that you?"

"Yes, it is. I tried to reach you at home and on your cell. Lucky your mother carries your lab number in her purse."

News to Margaret. Her mother had never used it, but then she never called, period. Susan expected her daughters to do the calling.

Certainly Dr. McElroy had never phoned. He hadn't been her doctor since she'd left town, so there was no reason to. Fearing bad news, Margaret leaned against the cinder block wall and bowed her head. She noted that her summer-weight slacks were creased from sitting so long and idly smoothed her hand over them. "What's happened to Mother?"

"There's been a car accident."

Margaret could hear the doctor's heavy breathing, as if he were struggling with the news. "And?" she prodded, gripping the phone.

"Your mother . . . she died."

"What?" Too shocked to fully absorb what she'd just heard, Margaret sank onto the floor. "When? How?"

Bruce stood, his face a mask of concern. Warning him off, Margaret shook her head and stared at her lap.

"She was broadsided by a pickup truck. Some teenage boy from out of town passing through. Wasn't his fault, though. According to eyewitnesses and Officer Washburn, your mother ran a red light because she took her attention from the road and leaned down.

Suzette was sitting in the passenger side, and we think she must've slipped off the seat. . . ." Dr. McElroy stopped and cleared his throat. "I'm sorry, Maggie."

"Suzette. Naturally." Feeling oddly disconnected, Margaret didn't tear up. But her sinuses ached and felt swollen the way they did when the weather was about to change. She squeezed the bridge of her nose. "My God."

Dr. McElroy made a sympathetic sound. "Would you like me to call your sisters?"

"No, I will." Margaret hadn't talked to either one in nearly six months, since Christmas. She dreaded sharing the grim news, but someone had to. Better she than their old family doctor. "It'll take me five hours to drive over, but if I leave in the morning I'll be there by mid-afternoon," she said. "Rose lives in Sacramento and Quincy's in Las Vegas, so it may take them awhile longer."

"As long as you all come home, Maggie. Anything you want me to do?"

"Start calling me Margaret. And please get hold of Mrs. Overman. Ask her to make up the beds and leave the key under the mat."

"You know we don't lock our doors in Shadow Falls, Magg—Margaret. Mrs. Overman is over at the house now, getting it ready for you girls."

Margaret hung up. Her mother's death still hadn't hit, and for a few moments she stared numbly at the receiver. Then with a sigh, she pushed to her feet.

Bruce headed forward. "You look as white as a lab coat," he said when he reached her.

"My mother was killed in an accident to-night." Saying it felt surreal and horrible.

"I'm sorry."

His hands curled and opened at his sides, and she knew he wanted to comfort her. In the past he'd asked her out, but she always turned him down and he'd stopped asking. Odd that now, feeling numb as she did, she wanted him to put his arms around her. She wouldn't let him know, though. What if she lost control?

Margaret was a private person. She kept her feelings to herself. Sometimes she pushed them so deep she could pretend they didn't exist. But now . . .

Needing to hold herself together, she fell back on what always worked—focusing on practical issues and decisions. "I'll need a week off, starting tomorrow," she said. Even that was too long away from the lab, but with a funeral, the house, and who knew what else to deal with, she didn't have much choice. "Can you handle things without me?"

"Don't worry about a thing. Just take care of yourself. I'm real sorry, Margaret," he repeated.

The tears she didn't want to shed just yet gathered behind her eyes. Blinking and afraid to speak, she ducked her head and nodded.

And concentrated on what to do next, who to call first.

Rose or Quincy? Margaret wasn't close to either one, and hadn't been in what seemed forever. By age seemed fair, and Rose was older than Quincy by eleven months. Unfortunately, both had unlisted numbers that were neither stored in Margaret's sharp memory nor programmed into her cell phone. They didn't talk often enough for either. She would have to drive home, when what she wanted was to stay here with Bruce and escape into her work. Or at least try.

She looked up and caught Bruce's concerned frown.

"Go on, Margaret," he said, shooing her out.

Mind whirling, feeling as if she'd been stabbed in the heart, she grabbed her purse and left.

With a heavy heart Rose Abbott trudged from the bathroom and returned to the living room. Danny hadn't moved from the sofa. He was flipping through the latest *Enology Today* magazine and eating the popcorn she'd made for their Saturday night movie fest.

On the TV screen the *Sideways* DVD they'd been watching—for what? The third time in as many years?—was on pause while Rose used the facilities. It showed Paul Giamatti, his expressive face frozen in sadness. How fitting.

"Ready to watch the rest of the movie?" Danny tossed the magazine onto the end table, but it didn't quite make it and landed on the floor. Ignoring it, he shoved a handful of popcorn into his mouth.

The buttery aroma that five minutes ago had made her mouth water now sickened her. She picked up the magazine and set it on the rack beneath the table, then straightened.

"I started my period," she said, slipping her antsy hands into the lace-trimmed pockets of her favorite dress, which she'd sewn from Laura Ashley fabric.

Her husband's round, friendly face fell before he caught himself. "That's okay, honey." Grabbing a napkin from the pile on the coffee table he wiped his hands. "We'll try again next month."

He'd been saying that for nearly two years now. They both had.

"I'm not getting any younger," she said, sounding shrill to her own ears. With reason. At thirty-one her biological clock was ticking right past the best childbearing years.

"Maybe it's time to make an appointment with Rachel Grant, that fertility doctor Mike and Linda used."

Rose recalled the cadre of questions Linda had had to answer, and the myriad tests that left no secrets untold. The very thought terrified her. What if Dr. Grant somehow could tell what had happened in college? She'd want to tell Danny. The panicky feeling Rose hated but couldn't ignore squeezed like a boa constrictor. *No!* She couldn't. Wouldn't. No matter how badly she wanted a child.

Oh, the irony. Here she was, a home ec teacher who couldn't create the home she longed for. A woman who loved her husband, but sometimes hated him, too, who was honest, but afraid to tell the truth. Her life was one big contradiction. If that didn't make her her mother's daughter . . .

"It'd be easier if you got tested first," she argued, knowing that Danny wouldn't, and that she was safe. For now.

Predictably, his jaw tightened. "We've already discussed this, Rose."

She crossed her arms. "Grow up, Danny. Finding out whether your sperm count is low is not a threat to your masculinity."

"I don't need any test to know I'm fine," he insisted, looking threatened all the same. Now his arms, too, were crossed. He studied her through slightly narrowed, slightly accusing eyes that spoke volumes.

You're the faulty one.

Rose feared he was right. The sins of the past and all that. Guilt and remorse churned in her gut, twin plagues she'd harbored for twelve years. Between the panic and the regret she sometimes thought she'd go mad. "I don't want to talk about this," she snapped. "I'm going to bed."

The ringing phone startled them both. Rose glanced at her watch. It was nearly eleven o'clock on a Saturday night. Nobody called this late, even on a weekend.

Danny stretched toward the end table and picked up. "Hello." He listened. "Maggie," he mouthed to Rose. "It's been a long time, *Margaret.*"

Both Rose and Danny thought the formal name, which Maggie insisted they use, pretentious. What was wrong with plain old Maggie? And why call now? Rose sent Danny a curious look.

Equally puzzled, he shook his head. "Rose is right here. Hang on." He handed over the phone.

Forgetting she was mad at her husband, Rose sank onto the arm of the sofa. "Hello, Margaret."

"Mother's dead," Margaret said in her usual no-nonsense fashion.

"Mother is dead?" Rose repeated, exchanging a shocked look with Danny. "But she's only fifty-one, and really healthy." Physically, anyway.

"I know."

She heard Margaret sniffle and her own eyes filled.

Danny scooted over and held out his arms. She batted him away. "What happened?"

"Car accident. A kid passing through town plowed into her."

Despite the tears running down her face,

Rose couldn't feel much quite yet. "A kid." She shook her head. "Was he drinking?"

"Not that I know of. Apparently Mother was at fault. She ran a red light. Something about leaning down to pick up Suzette while she was driving."

"Of course Suzette would be involved," Rose muttered.

"Exactly what I said," Margaret replied.

"Suzette." Danny rolled his eyes and snickered.

"When did this happen?"

"Earlier this evening."

"Who called you?" *Why didn't they call me instead?* Jealousy reared its ugly head. Petty in light of her mother's death, but Rose couldn't help her feelings. After all, she was the middle child. What with Margaret's brains and Quincy's stunning beauty, the invisible one.

"Dr. McElroy. I suppose he contacted me because I'm the oldest. I would've called sooner, only I was in the lab and didn't have your number with me."

That her own sister didn't know her number by heart stung. Even though Rose rarely called Margaret or Quincy, she knew their numbers. "Does Quincy know?"

"Not yet. I'm about to call her."

At least she knew before Quincy. That felt good. Also small-minded and awful. Here she was, gloating over knowing first, when their mother was dead.

It finally sank in. *My mother is dead.* Pain welled in Rose's chest, filled her heart, and clogged her throat. Crying noisily she tumbled from the sofa arm into Danny's embrace. His solid warmth comforted her, and she burrowed against his chest.

"I'm leaving for Shadow Falls in the morning," Margaret said. "How soon can you get there?"

Rose swiped at her eyes. "I'll book a flight out as soon as we hang up." The plane trip from Sacramento to Seattle took nearly three hours. From there she'd need a car to get to Shadow Falls, a five-hour drive that meant crossing the Cascade Mountains. "But summer school starts a week from Monday, and the kids and district are depending on me, so I can't stay long."

"Me, either."

Susan is dead. *Mama.* A name Rose and her sisters had been forbidden to use since their father had run off with a blond bimbo.

Rose raised herself from Danny's chest and slowly shook her head. "I can't believe this."

"It hasn't sunk in for me, either," Margaret said, sounding tired and sad.

Fresh tears rolled down Rose's cheeks. Danny handed her a paper napkin. She dabbed her eyes, then crumpled it in her fist.

"Mrs. Overman is making up the beds," Margaret said. "You and Danny can sleep in Susan's room."

Danny barely knew their mother. They'd met exactly twice, at their spring wedding four years ago and again at Thanksgiving that same year. The worst holiday of Rose's life, which said a lot. That her sisters agreed said even more. None of them had gone back to Shadow Falls since.

Rose didn't want Danny to come with her, not now. Maybe in time for the funeral. "Um, Danny won't be with me."

He looked confused and hurt. She covered the mouthpiece. "You can't afford to miss the enology conference in San Francisco." Which started tomorrow. "Just come for the funeral. I'll manage." Sniffling and wriggling off his lap, she stood.

"If that's how you want it," he said, pouting like a little boy.

Now was no time to worry about soothing his feelings. She carried the phone into the kitchen. "I suppose I should call Quincy," she mused to Margaret. "We can meet in Seattle and rent a car together for the drive."

"Oh, that sounds fun. You'll probably kill each other before you leave the airport."

Which could happen, since she and Quincy were as different as cotton and Lycra. Margaret was permanent press. None of them got along. Now their bitter, self-absorbed mother, whom they all hated, was dead.

How wretchedly empty that felt.

"Even if we fight the whole time, sharing a

rental car is a good idea," Rose insisted. "I'm calling her."

"Fine, but give me ten minutes to break the news."

Breathing hard, Duke rolled off Quincy. "That was great."

If you liked men interested only in satisfying themselves. Quincy pasted a fulfilled smile on her face. "It sure was."

Duke, who was old enough to be her father, pulled her tight against his flabby side. She tried not to grimace. Every night for the past two weeks he'd shown up at the Blue Dove, the cocktail lounge where she worked. Or had until her boss had fired her earlier tonight. A drunken customer had pinched her behind one too many times and she'd lost her temper and slapped him.

Barely able to pay the rent and other bills as it was, especially since Chuck had moved out, she was in a world of trouble now. Quincy hated being alone. So when Duke, who'd witnessed the whole thing, grabbed her hand and said, "Come on, doll baby, let's go someplace," she had.

He'd treated her to dinner, which was sweet. Trouble was, instead of eating he guzzled gin and tonics. Her second husband had been an alcoholic, and Quincy wanted nothing to do with another drunk. Before she finished her dinner salad she'd decided to ditch Duke.

Yet here she was, in bed with him, and as lonely as ever. Without a job and broke to boot.

Disgusted with herself and her life, she pulled out of his arms. She'd clean up and grab a robe. Then she would send him home. "Be right back, sugar."

Knowing he was watching, she fluffed her red hair and sashayed her perfect rear end across the room. The wrong thing to do when she wanted him gone, but second to her face, her body was her best feature, and she simply couldn't stop herself.

She was out of the bedroom and halfway to the bathroom down the hall when the phone rang. That it was after eleven on a Saturday night was no big deal. This was Las Vegas and the night was just beginning. Quincy pivoted around, returned to the bedroom, and snatched the phone from the dresser.

"This is Quincy," she said, putting a purr into her voice. She winked at Duke, whose eyes were clouded with booze and lust, and again paraded toward the hallway and bathroom.

"It's Margaret. Did I wake you?"

"Who's that, doll baby?" Duke hollered.

"Are you kidding?" Of all the people to call now when she'd lost her job. Quincy forced a laugh. "I have company, Mags, and he's hung like a—"

"Quincy, please," her sister said.

Margaret hadn't been laid in years. Quincy could hear the contempt in her voice. Or was it jealousy? Either worked for her. She grinned. "Sorry about that, Mags."

"My name is Margaret."

She sounded as if she were gritting her teeth. Getting to her was fun and so easy. "What in the world are you doing up at this hour on a Saturday night?" Quincy asked.

If Margaret heard the dig—outside her work with lichen, *lichen*, for God's sake, she didn't have a life—she didn't let on. "Mother's dead."

Quincy's smile faded. "No way." She carried the phone into the bathroom. "What happened?"

"Dr. McElroy said it was a car accident. Her fault. She drove through a red light. Witnesses say she was leaning down, probably distracted by Suzette. A poor kid driving through town on his way someplace else smacked into her."

"Wow." Overwhelmed, Quincy sat down on the toilet. "Suzette, huh?" She shook her head. "So Susan's favorite caused her death. How fitting."

"Baby doll?" Duke called out.

Quincy covered the mouthpiece. "Shut up!" She kicked the door closed, which, since the bathroom was small, was easy to do from the toilet, and returned her attention to Margaret. "I'll have to ask my boss for time off," she lied.

"He won't let me take more than a week." She could barely afford that. "What's the plan?"

"There isn't one yet, but we're all busy with our own lives, so we'll get things done fast." Margaret sniffled. "We can decide how to do that when we're together. I'll be driving to Shadow Falls in the morning. Rose will fly in as soon as she can. You should, too. She mentioned the two of you renting a car at the airport and driving over together."

"Rose and me alone in a car for five hours?" Despite her grief, Quincy laughed.

"Well, it does make sense from a practical standpoint."

Practical. That was Rose. Margaret was, too, and look where it got them? One sister spent her life isolated in a lab and the other taught home ec to high school kids and was married to a man without an ounce of imagination. Boring. Quincy was the only one who enjoyed life to the fullest. Though at the moment, "enjoy" seemed a tad exaggerated.

My mother is dead. As lousy a mother as Susan was, her passing hurt unbearably. Tears spilled from Quincy's eyes. Her chest felt heavy and way too full. Or was it empty? She couldn't wait to send Duke home and bawl like a baby. "I'll make a plane reservation right away," she said.

"You might wait until you hear from Rose, so you can coordinate. She'll probably call as soon as we hang up."

Despite her grief and fierce need to cry,

Quincy changed her mind about sending Duke home just yet. She wanted him all hot and bothered when Rose called. Just to get her goat.

After all, grieving or not, she had a reputation to uphold.

Chapter 2

Sunday

Sick of driving and sicker for the reason why, Margaret turned onto Mayfair Street, where her mother had lived for thirty-odd years. Thanks to the usual hot, dry June weather, every yard in the modest neighborhood was more brown than green, probably due to water rationing. Like Susan, many of the residents had raised their children here, paid off their mortgages, and stayed to grow older. The once kid-busy neighborhood now was quieter and more sedate. Especially on a scorching Sunday afternoon, when most people were napping off their after-church supper.

Susan's bungalow sat in the middle of the block. Since there was no driveway, Margaret pulled to a stop in front, parking under the shade of the big magnolia. The place looked the same as it always had—white vinyl siding and black vinyl shutters. Black and white. That was Susan.

Someone had cut and edged the browning lawn and weeded and watered the flower beds. Rose bushes, dahlias, and snapdragons, all in variations of white, lined the front of the house on both sides of the front stoop.

The instant Margaret opened the door of her air-conditioned car the heat assaulted her. Despite the dry air, sweat beaded her lip. She pulled her bag from the backseat and hurried up the cracked walkway.

Holding the screen door wide with her hip she opened the unlocked door and stepped into the dim stillness. Here the air was blessedly cool. The entry, really just a three-foot square patch of tile, led straight into the living room.

Margaret set down her purse and suitcase. Nothing in the room had changed for as long as she could remember. Same old pleated beige drapes pulled against the bright light of day; worn, beige carpet; eggshell colored walls; and thirty-year-old tan furniture. Thanks to the ever-changing tastes of fashion, the burlwood coffee table, sofa, and chairs looked hip and stylish— or would have if they were recovered. The fireplace, used only for company, was clean and bare, with a large painting of Suzette on the wall above the mantel. Margaret thought it tasteless and unattractive. The white mantelpiece was adorned with the same impersonal knickknacks that always had been there—four porcelain dogs, a pair of gold-color candlesticks, and a small brass clock. No photographs. As if Margaret and her sisters didn't matter.

This slight had always hurt, and cut especially deeply today. As self-absorbed as Susan had been, Margaret couldn't help loving her or wishing things might have been different. Too late now.

Squeezing her eyes against an onslaught of regret, she wandered aimlessly through the main floor. Mrs. Overman, the woman Susan had hired to clean once her daughters moved out, had dusted and vacuumed. The soft whir of the central air conditioner drowned any neighborhood noises, making the empty house ominously silent. Margaret headed past the small dining room for the kitchen to turn on the radio.

She stopped in the doorway, gaping at the foil-covered cakes, pies, and breads that cluttered the counter and kitchen table. Susan, who disliked clutter, would not have approved.

Margaret didn't have to wonder how the food had gotten here. In Shadow Falls people walked into each other's homes all the time, a habit she found annoying.

Unable to find a classical music station, she tuned in to rock 'n' roll oldies. An early Beatles song filled the air. But her mother had just died, and the upbeat music felt sacrilegious. She switched to the gospel station.

She hadn't eaten since breakfast, and suddenly felt ravenous. The refrigerator bulged with casseroles, cheeses, and cold cuts. Margaret sliced two slabs of homemade bread and made herself a ham and cheese sandwich. Since the table was filled with food, she ate standing over the sink.

Halfway through the hurried meal, a staccato knock sounded on the front door, followed by, "Yoo-hoo, Maggie. It's Fiona."

Her mother's best friend. In no mood for company, but stuck, Margaret stifled a groan. She would get rid of Fiona, fast.

"Um, I'll be right there." She turned off the radio, brushed her hands together, and hurried down the hall to the living room.

Slightly overweight but well-groomed as always, Fiona looked impeccable in a modest dress, sandals, and a straw hat, no doubt the same clothes she'd worn to church this morning.

"Land, but it's hot out there today." Her carefully made-up face lined with grief, she held out a bouquet of flowers. "From my garden with love."

Margaret bit her lip. "Thank you."

"It's wonderful to see you, even under these circumstances."

Widowed at forty and left with a then-teenage son to raise, Fiona understood the wrenching pain of losing a loved one. And the need for comfort. She set her hat on the sofa, then opened her arms. Clutching the flowers,

Margaret walked into a warm, compassionate embrace. When they pulled apart, both were sniffling.

"How're you holding up?" Fiona asked, dabbing her eyes with her knuckle.

"I'm okay. It still hasn't sunk in, you know?" She decided she wanted Fiona to stay awhile. "I should put these beautiful flowers in water. Can I get you something to eat or drink?"

"I'm watching my figure, so nothing to eat, thanks. Now, I don't usually drink this early, but under the circumstances, a white wine would be lovely. I believe there's an unopened bottle of pinot grigio in the cabinet to the left of the sink, from that carton Rose and Danny sent last Christmas."

Wine sounded good to Margaret, too. "I'll join you," she said. "Please sit down."

In the kitchen she found a vase, arranged the flowers, and added water. She set it on the dining room table already crowded with floral arrangements from Spader Flowers, the local florist. When she returned to the living room with the open bottle and two crystal glasses, Fiona was seated beside her hat, legs crossed demurely at the knee.

Margaret filled the glasses. She handed Fiona one and set the bottle on the coffee table. The only chairs were the two beige and white striped Queen Anne armchairs. With hard seats and rigid backs they were less than comfortable, but it was either one of them or the ottoman. Margaret sat down.

"Here's to your mother." Fiona raised her glass.

Margaret somberly matched the gesture, and they each took healthy swigs.

"That's better," Fiona said, smacking her lips.

The imprint from her red lipstick colored the rim and brought to mind a magazine ad for cosmetics. Margaret didn't wear makeup, and her lips barely clouded the crystal. In comfortable khaki shorts and a loose, white T-shirt, she felt decidedly plain.

"Reverend Hill asked me to tell you that he has reserved Wednesday for the funeral," Fiona said. "He'd like you and your sisters to stop by tomorrow. Have you decided on the service?"

Margaret added visiting the minister to her mental to-do list. She shook her head. "Do you know what kind of funeral service Susan wanted?"

"Goodness, no. Your mother was far too young to worry about those things. Whatever you girls decide will be fine."

Margaret hoped for a short service. Get it over with and move on to the other chores. "I'll let you know."

"Please do. I'd like to help you girls any way I can, so feel free to call on me." Fiona downed the rest of the wine and refilled her glass. "What are you going to do with the house?"

Fiona owned a real estate company, Fiona Applebee Realty, so the question was not unexpected.

"Sell it, of course." With nothing but painful memories here, Margaret knew she also spoke for Rose and Quincy.

"When you're ready to talk about listing . . . well, I'm here."

"We'll definitely call you."

Tired of Fiona—tired period—and wanting to be alone, Margaret gauged the level of wine in her glass—a few sips meant what, five more minutes?—then pointedly corked the bottle. "That's all the wine I can handle," she said after draining her own glass. "Thanks so much for stopping by."

"I'm not ready to leave just yet."

With a stubborn set to her jaw and a mulish glint in her eyes, Fiona uncorked the bottle and replenished her glass. "When are Rose and Quincy expected?" she asked after a lengthy guzzle.

"Sometime late tonight."

"Well, shoot. I wanted to speak to all three of you, but you can tell your sisters later." Leaning forward, she lowered her voice. "There's something you should know, and you should hear it from me."

"What's that?"

"Over the years your mother had various . . . How shall I put this? Special male friends."

This was the last thing Margaret expected. Her jaw dropped. "That's impossible. Susan detested men."

Not a day went by that she didn't decry the masculine sex and advise each of her daughters to steer clear. Every boy who knocked on the door was filleted like a freshly caught fish. Which had made high school dating sheer hell.

To keep the peace Margaret and Rose had resorted to lying or sneaking out. Headstrong Quincy had flaunted their mother's warning in her face and had received a world of flack for it. So had the boys who pursued her, but for her, they'd have tolerated anything, and a steady stream of them had. Quincy had been and still was a walking male magnet.

"She's steered clear of men since my father left," Margaret said.

"There's where you're wrong." Fiona swirled the dwindling contents of her glass. "Susan didn't trust men, but she liked them. She had needs, Maggie. Sexual needs."

Not something Margaret wanted to know. "Ick!" She covered her ears. "She hasn't even been dead twenty-four hours. Her sex life is none of my business. And I go by Margaret now."

The older woman's lips tightened. "Regardless what you think, you need to know about it.

Now, she hasn't been involved with anyone in several years, but you can bet this house and everything in it that all her old flames will show up at the funeral. Your mother was very discreet, but people may talk. That's why I wanted you to know."

"*All* her old flames? Just how many were there?"

"Let me see." Fiona glanced at the ceiling. "There was Matt Greenwald. That was quite awhile back. You must have been about ten. Matt had just gone through a rough divorce. He and Susan were together about a year." She stroked her chin. "I believe she waited another few years before she started up with Tom Brewster. That's right, because his wife, Maybelline, had been dead eighteen months. Remember that horrible accident at the cannery? Susan and Tom were together for about six months. Frank Vale was next—at the time he was between wives. As I recall, by then you were in high school. That lasted, oh, three years. Her final and longest relationship was with Eric DelVaio. They saw each other for nearly eleven years. But Eric wanted to get married and your mother refused." Fiona shrugged. "So he broke things off, what? About four years ago, right before Thanksgiving."

The year of the worst ever—and last—family holiday. Susan had been bitter, manipulative, and downright nasty to everyone. Was the breakup part of the reason why? Wait till Rose and Quincy heard about this.

"That many?" Margaret shook her head. "We're adults now and have been for some time. Why would Susan hide that from us?"

"At first because you'd already been through so much. She never intended to settle down with any of those men and didn't want you to get attached, so why take the chance? And later . . . it could be, she was used to keeping her romantic life a secret, or maybe she felt uncomfortable talking about lovers with her own daughters. Who knows?"

Margaret absorbed this without fully processing it. She would save that for when she was alone. "How in the world did she see those men without our knowing? And when did she have the time? She was always either working, sleeping, or meeting you for coffee." Susan had worked as a paralegal at a local law firm for years before going into business for herself.

"All that overtime led to half-days off— comp days she called them—that you never knew about. Or sometimes she took a long 'lunch' at the motel outside town. And sometimes when she said she was meeting me, she wasn't."

That her mother had chosen to spend her rare free time with lovers rather than her attention-starved daughters wasn't surprising. But it hurt. Margaret said nothing. More than ever she wished Fiona would leave.

"So, now you know."

The second Fiona drained her glass, Margaret stood. "If you don't mind, it's been a long day and I'm exhausted."

"Now that I've said what I needed to, I'm happy to let you rest."

After securing Margaret's promise to call if she needed anything and enfolding her in one more hug, Fiona left.

Silence at last. Despite being preoccupied with Fiona's startling disclosures, Margaret felt the first twinge of a bad headache. She swallowed two extra-strength pain relievers and decided to lie down. She wandered past the bathroom, toward Susan's bedroom, the one bedroom on the main floor.

The beige pillows on the matching satin comforter were perfectly arranged, exactly as they always had been. Precisely in the middle of the bed, between two small, decorative pillows, sat Suzette in all her fawn-colored, freeze-dried glory. Mrs. Overman must have placed her there when she cleaned.

Once Glory Lansing had walked out, the Chihuahua, at the time a pup, had become the love of Susan's life. Her stingy heart carried only a limited supply of love, which she showered on her pet and namesake, and apparently Matt, Tom, Frank, and Eric. Margaret, Rose, and Quincy were treated as nuisances to be fed and clothed, shushed and pushed aside, but the dog was pampered like a princess.

After her doggie death at the age of seventeen, the grieving Susan had paid a fortune to freeze-dry Suzette, preserving her for eternity. She brought the stuffed dog everywhere with her: a trusted, though dead, companion. When at home, her namesake stayed on the bed to lord over the bedroom as she did now, as proud and smug as when she'd been alive.

Margaret grimaced. No way was she sleeping in there. Rose or Quincy could use the room.

She shut the door on the dog. But not the memories.

They rasped through her brain as she carried her bag upstairs to the tiny sunroom she'd moved into when Quincy was old enough to share a room with Rose. The week Margaret had left for college (good-bye, Margaret, and don't come back) Susan had moved her then fledgling freelance paralegal business from the dining room table into this room. A computer, bookcase, and desk now filled the space.

The only other room upstairs besides a miniscule bathroom was the dormer-style bedroom Quincy and Rose had shared. A room so bright it hurt your eyes, with bedspreads, ruffled curtains, and shag carpet all the same cotton candy pink, and the walls a paler version. The framed pictures of clowns who looked more sad than happy still hung on the wall, but the punk rock posters Quincy had rebelliously taped everywhere had disappeared.

Posters aside, the room remained virtually unchanged. Margaret understood the not-so-subtle message loud and clear: Quincy and Rose were welcome back, provided they behaved as Susan dictated. Margaret was the one she wanted out for good.

She was over all that and had been for years. Yet the old jealousies flooded back. She was the one with the brains, the one who earned good grades, kept her room and the entire house tidy, and had done everything possible to please Susan. Her mother had failed to appreciate her efforts, and though long ago Margaret had realized she never would, she'd always hoped . . . Now there was no chance of earning Susan's approval.

But then, it was partly Margaret's fault that Glory Lansing had left when he did and never come back. And Susan knew it.

For a moment Margaret's world darkened. The memories always hit hardest when she was in this house. She refused to let them make her even more miserable. Gritting her teeth, she pushed away the pain.

If only she didn't have to sleep here. She didn't want to be in Shadow Falls, period. But here she was, and the twin beds here were freshly made up and invitingly turned down.

So she set her bag beside the bed nearest the window, slipped off her sandals, and sat down. The mattress sagged under her and the springs groaned, but the pain reliever had begun to work, and Margaret was too sleepy to mind. Unable to keep her eyes open one more second, she lay down. She was just drifting off when a noise woke her.

"Helloooo, Maggie! It's me, Ruth Adele Johanssen."

A neighbor from up the block. Footsteps on the stairs meant she was headed up. Margaret did not want to be trapped in this hideous sea of pink with a talkative neighbor.

"I'll be right down," she called out.

So much for a nap.

"Wake up, Quincy," Rose said as she pulled to a stop under the streetlight near their mother's house. "We're here."

"Finally." Quincy stretched and yawned, reminding Rose of a sleek, graceful cat. "How many days did it take?"

"Very funny." Tired and crabby, Rose glared at her sister who managed to look beautiful even after sleeping hours in the car. "At least *I* didn't get a speeding ticket and try to flirt my way out of it." After which she'd traded places with Quincy and had driven the rest of the way herself.

"Would've worked, too, if that policeman hadn't had a female partner." Quincy tugged down her form-fitting, leopard print tank top. "Anyway, what do I care about a silly ticket? I'll never be back this way again."

Her comment worried Rose. "You're not going to pay it?"

"Nope." Quincy fluffed her long, red hair, which was a different color every time Rose saw her.

"Dammit, Quincy, my name is on that car rental agreement. I'm responsible for this car and I don't want any marks against me or my driving record. I'm not bailing you out by paying that ticket."

"So don't. I get it, Rose. You're perfect and I'm not."

"Where in the world did you come up with that? I'm nowhere close to perfect."

"You're the one with the adoring husband and her very own house."

A husband Rose didn't want with her, who she now questioned whether she even loved. She wondered whether Danny loved her. They argued often and seemed to grow further apart by the day. Not a baby in sight, either, which was her fault. Oh, she was perfect, all right. She said nothing.

"You probably never had a speeding ticket in your life," Quincy added in the silence.

"If I did, I wouldn't stick my sister with the bill."

Quincy shook her head at the car ceiling. "All right, all right, I'll take care of it. Now can we puh-lease get out of the car and go inside? I'm tired and I have to pee." She opened the door.

"Tired?" Rose followed her out. "You've been asleep for hours."

"Yes, but I didn't sleep a wink last night. I had company, remember?" Quincy licked her lips. She smoothed her hands over the hips of her skintight capri pants. Her rhinestone mules winked under the artificial light. "Company who kept me very busy."

This was too much. Rose blew out an exasperated breath. "Mother just died, Quincy." She clicked the remote to open the trunk. "For God's sake, show some decency."

"Geez, Rose, lighten up." Grunting, Quincy pulled two gigantic, scarlet suitcases from the trunk.

"We're only here a week. What'd you do, bring your entire wardrobe?"

"At least I *have* a wardrobe." Quincy frowned at Rose's short sleeve empire dress and smirked. "All you have are baggy, homemade dresses with lace on the collars and little flowers all over them. I'll bet Danny just loves those."

Danny never seemed to notice what she wore. Rose raised her chin. "He likes my clothes just fine. What's wrong with sewing?"

"Not a thing, if you like wholesome."

"I'll take wholesome over sluttish any day."

"Ouch," Quincy said, her satisfied smirk irking Rose no end.

She always had enjoyed pushing Rose's buttons. Knowing that didn't help, and anger bubbled up just as it had during her teen years. Rose snatched her medium-size, flowered suitcase from the trunk and slammed it shut.

"Shh," Quincy cautioned. "It's after one. Don't want to wake the neighbors." She turned toward the house, her mules clicking smartly on the pavement. "Speaking of sleep, looks as if Margaret went to bed instead of waiting up for us. You'd think that now, with Susan dead . . ."

She swallowed and seemed to choke up. Rose's eyes, too, filled. Her anger faded and feelings for her sister softened. The one thing they shared was their grief.

"She's probably as exhausted as we are," she said. "Don't worry, we have a whole week of togetherness ahead."

Feeling queasy, Quincy stood at the door of Susan's bedroom. The rheostat was turned on low, and in the dim light Suzette's big, brown, fake eyes glittered. She shuddered. "That dog gives me the creeps. You couldn't pay me to sleep in there." She reached in and flipped off the light.

"That makes two of us," Rose said. "Remember when we were kids and Mother wouldn't let us in here no matter how much we begged? Her bedroom was off-limits. Now we'd rather stay out. Ironic, isn't it?"

"I went in there plenty of times when nobody else was home," Quincy said. "When I was seventeen I had sex in Susan's bed."

"You did not. You're just trying to shock me."

Quincy was, but she also was telling the truth. "I really did, with Jeff Murdock." At the time, Shadow Falls High School's star quarterback. "Susan was at some meeting with one of the lawyers she worked for, you were babysitting, and Margaret was working on some science project at school. That was a good five years before Suzette died. Remember how hyper and obnoxious she was? She kept barking and trying to jump on the bed, so I locked her in the kitchen. Then Jeff and I did the deed."

"That's disgusting," Rose said, looking revolted.

It had been. Quincy had lost her virginity that very day. Jeff had been so warm and convincing with his declarations of love, and Quincy had craved the attention. So she'd let him have his way. He hadn't known how to get a girl ready and the sex had hurt. After he finished, the words of love had stopped. He'd stayed around all of fifteen minutes, a painful experience that had left her feeling degraded and filled with self-loathing. She hadn't had sex again for three years, a little secret nobody but her knew.

"It only happened once in Susan's bed," she said. "And I washed the sheets and towels after and got rid of the sex smell with a spritz of mother's My Sin perfume."

"I get the picture." Her sister wrinkled her nose. "Now, would you please stop?"

"Okay." Quincy shrugged. "Back to sleeping arrangements." She gestured toward the now-dark room. "That's the only queen-size bed in the house. You should take it. Then when Danny comes, you won't have to move."

"I am not sleeping in there." Rose shut the door on the room with a firm click. "I'll figure out where to put Danny later."

The second she mentioned Danny, her eyes filled with shadows.

"Are you two having problems?" Quincy asked.

"What makes you think that?"

"Just a hunch. Listen, I've had lots of experience with men. Maybe I can help."

"With two divorces and dozens of boyfriends who never last more than a few months? I don't think you know much about men at all."

"You're probably right," Quincy admitted. "But I do know how to keep a man interested. It's all between his legs. There are things you can do with your mouth and your hands . . ."

Her sister snorted. "It's always sex with you, isn't it? I feel sorry for you, Quincy."

The last thing Quincy wanted was Miss Perfect's pity. She straightened her spine. "Then we're even, because I feel sorry for you, too. Forget I asked."

Standing outside Susan's closed door they

glared at each other. Until Rose caved with a sigh. She always gave in first.

"I apologize. You're right, there are some issues between Danny and me. But I don't want to talk about it."

"No big." Quincy never shared that stuff, either. She didn't trust anyone enough for that. "So. If neither of us sleeps in there"—she gestured at the closed door—"that leaves two choices. The twin bed upstairs or the lumpy hide-a-bed in the living room. I'll flip you for it."

"I don't mind the hide-a-bed," Rose said.

She always put herself last. Tonight for some reason Quincy felt guilty about that. "Are you sure?"

"I'm an early riser and you're not. If you slept down here I'd wake you up when I came down to make coffee. And you know how nasty you are when that happens."

"Good point. Okay, I'll lug my bags upstairs."

By the time Quincy retrieved her suitcases from beside the front door, Rose had removed the cushions from the sofa and opened it.

"Sweet dreams," she said.

"One can hope."

Quincy plodded upstairs, wondering why she'd felt the need to bring two heavy suitcases. But dressing a certain way was part of her image and required multiple changes and outfits.

Margaret was out cold, so still that at first Quincy didn't notice her. She'd always been like that—quiet, making no waves—while that smart brain of hers stayed busy doing its thing. She'd left on the night-light, which toned down the putrid pink everywhere. Quincy dropped her bags beside the very bed she'd slept in until she'd moved out when she turned eighteen.

Since then she'd stayed here a handful of times and believed she'd moved past the bad memories. Yet standing here tonight she felt like a child again, stranded in a bright pink world that was dark and bleak underneath. Emotions she preferred to ignore deluged her—loneliness and longing for the father who had run away on her fourth birthday without so much as a "Happy Birthday, Quincy." He'd never come back, either.

Glory's desertion had devastated Susan, and she never did celebrate Quincy's birthday. While Susan had holed up with Suzette in her bedroom with the door locked, Margaret and Rose had taken pity on Quincy and brought the gifts and the cake to this very room for a sisterly celebration. Since then Quincy had become a thorn in her mother's side, an irritation to be picked on and yelled at.

Now Susan was dead, and Quincy had forever lost the chance to get any positive attention. Tears flooded her eyes. A sob burst from her chest.

Mumbling, Margaret turned over. Quincy froze. *Silly girl, that was a long time ago.*

Blinking away the tears and tamping down her feelings, she changed into a cotton nightshirt. She tiptoed into the bathroom down the hall to wash her face and brush her teeth.

Then stripped of makeup, feeling small and lost, she padded softly back to the bedroom.

Chapter 3

Monday

After a solid night's sleep, rested, showered, dressed, and starting her third cup of coffee, Margaret at last felt human again. She was ready to plan the funeral, tell her sisters about their mother's secret sex life, and start taking apart the house. But not until they were all three here. Quincy wasn't up yet.

Despite arriving late, Rose was awake, but she'd always been an early riser. She, too, was dressed and on her second cup. She claimed she'd slept well on the hide-a-bed, but the circles under her eyes told a different story. Her face, never heavy, was thinner than Margaret remembered. She couldn't tell for sure whether Rose had lost weight, though, because of the loose, feminine shift that hid her body. The navy blue color and white lace collar only emphasized her too-pale skin.

Concerned, wondering whether her sister was ill, Margaret eyed her. "How are you, Rose?"

"Fine, thanks."

The bright smile didn't fool Margaret. "No offense, but you don't look so great. If you're sick or something—"

"What is it with you and Quincy? If I say I'm fine, I mean it. Of course I look bad. We just lost our mother. Honestly!"

Margaret was certain that prickly, defensive attitude covered more than their mother's death. "I know," she said. "I just thought . . . If you need help or advice or anything . . ."

"Well, I don't." Rose narrow-eyed her. "Are you even grieving?"

Aside from sporadic tears and a heavy feeling in her sinuses, Margaret hadn't truly cried yet—for some reason she couldn't—but she definitely felt the loss. "Of course I am. Just because I disliked Susan doesn't mean I'm not sorry she's gone."

At that moment Quincy wandered into the kitchen, her feet bare and a short, butter-color robe tied over an oversize T-shirt. "Coffee. I need coffee."

Even with her shoulder-length hair a tangled mess and no makeup she looked beautiful. Margaret regarded her with envy before she compressed her lips. Beauty was overrated.

"What happened to 'good morning, Margaret and Rose, it's nice to see you after four years'?"

For an instant Quincy looked taken aback. "I'm saving the small talk for after I get my coffee."

Rose, who as the middle child strove to resolve conflict even though she often fomented and participated in it, jumped to her feet.

"I just made a fresh pot. Sit down and I'll pour you some." Busy trying to please, she bustled to the now neat counter she'd organized before Margaret was up, where the coffeepot sat.

"Thanks." Quincy sank onto an empty seat at the old birch table, which Rose had also cleared. She pulled the milk pitcher and sugar bowl Rose had set out toward her.

"If you want breakfast, there's food in the fridge," Margaret said.

"Or I could make you something." Rose had cooked for the family since the age of nine. "Eggs? Toast?"

"All I want is coffee."

Rose set a steaming white mug in front of her. Quincy added a dash of milk. Sipped, closed her eyes, and sighed. "That's better. Why are you all dressed up, Rose?"

"Because people will be stopping by to pay their respects."

"So? That's no reason to wear your funeral clothes. Don't you want to save those for the actual funeral?"

"I brought another dress for that, something more appropriate," Rose said.

"More somber than what you're wearing

now?" Quincy snorted. "I can't wait to see that."

"Must you always pick at me?"

"I wouldn't if you dressed your age. You look old in that thing, like you're somebody's grandma."

"At least I dress like a mature adult, not a wannabe slut teenager."

Margaret saw the flash of hurt in Quincy's eyes.

"We're back to that, are we? Sticks and stones and all that crap." Quincy tossed her head. "You're just jealous of my body."

"I am not."

"You don't lie very well. Isn't that why you wear those baggy clothes, to hide what you don't have?"

"Ooh." Rose clenched her teeth. "One of these days . . ."

"What, Rose?" Quincy taunted. "One of these days, what?"

"Give me back that coffee. You get your own."

Acting like children, they both grabbed the mug. Coffee sloshed over the rim and splashed the table.

Enough was enough. Slipping into her oldest sister, in-charge role Margaret yelled. "Both of you, stop it!" That silenced her sisters, and she lowered her voice to normal. "Rose, sit down. Quincy, drink your coffee."

"Fine." Eyes narrowed, Rose dropped to her chair.

Quincy silently wiped up the spill with a napkin, then sipped from her mug with lowered eyes.

Margaret released a sigh. She'd been in her sisters' company less than ten minutes and could hardly wait to go back to the peace and quiet of her Seattle condo.

After a few minutes of silence, when both women had regained a measure of composure, Quincy glanced from Rose to Margaret. "So, what were you two talking about when I walked in?"

"Nothing much yet," Margaret replied. "We were waiting for you. We have a lot to do in a short time. Fiona stopped by yesterday and offered to list the house if we want to sell. What do you think?"

"Absolutely," Rose said. "Sell the place."

"And everything in it," Quincy added.

Margaret nodded. "I thought so. We can talk more about that after we plan the funeral. Fiona said that Reverend Hill has reserved Wednesday for us. Have either of you thought about the service?"

"Can't we leave that to Harold?" Quincy asked.

And earned a scowl from Rose. "Show the man some respect. His name is Reverend Hill."

"Actually, it's Harold Hill, the same as that guy in *The Music Man*." Quincy got up and refilled her cup. "I've always called him Harold. He never seemed to mind."

No doubt because Quincy's beauty had dazzled him into submission, Margaret guessed.

Rose shook her head. "You're thirty years old, Quincy. When are you going to grow up and act your age?"

"I wish you'd stop telling me what to do."

"And *I* wish you'd both stick to the subject," Margaret muttered. "If we want the funeral Wednesday, we need to make the arrangements now."

"Yes, ma'am, Miss Taskmaster." Quincy saluted. "Are we burying Susan or cremating her?"

"Knowing her, she'd want a burial, with her makeup in place, her hair fixed, and her best dress," Rose said. "If the funeral people can hide the bruises and gashes." She swallowed and paled.

Margaret felt sick at her stomach. "I hope she didn't suffer. Dr. McElroy never said . . ."

"Well then, we'll just believe that she didn't," Quincy said. "As for bruises, makeup and a deft hand can hide a multitude of sins. Isn't that part of what the funeral people are paid for?"

"That's true." Rose nodded. "She should be buried with Suzette at her side."

"That solves the problem of what to do with the ugly thing," Quincy said. "Unless you have other ideas, Margaret?"

Burying the already dead dog with her master suited Margaret fine. "Burial it is, and an open casket for viewing. Are you taking notes, Rose? Because someone will need to notify Reverend Hill, and you're dressed for the occasion. What else?"

Everyone went quiet, Quincy fiddling with her cup and Rose dabbing a drop of spilled milk with her napkin. Uncertain what she wanted, Margaret rubbed a scar on the tabletop and waited for one of her sisters to speak.

Quincy broke the silence first. "I don't know how to plan a funeral, especially my own mother's. But I know what I *don't* want—a long, sappy service."

"That would be awful," Rose said.

"And I don't think we should ask people to share their fond memories," Margaret added. "Can you imagine?"

"That *would* make for a very short service, though." Quincy's lip curled. "Since no one would be able to think of anything nice to say. Except maybe Fiona."

This was the perfect time to drop the bomb, and Margaret leaned forward. "Speaking of Fiona. . . . You won't believe what she told me yesterday. Apparently there are four men who'll have plenty of good things to say."

Rose looked puzzled. "I don't understand."

"Susan hated the entire male population," Quincy said.

"Not the four she slept with."

Her sisters gaped at her, both looking as

shocked by this news as Margaret had been. It was funny, really, and she couldn't stop a smile.

"Get out!" Quincy hooted. "Sex is much too earthy for Susan. All those juices and smells, not to mention messing up her hair . . ."

"That's enough, Quincy!" Rose shrieked.

Obviously enjoying herself, Quincy grinned. "Well, it's true. Mother was as sexless as her freeze-dried dog. It's a wonder she conceived any of us. That has to be the reason Daddy ran off with Tiffani-with-an-i-not-a-y," she said in the sarcastic tone their mother had used the few times she'd mentioned the woman's name.

Neither of her sisters knew the *real* reason, and Margaret wasn't about to divulge it. It was too painful to share, though God knew, she deserved their condemnation.

"If Susan had slept with anybody, we'd have known," Quincy said. "We weren't that naive."

Rose nodded. "She's right. Mother never looked at men, period."

"Exactly what I thought," Margaret said. "Until Fiona enlightened me after she finished half a bottle of wine. According to her, Susan took her first lover when I was ten. She ended her fourth affair just before that god-awful Thanksgiving four years ago."

"That could explain why she was such a witch that year," Quincy said. "Did Fiona mention any names?"

"Oh, yes." Margaret used her fingers to count. "In chronological order, Matt Greenwald, Tom

Brewster, Frank Vale, and Eric DelVaio. The relationship with Eric lasted the longest, eleven years. They all either were single, divorced, or widowers."

"At least she didn't mess with married men," Quincy said.

Rose rubbed the back of her neck. "That's something, I guess, but I still don't get it."

"Fiona said Mother had needs that those men filled," Margaret said.

"Filled, eh?" Quincy waggled her eyebrows. "Nice pun there."

Rose's mouth twitched. She and Quincy looked at each other and started to giggle. It *was* funny. Margaret joined in. In no time they were laughing so hard, tears filled their eyes.

Rose and Quincy soon sobered and dried their eyes, but the tears that flooded Margaret's eyes refused to stop.

At last, in the company of her sisters, she cried.

Though Rose hadn't lived in Shadow Falls for thirteen years, she'd grown up here. She knew that starting today, people would stop by to pay their respects, even those who'd already brought food or sent flowers. Neighbors, friends, and acquaintances started showing up at noon, right after she returned from making the funeral plans with Reverend Hill.

Rose couldn't get over the steady stream. Susan hadn't had a large group of friends, and she suspected curiosity brought in some of the visitors. None of Susan's ex-boyfriends showed up, though. Since Rose wasn't sure how she should act around them, that was a relief.

She put herself in charge of making visitors comfortable and seeing to their needs, a role that always had been hers.

As kids, Margaret oversaw the decisions and kept the house clean. Rose took care of grocery shopping and cooking. Quincy did the laundry, mowed the lawn, and kept her sisters on their toes with her embarrassing antics.

Today, in a show of rebellion, Quincy had opened the drapes, something their mother had frowned upon. Sunshine flooded the living and dining rooms, the bright, cheery light at odds with the occasion.

Rose didn't mind the sunlight, but she did mind Quincy's outfit. Her sister was dressed in a bronze jumpsuit that clung to her body and revealed her deep, creamy cleavage. Not at all appropriate, and neither were the bronze, three-inch heel, thong-toed sandals or the silver ankle charm bracelet that spelled out the word *sexy*. How inappropriate was that?

Margaret, who never seemed to notice her own clothes, was dressed in wrinkled Bermuda shorts, a sleeveless blouse, and Birkenstocks. Perfect for taking apart the house later, but not for receiving guests.

Rose was the only one dressed for the occasion. In a mid-afternoon lull between visitors she caught Quincy on the way into the kitchen. "Honestly, Quincy, the way you're dressed, you'd think you were at a party. Our mother just died."

Quincy rolled her eyes. "And I don't need another one, thank you very much."

"Apparently, you do. At least take off that ankle bracelet."

"I will not. Lighten up, Rose. You need a kid or two of your own to pick on."

She'd hit Rose right where it hurt. "You are such a brat," she said, squinting menacingly.

"Will you both please stop it," Margaret wailed from the living room. "I can't—"

"Helloooo!" a woman called out.

They both shut their mouths.

By this time Rose, Quincy, and Margaret were cranky and tired of making conversation with people they barely knew.

Having slept badly, Rose longed for a nap. In another lull between visitors, she said, "I wish they'd all just go away."

"Why don't we pull the drapes, lock the door, and hide," Quincy suggested.

Never mind that she'd been the one to open them.

"Let's, because we have a ton to do." Margaret headed for the door to lock it. "We have to sort through each room and figure out what we want to keep."

"Susan left me with enough baggage to last a lifetime. I don't need or want any other mementos,"

Quincy said. "I say we hold a garage sale and split the proceeds. As soon as possible, so we can leave this hellhole of a town in one week, as planned, and never come back."

"I like that idea," Rose said. "Quincy and I should change our clothes first, though."

"Okay." Margaret nodded. "I say we start with the hardest room in the house—Susan's bedroom."

Chapter 4

Quincy stared in disgust at Suzette. "I refuse to touch that freeze-dried freak."

"She's not infected or anything," Rose said. "If she was we'd have known it long ago. I'll do it."

"I don't care. She gives me the creeps." Quincy offered her sister a pair of latex gloves from a box she'd found under the kitchen sink. "Here, put these on. I'll empty the dresser."

"That reminds me," Margaret said. "Someone needs to take Suzette to Bushell's Mortuary."

The very thought of driving anyplace with Suzette creeped out Quincy. "Would you do it?" she asked Rose. "Since you already met with the people there."

Rose had explained that after meeting with Reverend Hill she'd visited Leonard Bushell, grandson of the late Harold Bushell, the eighty-year-old mortuary's founder. Leonard had assured her that his people would banish any cuts and bruises and make Susan look as if she were "sleeping peacefully without a care in the world." And that yes, they would happily bury her with Suzette. Which was a huge relief to Quincy. The sooner the dog was out of the house, the better.

Rose sighed. "All right, I'll deliver her first thing tomorrow morning."

"Thanks," Margaret said. "If Quincy's taking the dresser, I'll empty the closet."

"That leaves me with the two bedside tables and the pictures." Rose glanced at the bed. "Guess I'll put Suzette out of harm's way."

She slipped on the gloves, proving that she didn't like the idea of touching Suzette any more than Quincy. Nose wrinkled and arms stiff in front of her like a zombie in a B-grade horror film, she carried the dog out of the room and deposited her beside the front door.

While Rose had visited with Reverend Hill, Margaret had picked up boxes to store items for the garage sale, and also had bought jumbo plastic bags for trash. Quincy grabbed several of both.

For a time she and her sisters worked in silence. On the off chance she might find something of value, Quincy concentrated on her task. The dresser was filled with the usual— socks and pantyhose, pajamas, shirts and sweaters, underwear. Items that any woman might own. As Quincy dumped the underwear and pantyhose into a trash bag she felt nothing remotely sentimental. She was folding sweaters and placing them in a garage sale box when Margaret made a sound of surprise.

"I haven't seen this dress since I was little."

Quincy glanced at the hanger in Margaret's hands. The belted and dated seersucker shirt-waist was nothing special, but she remembered it all too well.

"I hate that thing," she said. "One morning before school when I was around six, I acciden-tally spilled milk all over the front of it. Susan went ballistic." Though it had happened twenty-plus years ago, she shuddered. "For a while I wasn't sure she'd let me live here anymore."

"I remember wondering the same thing," Rose said. "She said she wished she'd bought three more dogs instead of having us."

Margaret nodded somberly, and seconds ticked by while they each silently and privately recalled that painful morning.

Then Margaret shoved the dress into a trash bag. "There," she said, brushing off her hands. As if her actions could banish the memories.

"You were her favorite, Margaret," Quincy said.

A haunted, guilty look darkened Margaret's face, gone so fast, Quincy wondered whether she'd imagined it. Must've, since her sister had nothing to feel guilty about.

Quincy continued. "She never yelled at you."

"Because she was too busy heaping responsi-bilities on my shoulders. Starting in grade school,

I pretty much ran the house and watched over you two."

Quincy hadn't thought about this. "She made you grow up fast."

"Yep."

"I wonder what the Children's Protection Society would have said about her?" Rose asked.

"Not much," Quincy said, "since most of her abuse was of the mental variety."

"Well, we all survived and turned out to be strong women despite our mother." Rose's bright tone sounded forced.

Quincy certainly didn't feel strong. She felt scared. Here she was, out of a job, with a stack of bills that wouldn't wait. A panicky feeling settled in her chest and she went cold inside. *Don't think about that now.* She inhaled a deep breath. "Anybody want a glass of wine?"

"I do," Margaret said.

Rose shook her head. "None for me."

"White okay?"

"Sure."

Quincy headed for the kitchen. When she returned with a bottle and two glasses her sisters were back at work. She and Margaret helped themselves and left the bottle on the bedside table closest to them. Quincy set her glass on the dresser, then pulled open the pajama drawer. Nothing here but assorted flannel and lightweight nightgowns, too old for anything but rags.

"You got all Susan's attention, Quincy," Rose commented minutes later.

"I did if you mean the yelling and getting in trouble."

"But attention all the same." Margaret made her I-know-what-I'm-talking-about-because-I'm-the-oldest-and-smartest face. "Which is exactly why you caused all that trouble."

"That's not true!" But as Quincy thought about it, she had to agree. "Maybe you're right."

"You bet I am." Margaret opened an old purse, peered into it, and tossed it into a box. "Even though I understood that, I was still jealous of you because it worked. Rose and I were the good girls, yet you were the one Susan noticed."

"Not always." Rose shoved a stack of magazines from the bottom of one bedside table onto a trash bag, wiped her hands on her denim shorts—thank God she owned something besides dresses—and reminisced. "Remember where she took us every August, right before school started? School shopping and lunch at Hal's Steakhouse? That was always fun."

Quincy had to agree. Despite tough financial times, Susan had managed to save enough to buy each of them new shoes and a few new outfits. If Quincy was half as good with money, she wouldn't be in the mess she was in now. . . .

She finished the contents of her glass, the

liquid sliding down her throat as smooth as velvet. Which reminded her . . . "This is great wine," she said. "My compliments to Danny."

Rose nodded, but said nothing. Quincy was dying to know what was wrong between them. "Issues," Rose had said. What issues? Determined to find out, hopefully tonight, Quincy refilled her glass.

Margaret held out hers, too. "The hard part about living with Susan was, we never knew what might set her off."

"Now that we know about the lovers, maybe they had something to do with her mood swings. A breakup or bad sex, or too long without it?" Quincy took a drink. "Those things always put me in a foul mood."

Rose closed her eyes and shook her head, but Margaret looked thoughtful. "You could be onto something."

Seconds later Rose held up a faded color photo. "Hey, look what I found in the back of the bottom drawer. Us when we were little."

Quincy and Margaret moved closer for a better look. In the picture the three of them were sitting in an inflated swimming pool, laughing. Suzette was in the picture, too, a tiny, frolicking puppy.

"That looks like one of the good times," Quincy said. "I wish I remembered it instead of all the bad stuff."

"You look about three years old, so you

wouldn't," Margaret said. "That means I was six. I don't either."

"I have this dim memory of the three of us once being close." Rose frowned. "What happened?"

"Our dear mother didn't like us banding together," Margaret said. "So she pitted us against each other."

Quincy never had realized that, but it made perfect sense. The strategy had worked all too well, for she and her sisters had fought and competed with each other through middle and high school. They still did. She wished things were different, but had no idea how to fix it. Heck, she didn't even know how to fix her own screwed-up life.

Fortifying herself with more wine, she opened the bottom drawer and found more than a few pieces of sexy lingerie. "Would you look at this," she said, holding up a black teddy.

"I never knew Susan owned that kind of lingerie," Rose said.

Margaret tossed a navy blue suit into a garage sale box. "I wonder if she wore those things for her lovers."

"Why else would she have them? Though I still can't picture her doing the nasty with anyone." Quincy grimaced and so did her sisters. She stared thoughtfully at one nightie with the tags still attached. "This see-through number was never worn." The devil made her hold it up and look at Rose. "You ought to take it. It looks like it'd fit you, and Danny would love it."

As she'd hoped, Rose prickled. "Don't butt in where you're not invited."

Quincy widened her eyes. "I have no idea what you mean, Rose."

Her sister's face darkened. "I changed my mind. I will have a drink," she said, striding around the bed for the bottle.

Quincy's comments rang in Rose's head and her heart felt sore. How long had it been since Danny had noticed what she wore to bed? How long had it been since she cared?

Because there wasn't a glass for her and the bottle was two-thirds empty anyway, she lifted it to her lips. She didn't set it down again until every drop was gone. Danny would have been appalled. Rose herself was surprised, but she was too bruised to stop.

She knew her sisters were beyond curious and were bound to question her, but for a few blessed seconds neither reacted beyond twin dumbfounded expressions. It wasn't often that she shocked Quincy, and Rose tossed a mental *touché* her way. Swiping her mouth with her forearm she calmly sat on the floor in front of the bedside table.

Hands on her hips, Margaret gave her head a slow shake. "I knew something was wrong."

"This is worse than I thought," Quincy added

with a perplexed frown. "You said 'issues,' but they must be ginormous. What's Danny doing, sleeping with somebody else?"

"No, and I'm not talking about this."

"Maybe you should," Margaret said. "You might feel better."

Their faces were alive with sisterly concern, tempting Rose to trust them. It would be so nice to share her burdens and confess her awful secret. But she was sure neither would understand. Quincy would make some cutting remark about Rose's naivete, and Margaret would think she'd been stupid. In the end they'd both look down on her. Or worse.

No, Rose decided. She'd keep her troubles to herself.

"I'm not sure I love Danny anymore," she admitted before she knew it. And realized the wine had blurred the edges of her self-control. Dismayed, she shut her mouth.

"Oh, honey." Quincy bit her lip.

"You two used to be crazy in love," Margaret said with a forlorn expression.

Rose remembered those days of lighthearted joy and frenzied passion. Making love because they wanted to, instead of because they *had* to. Working the crossword puzzle in bed Sunday mornings, and later, combing flea markets just for fun. Laughing, always laughing. It seemed like ages ago.

Danny had been her best friend. She shared everything with him—except her secret. Deep sadness filled her and slumped her shoulders, and the wine burned in her stomach. "Lately, all we do is fight," she confessed, staring at her lap. "I just . . . I'm so confused."

Tears flooded her eyes and words that wanted out clogged her throat, but she would not let herself say any more. Biting the inside of her cheek she pulled a drawer completely out of the dresser. Nothing in here but two cheap ballpoint pens and a hand mirror.

"Been there, done that," Quincy murmured. "You know what Ann Landers used to say. Ask yourself, are you better with him or without him?"

Sometimes her baby sister surprised her. Rose eyed her before dumping the contents of the drawer into a trash bag.

"That's wise advice, Quincy," Margaret said, sounding equally amazed.

The compliment flustered Quincy, and for a moment she looked as pleased as a teenager who'd earned an A on a test. "See? I'm not so dumb. Have you asked yourself that question, Rose?"

At the moment, Rose couldn't think beyond right now. Hugging the empty drawer, she shook her head. "I might ask for a separation."

Margaret and Quincy shared distressed looks.

"This is a bad time to decide such a serious decision," Margaret said. "After we bury Susan and the dust settles, maybe you and Danny can talk things out, or see a marriage counselor."

"Maybe." Uneasy at the thought of talking over "things" with Danny, which meant telling him about her past, and tired of claiming the spotlight, Rose fitted the drawer into place and searched her muzzy brain for a new topic of conversation. "Did I hear you talking to Arthur Tremayne on the phone earlier, Margaret?"

"Now there's a name I haven't heard for a while," Quincy said as she pawed through another drawer. "Susan's old boss. I'm sure she would've slept with him if he hadn't been married."

Subject successfully changed. For once glad of her sister's fixation on sex, Rose released a breath. "You *would* think that," she said, forcing a disapproving tone.

"Anyway," Margaret went on. "Apparently Arthur was her lawyer even after she stopped working for him." She began piling pumps, sandals, and boots in a box. "He offered his condolences and scheduled a meeting Thursday afternoon to, and I quote, 'discuss your mother's estate.'"

"Estate?" Quincy licked her lips. "Wouldn't that be nice."

"So would finding a pot of gold at the end of the rainbow," Rose said. Or getting pregnant. "Mother's entire holdings consist of this house and the stuff in it, period, and neither are worth much."

"It's still an estate and has to go through probate—I think," Margaret said. "You need a lawyer for that, and it may as well be Arthur Tremayne. Our appointment is at three."

"Works for me." Rose opened the last drawer in the bedside table and discovered a stash of yellowed stationery. She scooped it out and tossed it. "I'm all through here."

"Me, too," Quincy said.

"Wow, so am I." Margaret shut the closet door, then wiped her hands on her Bermuda shorts. "We make a good team, don't we?"

"Now and then." Quincy frowned into her empty glass. "I need a refill."

"And I need food," Famished, Rose checked her watch. "It's nearly dinnertime. How about I stick a casserole in the oven, the one from Bootsie Haggerty? It's her chicken and broccoli specialty, the one she makes for the church socials every year. While it heats, we can start on the downstairs bathroom."

"I've been eyeing that very casserole." Margaret rubbed her stomach.

"It's been years since I tasted it," Quincy said, "but if it's anything as good as it used to be. . . . Yum. Shall I open a new bottle of wine?"

Rose considered that a great idea. "Yes, please. This time I'll use a glass."

As the aroma of the chicken casserole wafted into the first floor bathroom, Margaret's mouth watered. "That smells heavenly." Having had countless glasses of wine, she was slightly drunk.

"Certainly does." Rose swiped her brow with her forearm. "Can you believe we've been at this for over four hours? Wonderful idea to lock the front door."

No one had bothered them since.

"Didn't I tell you? People got the message that we want to be left alone. And look how much we accomplished." Margaret waved her hand around. "Susan's room and most of this bathroom." Her stomach rumbled. "Do you think the casserole's ready? Because I'm starved."

"Wine is an appetite enhancer," Quincy said. "At least that's what Danny says. Oops." She made a contrite face at Rose. "Sorry I mentioned him."

Looking blotto herself, Rose shrugged. "Nothing to be sorry about." She plucked a perfume vial from a shelf in the bathroom cabinet. "Look at this—an old, empty bottle of My Sin." She uncapped the stopper and sniffed. "Smells just like Susan."

Margaret caught a whiff and it unlocked an unpleasant memory. "Once when I was little, wanting to smell good like her, I dabbed some on my wrists before school. You'd have thought I robbed a bank."

Susan had yanked her into this very bathroom and scrubbed her wrists until they were nearly raw. Margaret still remembered feeling that she'd done something truly terrible. For months after she'd been careful to do everything right, hoping to get back on Susan's good side. Because she'd dared to use her perfume! Angry and sad for the little girl she'd been, she muttered, "There goes my appetite."

"It'll come back." Quincy reached out her hand. "Give me that My Sin bottle, Rose." She turned on the faucet and rinsed it out, then recapped it. "There," she said, lobbing it into the bulging trash bag. An instant later she cast a thoughtful look at the bag. "They don't make bottles like that anymore. I wonder if we can sell it on eBay. Hmm." She fished it out of the trash.

Very telling, indeed. Margaret arched her brows. "If you're that hard up for money and you want to drag that bottle and anything else home with you, feel free."

"This has nothing to do with my finances," Quincy said. She pocketed the bottle, no easy feat given her skintight cutoffs.

Margaret didn't believe her. Since her youngest sister often changed jobs and juggled multiple credit cards, it wouldn't be the first time. And the men she'd married and lived with—losers all—each one adding to the debt. But Margaret didn't want to know.

Suddenly the doorbell chimed. She groaned. "Not even a locked door keeps everyone away. We should've posted a note, too. I can't handle visitors, not tonight. Let's ignore it."

The chimes pealed again. Quincy sighed. "I

never could resist a ringing phone or doorbell. I'll get it and send whoever it is away. Besides, I'm sick of cleaning. I need a break." She fluffed her hair, then smoothed her snug tank top over her cutoffs. "A long break. Once this person's gone, we'll eat."

Grabbing her wineglass from the windowsill, she staggered around the boxes and bags filled with towels, Band-Aids, cosmetics, hair paraphernalia, and other items from the bathroom cabinet.

"You're walking like you're sloshed," Rose said. "I certainly am. I *hate* this feeling."

"I never get drunk," Quincy said. "But I may be a teensy bit tipsy."

"Well, I'm smashed." Margaret stuffed the empty wine bottle into a bag. She took the two bland watercolors from the wall and put them into a box, Then there was nothing left to do. "We're through here, anyway. Let's go rescue Quincy. Unless whoever came to the door went away before she answered it."

"In that case, she could be taking the casserole from the oven right now," Rose said.

"She'd better not start without us."

Margaret and Rose washed up, then headed for the living room, which led into the dining room and the kitchen beyond.

They found Quincy standing in front of an enormous bouquet of sweet-smelling, colorful flowers that sat on the coffee table.

"Look what just arrived," she said, waving

the card she'd opened. "This was addressed to you, Margaret," she said without a trace of shame for snooping. "Who's Bruce?"

"Bruce?" Margaret snatched the card from her and read it.

With deepest sympathy, Bruce. A generic message, likely something the florist thought up. Yet her heart lifted. She missed him. *Nonsense,* she told herself. Too much wine.

Now Rose looked as curious as Quincy. "Well, who is he?"

"The other researcher working on the lichen project." Margaret was proud of her neutral tone.

"That bouquet had to cost several hundred dollars," Quincy said. "This is more than just a guy from work."

Rose nodded. "She makes a good point."

Margaret didn't want a relationship with Bruce and he knew it. She didn't want a relationship, period. "You're wrong." She stuffed the card into her pocket. "He's a nice man, that's all."

"What a load of garbanzo beans." Quincy eyed her. "You never did have much of a poker face. Anybody can see that you have feelings for this guy."

"It's obvious," Rose said.

That her sisters saw what Margaret barely admitted to herself was unnerving. "You're both crazy. There's nothing between Bruce and me."

"If not, then you wish there was. By the look of those flowers, I'd say he does, too." Expression impish, Quincy angled her chin. "What does he look like? Is he tall, dark, and well-hung?"

To Margaret's chagrin her face warmed. "We're scientists, Quincy. Anything we share is between our ears, period."

Her baby sister winked. "'The dirtiest part of your body is your mind.' Frank Zappa."

"Hush, Quincy," Rose said without taking her eyes from Margaret. "If you like this guy and he likes you . . . maybe you should do something about it."

Since he'd stopped asking Margaret out, he couldn't be truly interested.

But what if he was? Margaret didn't want to think about that, not with her sisters scrutinizing her the same careful way she studied lichen under a microscope.

Doing her best to look intimidating, she frowned. "Since I *don't* have feelings for Bruce, I'm not going to do a damned thing. Something tells me that if we don't take that casserole out soon it'll burn. Would either of you care to join me for dinner?"

Without waiting for a reply, she turned toward the kitchen.

Chapter 5

Tuesday

Quincy set a glass of water and a bottle of aspirin on the table between the beds, then sat down on her own bed, which she'd made earlier. "Rise and shine, big sister."

Margaret cracked open one bleary eye, and Quincy grinned. Playing taskmaster was a new and enjoyable role. Especially when her goody-two-shoes sister was hungover, something Quincy had never seen. "We have things to do and places to go, and not much time," she said.

"You're horribly cheerful this morning. When did you get up?"

It had been a long night spent working into the wee hours, but Quincy had awakened early. "About an hour ago. I'm showered, dressed, and coffeed up—ready for the day. Rose is off taking Suzette to the mortuary and picking up more boxes and trash bags."

"She is?" Margaret groaned and closed her eyes. "I have such a headache."

"It's called a hangover."

"Ooh." She pulled the pillow over her head. "I need aspirin," she said in a muffled voice.

"Never fear, Dr. Quincy is here." Quincy opened the bottle she'd brought up and emptied out three tablets. "Take these."

Margaret meekly accepted the tablets and the glass of water Quincy handed her. "Thanks." After swallowing the pills she flopped again onto the pillow and closed her eyes. A moment later she opened them. "How come you aren't hungover?"

"I drank two glasses of water and popped a vitamin pill before bed." A trick she'd learned from an old boyfriend. "Worked like a charm."

She could hardly wait to see Margaret's face when she noticed the bouquet from Bruce, which Quincy had toted upstairs and set on the dresser. The colorful flowers trumped the disgusting pinkness and certainly made the room smell better than stale wine breath. Quincy wanted Margaret's nonalcoholic-induced reaction so she could find out how her sister really felt about Bruce. As Margaret struggled up on one elbow, Quincy watched her face.

Margaret noted the bouquet and frowned. "Why'd you bring *those* up here?"

"Because we're stuck in this room for five more nights and it needs help. Don't you think the whole space looks and smells fresher?"

Margaret moaned. "Don't mention smells." Her face was pale, and she looked ready to puke. "I'll be right back."

Holding her head she scrambled from her bed and raced for the bathroom, her cotton nightgown flying behind her. Seconds later the toilet flushed. The pipes protested, signaling the water had been turned on. When Margaret staggered back, her face was clean with a hint of color.

"Feeling better?" Quincy asked.

"No, but I will." The bed creaked and squeaked as she climbed back in. "Just give me a few minutes." She burrowed under the covers.

Not about to let her fall asleep again, Quincy sat on her own bed with her back against the wall. "Tell me about Bruce."

"Now?"

"Maybe if you talk, you'll forget about your hangover."

"If only. I told you, there's nothing to say."

"I still want to know about him."

Margaret peered at her from under the covers. "You aren't going to let me go back to sleep, are you?"

"Nope, so you may as well talk."

"All right." With a sigh she peeled back the covers so that her head and shoulders were exposed. She didn't sit up, though. "Bruce and I were in the same doctoral program at the University of Washington. That's where we met. We never socialized or anything. After we graduated we went to work for different companies. We didn't see each other again until three and a half years ago, when Hassell Pharmaceuticals hired both of us."

Despite the unexciting details, her sister's voice grew more animated with each breath. Quincy knew she was on to something.

"Obviously he's a brain, but what's he like otherwise?"

"As a researcher he's thorough, conscientious, and not afraid to take chances. Outside of work, I really don't know."

"Does he work as hard as you?"

"Yes, and I respect him for it." Margaret sat up and, like Quincy, leaned against the wall.

"What else?" Quincy asked.

"He likes to hike."

"You hike." Quincy raised her brows. "You could do it together."

A tiny pucker between her brows, Margaret stared at the bouquet.

"Next time you go, why not invite him along?"

"Stop with the questions."

"Hey, I'm only trying to make conversation." Quincy put on her innocent face. "I wish I knew what you were scared of."

"I'm not afraid," Scoffing, Margaret crossed her arms over her breasts. "I just don't want to get involved. Who wants the fuss?"

"I do." Quincy sighed. "I wish someone I admired and respected would send me flowers."

"What about that man you were with the night I called? Your latest boyfriend."

"He's not a boyfriend," Quincy said. "I'm talking about a man who likes me for *me*, not for my face and body. Sometimes I wish I'd been born ugly."

Fearful that she'd exposed herself, she tossed her head and laughed. "But then, who can argue with gorgeous?"

Margaret stared at her openmouthed. "You don't like your looks? I had no idea."

"You misunderstood. Who wouldn't want big eyes and pouty lips, these breasts and this behind?" She thrust out her chest, magnificent in a blue tank top, and pointed to her tush, equally fabulous in snug little shorts.

But she couldn't fool Margaret.

"If you want a man to like you for yourself, you should stop with the I'm-easy clothes and sex kitten behavior."

They were treading on dangerous ground here. Quincy frowned. "Don't try to change the subject, Mags. We were talking about the flowers Bruce sent you. Admit it, you liked seeing them when you first opened your eyes because they made you think of him. Since he isn't in your bed or anything."

"My name is Margaret." Her sister's head lifted like a snob and a half. "And I am not interested in Bruce Cropper."

"Cropper, huh? Hmm. Mags Cropper. Has a nice ring to it."

"Knock it off, Quincy."

"God you're funny when you get all high and mighty."

"Sometimes you are such a bitch."

That stung. Quincy widened her smile. "That's me, Miss Bitch."

"Can't you ever be serious?"

"I guess not. Bet I made you forget that hangover though, huh?" Feigning indifference, she stretched. "I think I'll head downstairs for another cup of coffee and put an ad in the paper for our garage sale."

As she strutted out of the room, careful to put extra swing into her walk, Margaret's glare burned her.

Barreling her shopping cart down the aisle of the local Wal-Mart, Rose headed for the packaging supplies aisle. She hadn't been gone long, dropping off Suzette at the mortuary and coming straight here, but there was still so much to do at the house and she was anxious to get back.

No doubt by now Margaret was up. Oddly out of character, she'd slept in while Quincy had awakened shortly after Rose. But then, Margaret had drunk the most last night. Since Rose had stopped after dinner she wasn't the slightest bit hungover. But she *was* tired. She wasn't sleeping well.

Small wonder, given all that was going on and so much to think about. Tomorrow's funeral, emptying the house, the mostly bleak memories and stories she and her sisters had shared. Last night Rose had felt closer to them than she had in a long time. Not that she trusted either one. But she'd never realized that Susan had treated them equally badly, only in different ways. They had that in common, along with the need to needle and pick at one another.

Rose hated that. She hated fighting, period, though lately her behavior proved otherwise. She and Danny were always arguing. Her heart contracted and her stomach knotted. *Don't think about Danny. Get the boxes.*

She knew exactly where they were. Maneuvering around several shoppers she chose the largest boxes: flat, six to a package. There were only three packs left, and she stuffed them all into her cart. They stuck up so that she could hardly see in front of her. The trash bags were on a different aisle and she moved that way, her wayward thoughts returning to her husband.

Danny had called last night with his travel information. By the time he landed, picked up his rental car, and drove over, he guessed he'd arrive around dinnertime. Once they exhausted that subject, the conversation had turned awkward and stilted. As if they were strangers.

It had only been two days since Rose had seen him, but she felt years distant. She wasn't sure she wanted him here at all.

Maybe they *should* separate. But the mere idea made her feel sick, and she went cold with apprehension. Shuttering her mind against further thought, she reached the garden supplies aisle and the jumbo lawn bags.

She paid no attention to the people milling around her until a woman with a young child in her cart wheeled to a stop beside her.

"Rose Lansing? Is it really you?"

She recognized the woman right away—Camille Suarez, who had gone to grade and high school with her. They'd never been good friends, but weren't enemies, either.

"It's Abbott now," Rose said, forcing a smile. "Hello, Camille."

"I'm not Suarez anymore, either. Remember Al Mooney? We got married seven years ago. I heard about your mom. I'm so sorry."

The sympathetic look on her face was all Rose needed. The tears that were always near the surface crowded her eyes. "Thank you."

The child, a chubby little boy with golden ringlets and big, blue eyes, smiled at her. "Don't cry, lady."

Now her heart literally hurt. Would she ever hold a baby of her own? A gaping hole opened inside of her and the dam holding back her tears crumbled. She sobbed openly, embarrassed but unable to stop.

Looking alarmed, Camille touched her forearm. "Are you okay?"

"N-no," Rose blubbered, hiding her face in her hands.

Instead of hastily backing away, Camille stayed and patted her shoulder until she quieted.

"Here." She pulled a packet of tissues from her purse and handed them to Rose.

"Th-thanks." Rose blew her nose. "I'm sorry. I don't know why I did that."

"Because your mother just died. I so understand." Camille dabbed her own eyes. "I lost mine when I was twenty."

Rose wasn't crying only for Susan, but she couldn't tell Camille. It was too personal. "I didn't know. I'm sorry."

"We were best friends. I still miss her. But you learn to live with it, and in time it really does get better."

Rose had missed her mother all her life. She couldn't imagine being friends with Susan. But to be a mother herself . . . She shot a longing gaze at the child. "He's adorable. What's his name, and how old is he?"

"This is Carter. Tell Mrs. Abbott how old you are, sweetie."

"Thwee and thwee-quarters," he said proudly.

"He'll be four in August."

"I'm jealous," Rose admitted. Again her eyes flooded. "I . . . We're trying to get pregnant." Why she could tell a virtual stranger and not her sisters was something to wonder over. "So far it hasn't happened."

"Al and I went through the same thing. Carter's adopted. We got him two years ago from Romania. I read about the orphanages there and had to see for myself. Al and I fell in love with this little guy the second we saw him."

"Was it hard to get him here?"

Camille nodded. "Lots of red tape and some big ups and downs, but with help from the Hope Adoption Agency, we finally brought our baby boy home." She smiled tenderly at her son. "Adopting him was the best thing we've ever done. We're getting ready to do it again. If you want, I'll give you the number of the Hope Agency."

"Please do," Rose said, knowing she'd never call.

Danny didn't want to adopt. They'd argued over that, too. He wanted a child with his genes, period. Maybe he'd settle for a surrogate mother, only that came with huge risks. And anyway, the way things were going, he and Rose would probably separate. She'd never be a mom. Feeling bluer than ever Rose exchanged cell phone numbers with Camille. They hugged.

"You take care of yourself," Camille said. "And please send our condolences to your sisters."

"I will. Tell Al hello."

The sunlight was harsh and hot, and the trek across the crowded parking lot seemed to take forever. By the time Rose reached the car her hands were sticky and sweat trickled down her temples. Squinting despite sunglasses, she opened the trunk to stow the supplies.

The parking ticket in the middle of the trunk was hard to miss. Quincy must have tossed it in here the other night. After she promised to pay it right away, too.

Irritated and glad to have someone besides herself or Danny to be upset with, Rose stuffed it into her purse. Irresponsible—that was Quincy's middle name. Would she never grow up? Rose vowed to make sure her baby sister paid, if she had to stand over her shoulder and watch her write the check.

Chapter 6

No longer hungover, Margaret hunkered down near the coffee table and opened one of the two dusty boxes Quincy had brought from the attic.

"Nothing but high school yearbooks in here." She noted the year on the top one. "Looks like our stuff. I already have mine. Anyone want theirs?"

Rose shrugged without glancing up. "I have the ones I want." She was sitting cross-legged on the floor, folding the flat cardboard she'd bought into boxes. Like an automaton.

"Quincy?" Margaret asked. "Do you want these?"

"I have a similar box at home, under the bed, that I never look through. Believe me, that's a walk down memory lane I can do without."

She wouldn't make eye contact. Their harsh exchange this morning weighed heavily on Margaret. But Quincy should have known better than to taunt her about Bruce, especially when she was hungover. What she couldn't know was that Margaret was raw from last night, the memories and her guilt and sorrow as fresh as a scar that had been ripped open. She'd needed to strike out, and Quincy had been there.

Contrite but not about to apologize—she couldn't without stirring up questions she refused to answer—she closed the lid and stood. "What's in the other box, Quincy?"

"Strings of Christmas lights and an old leather case with some weird-looking tools inside." She opened the case and held it up to reveal eight wood-handled tools, one a chisel of some kind and the rest with silvery blades of varying lengths and curvatures. "I wonder where she got these, and what they are."

"I've never seen them before and don't have a clue," Margaret said.

Rose's shoulders drooped and she seemed less than curious. "Me, either. The high school might want those yearbooks."

She'd been disengaged since coming back from Wal-Mart. Not at all like herself—more like a fragile, wounded waif. A gut feeling told Margaret that the red, puffy eyes and unusually pale face had a lot to do with Danny.

Who knew, maybe he'd called her while she was running errands. Whatever they'd said to each other, it hadn't been good.

Margaret hurt for her sister and wanted to know more about the situation to try to help.

But if Rose didn't want to share, there wasn't much she could do. Still, she wished she could think of something warm and loving to say and do to brighten Rose's spirits.

Of course, she couldn't. She wasn't the warm, fuzzy type. Her talents lay in scientific research. Which reminded her that she needed to check in with Bruce later today. Without letting her sisters know. Quincy'd have a field day with that.

"I wish one of us remembered something about these tools," she said. "Now we'll never know who they belonged to or what they're used for."

Not knowing her mother's history was unbearably sad. Susan had told them so little. Only that her own mother, whose husband disappeared before she was born, had died young and that she'd been raised by her spinster aunt Ella.

"Whatever these tools are, they're in mint condition, and somebody at the garage sale or on eBay will pay big bucks for them." Quincy rubbed her hands together.

"That reminds me." Rose pushed to her feet. She retrieved her purse, pulled out what looked like a parking ticket, and waved it at Quincy. "I found this in the trunk of the car. You weren't planning on paying it after all, were you?"

"So-ry." Quincy took the ticket with reluctance. "I must have dropped it."

Or she was too broke to pay it. Margaret stifled a snort of disapproval. What mess had she gotten into *this* time?

"You dropped it. Right," Rose said, crossing her arms. "Just get out your checkbook and pay the damned thing."

"Yes, ma'am." Quincy stuffed it into her pocket. "Oh, and *I* just remembered something, too. While you were out, Rose, and Margaret was in the shower, Leonard Bushell called. Susan will be ready for viewing in the morning before the service." She sucked on her bottom lip. "Do we want to 'view' her?"

"I do," Margaret said.

"Me, too." Her face pinched, Rose wandered toward the leather case, picked it up, and absently ran her fingers over its smoothness.

"Then I guess I'll go, too." The doorbell chimed. Quincy glanced at Rose. "Maybe that's Danny."

"Dear God, not yet," Rose pleaded, dropping the case onto the table to hug herself. "I'm not ready."

Her desperate expression tore at Margaret's heart. Right then and there she made up her mind to stick close by when the man showed up. "It's way too early for Danny," she soothed, "but if by some miracle he's here we'll put him to work. There's enough trash for several trips to the dump."

"Or if you want, we can take *him* to the dump and leave him there," Quincy cracked, her teasing tone at odds with her worried frown.

"Stay put, Rose." Margaret picked her way past boxes and trash bags. At the door she peered through the peephole. "It's Fiona."

A shaky breath rushed from Rose's lips and she sank onto a chair.

"Hello, Fiona." Margaret unlocked the latch and opened the screen. "Come on in."

Wearing a yellow blouse, matching yellow skirt, and the same straw hat as before, Fiona blew through the door with a blast of heat. "I stopped by to see how you're doing and say hi to your sisters. Why on earth would you lock the door?" She pulled off her hat and set it on the back of the sofa.

"We have a lot to do, that's why. Hi, Fiona." Quincy flashed her teeth. "That's a sharp hat and outfit."

"Thank you, Quincy."

"It's been a long time," Rose murmured with a weak smile.

As she had the other day, Fiona opened her arms. "Come to Fiona, darlings."

And as before, all eyes were wet when the women let go of each other.

"Crying is good for the soul," Fiona said, sniffing. "How're you all doing?"

Between the emotional turmoil of losing their mother, living under the same roof with sisters who didn't understand each other and never would, and taking apart the entire house in record time . . . Margaret glanced at her somber-faced sisters and assumed her role as spokesperson. "We're managing as best we can."

Fiona glanced around at the chaos. "My land, you certainly have been busy."

"And we still have so much to do. It's slow going, but somehow we'll empty the house by Sunday." The day they were leaving.

Quincy nodded. "We're hosting a two-day garage sale that starts Friday. I placed the ad this morning. We hope to sell it all, but anything left will go to charity."

"I don't know how you'll get it all done." Fiona gave her head a doubtful shake. "Couldn't you stay longer?"

"No—"

"Can't—"

"Not possible—"

Margaret and her sisters replied rapidly and at the same time, for once all in agreement.

"I understand," Fiona said, but she looked disappointed. "You're busy women with your own lives. I'm happy to step in and tie up any loose ends for you."

"That'd be wonderful," Margaret said. "In case you're interested, Susan will be 'on view' at the mortuary before the funeral tomorrow. Please pass the word."

"I certainly will. That reminds me, did you see the nice obituary in this morning's paper?"

Bushell's Mortuary had handled the death notice. Margaret hadn't so much as glanced at the paper and neither had her sisters. They shook their heads.

"I thought not." Slipping a hand inside her purse, Fiona extracted three laminated sheets. "I made a copy for each of you."

The obituary was short and to the point, listing Susan's birth date and place of birth and her various jobs. Also included were brief references to Glory, Margaret, and her sisters. The piece ended with the time, date, and location of the service, which was open to all.

While Margaret and her sisters read, Fiona wandered toward the boxes on the coffee table. She picked up the leather case. "Goodness me, I haven't seen this in nearly thirty years. I thought your mother gave it away long ago."

"It was in the attic, along with that box of yearbooks," Quincy said. "What's it for?"

Margaret hefted the boxes off the sofa and onto the floor so Fiona could sit down. "We're fresh out of wine," she said, relieved despite her earlier hangover that she and her sisters had polished off the last of Susan's supply. "But we can make a pot of coffee or mix some iced tea."

Fiona dropped her purse and sat. "Since I don't want to take too much of your time, I won't be staying long enough for coffee. And I don't drink tea. How about a glass of ice water?"

"Coming right up," Rose said. "Don't say a word until I get back." She scurried toward the kitchen.

Fiona's arrival had worked wonders on Rose's desolate mood. A fresh face, or was it simply that the company of her sisters depressed her? Given that they weren't close and didn't get along, probably the latter. Margaret told herself she didn't care, that soon enough they'd all head back to their respective lives and not see each other again for ages. But the thought left her feeling empty and sad.

"Are those yearbooks?" Fiona dug into the box on the table. "I love those things." She pulled out the annuals and piled them on the already crowded table. "I knew it!" she said as she grabbed the one on the very bottom. "This is from your mother's and my senior year."

"Susan's yearbook?" Quincy reached for it. "Give that here. I want to see Glory." She settled into a chair and opened it.

"You'll want to see your mother and me, too," Fiona said as she cast a wistful glance at the book in Quincy's hands. "And my Jerry, may God rest his soul."

"Yes, but we know what you look like," Margaret said. There were no family pictures of Glory in the house, and she could barely remember him. Eager for a look, she leaned over Quincy's shoulder while Quincy leafed through the pages.

"Look what Fiona found," Quincy murmured as Rose returned with the water. "Susan and Glory's senior yearbook."

"Let me see."

Rose quickly handed Fiona her water, then squeezed in beside Quincy.

Margaret continued to look over their shoulders, impatience making her pushy. "Hurry up and find the senior pictures, Quincy."

"That's what I'm trying to do." Her sister paused to frown up at her. "They're not in the same place ours were—"

"There he is!" Rose said, pointing. "I had no idea he was so handsome."

Margaret hadn't, either. The impish gleam in his eyes and the dimple in his cheek reminded her of someone. She glanced at her youngest sister. "You look like him, Quincy."

"I do not."

"Yes, you do," Fiona said, leaning forward to peer at the picture. "Read what it says under his picture."

"'Voted sexiest man in his class, Glory Lansing plans to travel the world and seek his fortune, whatever it may be. Hobbies: woodcarving and girls.'"

"Woodcarving?" Margaret gestured at the tools on the coffee table. "Were those Glory's?"

Fiona nodded. "He loved to carve," she said, grasping the case. "I wish your mother had saved the figurines he made after each of you girls was born."

This startling information wiped the rest of Margaret's questions from her head. A dim memory floated into her mind and she sank onto the ottoman. "I vaguely remember a wooden rocking horse about the size of my hand."

"That was one of his."

Trying to recall details, Margaret rubbed her forehead. None came to mind, and she frowned. "I wonder what happened to it."

A pained sigh slipped from Fiona's lips. "I'm afraid your mother threw all his carvings away."

"She had no right!" Quincy cried. "They belonged to us."

"Susan was so hurt and angry she destroyed everything related to your father."

"She shouldn't have." Quincy's lips flattened.

Margaret agreed. But it had happened long ago. There was no point getting upset now. Besides, she wanted to learn more about her parents, not get sidetracked on the subject of Susan's destructive behavior. She turned toward the older woman. "The rocking horse was mine. Do you remember what Glory made for Rose and Quincy?"

"Well, now." Squinting as if trying to visualize the carvings in her mind, Fiona stroked her chin. "I believe Rose's was a teddy bear. Quincy got a bird." She glanced at each of them. "Jerry's father hired your father to work at his construction company, and Glory worked long hours. He came home exhausted. Carving took valuable time he could have spent sleeping. But he was so proud and overjoyed when each of you was born that he didn't mind taking the time."

"So filled with pride and joy that we haven't

seen him in twenty-six years." Quincy tossed her head as if she didn't care.

But Margaret saw the pain beneath her blasé expression. And winced. Their father had deserted them, and she was partly to blame. Eyes squeezed shut, she pinched the bridge of her nose. When she opened her eyes, Fiona looked helpless.

"I'm truly sorry."

"It's not your fault he walked out on us." Rose's lips curled into a reassuring smile belied by the bleakness in her eyes.

In the silence that followed, Margaret absently smoothed her shorts. If only she'd been nicer that last morning, Glory might have stayed for a while longer. Though it had been ages, the regret and anguish that cut through her were as sharp as a gash from one of the carving knives.

"Susan never told us anything about Glory," Quincy said. "Except that he was a worthless bum who left us high and dry."

"She didn't always feel that way." Fiona sat back and folded her hands in her lap. "At one time she was crazy in love with him."

"Until he ran off with Tiffani-with-an-i-not-a-y." Quincy smirked. "After that she loathed him."

"Yet she held on to his carving tools." Rose looked to Fiona. "Why?"

"Who knows? Your mother was a complicated and private woman. Once your father left, she wouldn't talk about him or her feelings, not even with me."

"Do you think they're worth much?" Quincy asked.

Margaret wasn't certain she wanted to sell them. Even though her father had dropped out of her life long ago and she ought to hate him, deep down she loved him. "One of us should keep his tools," she said.

Rose chafed her arms. "I don't want them."

"Me, either." Quincy stood, picked up the case, and snapped it closed, then lobbed it at Margaret. "Guess they're yours, Mags."

Ignoring the horrid nickname, Margaret caught it. "I'm keeping it for all of us."

"If you change your mind and decide to sell it, you have my permission." Quincy cleared off the other chair and sat down, tucking her bare feet under her. Then she turned a questioning look Fiona's way. "Exactly why did Glory run off with Tiffani, anyway? I always figured because Susan hated sex, but with four lovers . . . boy, was I wrong."

Did Fiona know the part Margaret had played in their father's leaving? Hoping she didn't, Margaret shifted on the hard ottoman. "That's really not our business."

"Baloney." Quincy scoffed. "We're talking about our parents here. They screwed us over and we deserve to know why."

Margaret glared at her. "Personally, I don't care."

"Then don't listen. I'm not saying anything Fiona doesn't know. Susan and Glory were lousy parents. They both deserted us, only in different ways."

Ever the loyal friend, Fiona stiffened defensively. "Your mother did the best she could. She never had parents of her own, and her aunt Ella wasn't exactly warm and cuddly. Not much of a role model."

"You'd have thought Susan would want to improve on her own upbringing," Quincy said, smirking yet again. "Not."

"At least she kept a decent roof over your heads. Did you know she paid cash for this house out of the money she inherited from Aunt Ella?"

"Really?" Margaret saw by her sisters' faces that they were equally surprised. "She never said."

Fiona knew more about Susan than her own daughters. How sad was that?

"No monthly payments." Quincy shook her head in amazement. "What I wouldn't give for that . . . No wonder she was able to hold on to this place after Glory left."

"Please help us understand our parents," Rose said. "I want to know how they got together and what went wrong—everything."

"It's not a pretty story." Fiona pushed a strand of hair behind her ear.

"We deserve to hear it anyway. Except Margaret." Quincy gave an exaggerated wink. "Who'd rather not."

Margaret wanted the information. She also

wanted to slap the smirk off her sister's face, but that wouldn't do anything but divert Fiona from the subject. "I changed my mind," she said to Fiona. "If you're willing to share."

Fiona glanced at each of them, narrowed her eyes in thought, and at last nodded. "I believe I'll have coffee after all."

Chapter 7

Curled into the corner of the uncomfortable chair, Quincy hugged her shins, propped her chin on her knees, and waited for what seemed ages for Fiona to fix her coffee. First she added milk, then she stirred. Then a packet of Equal, stir, then a second packet. Either she was a master at delay tactics or she didn't want to dish.

Come on, come on.

Strange how she felt—anxious and a little scared. She'd always blamed herself for Glory's leaving—one too many children. Or so Susan had intimated. Of course she'd also frequently stated that even one child was too much.

Her sisters were just as interested and scared, Margaret stiff and tense but pretending she wasn't, and Rose fidgety and haunty eyed. Which wasn't all that different from before Fiona showed up. Things with Danny must be worse than ever. Quincy was plenty worried and would personally strangle the man if he hurt her sister in any way.

At last Fiona set her spoon on her saucer and cleared her throat. Quincy let out a breath and swore she heard her sisters do the same.

"Your parents met their senior year of high school, when Glory's family—no brothers and sisters, just him and his parents—moved to Shadow Falls. As you saw by his senior picture, he was a real looker. Also a star athlete. Those two things made him instantly popular. Boys wanted to be his friend, and every girl in school fantasized about him. Not me, as by then Jerry and I were going steady and talking marriage, but certainly your mother."

Fiona paused to sip her coffee, leaving Quincy hungry for more. Luckily she didn't have to wait long.

"Susan was absolutely tongue-tied around him, unable even to say hello. Of course with so many kids always crowded around, he never noticed her. We were on the way to homeroom one morning when he sauntered past, for once alone, and smiled. She was so flustered, she dropped an armful of books. Her face turned red as a tomato." Smiling into space, Fiona shook her head. "I thought for sure she'd fall to the floor and die.

"Glory thought she was cute. He sat with her at lunch that day and when school let out, walked her to the bus. When he called that evening, she was over the moon. She'd never been part of the cool crowd and here she was, involved with the most popular boy in school." Clearly lost in memories, Fiona smiled. "You can imagine."

Quincy could. Appearances always had been important to Susan—far more important than her daughters.

"I know you girls never met Aunt Ella, but she must've been eighty at the time, and stern and strict as they come. Land." Fiona laid her palm over her bosom and shook her head. "Anyway, your mother didn't date because Aunt Ella didn't think any of the boys were good enough. But Glory wowed the old bat with his charm. She liked him so much, she actually encouraged your mother to go out with him and filled her head with thoughts of marriage and settling down.

"Of course, Glory was never interested in either. As it says in the yearbook, he wanted to travel the world with a backpack, using his charm to get by. Your mother invited him to the autumn tolo. Since Jerry was on the football team, too, and he and Glory were friends, we double-dated to that dance, the first of many more double dates."

"So they went steady, like you and Jerry," Margaret said.

"No." Fiona shook her head. "Your mother would've, only Glory never asked. From the start he told her he wasn't interested in long-term relationships and that once he graduated, he was leaving. But he wasn't seeing anyone else, and your mother figured she'd change his mind and eventually get him to marry her. Around Christmas he started to get restless. She didn't want to lose him, so she slept with him."

Quincy had done the same with Jeff Murdock, also a quarterback, in her mother's very bed. This apple hadn't fallen far from the tree—a thought that spooked her. She hated that she was like her mother in any way. Shoving the thought aside, she quipped, "It's a well-known fact that the way to a man's heart is between a woman's thighs."

Groaning, Margaret covered her face with her hands.

Rose grimaced as if she smelled rotting garbage. "I still can't picture my mother having sex."

"Well she did, and it worked. Glory stayed with her." Fiona slurped more coffee. "That spring she got pregnant. She'd told him she was on the pill, you see, but she'd lied. Glory was livid. I remember Jerry taking him to a tavern out of town that didn't check ID and the two of them getting stinko drunk over it.

"Glory didn't want to get married, and for a while we didn't think he would. But when his parents relocated to some other town right after graduation he did the honorable thing and stayed behind. The following week he and your mother were married."

Wondering whether she'd heard right, Quincy frowned and fiddled with the huge gold hoop in her earlobe. Rose hugged her waist and looked as if she'd been stabbed in the heart, which was odd. She wasn't the one responsible for Susan getting knocked up.

"You mean they had to get married because Susan was pregnant with me?" Margaret's brow furrowed. "I never knew."

"My big sister, a bastard love child." If Quincy hadn't heard it from Fiona, she wouldn't have believed it.

"That's not quite what happened." Fiona's smile reminded Quincy of the *Mona Lisa,* only Fiona was telling all. "Turned out she wasn't pregnant after all, but she didn't tell Glory until a few days after the ceremony. Plain out trapped him, you see. At least that's the way Glory saw things. Back then they didn't have those take home pregnancy tests you can buy in any drugstore, but Susan swore up and down that her period was late and she truly had believed she was pregnant." Glancing at her cup, Fiona shook her head. "She never did convince him."

"Heck of a way to start a marriage," Margaret said. "If that's how he felt, why not get an annulment?"

Quincy nodded. "That would've saved everyone a boatload of misery. Of course then the three of us wouldn't be here. . . ."

"Glory talked about doing just that," Fiona

said. "But before he could, your mother really was pregnant. With you, Margaret, so you see, you were totally legitimate. Glory couldn't leave her alone and pregnant. To help make ends meet your mother got a part-time receptionist job with Arthur Tremayne, who back then was a brand new attorney. By the time you came along two years later, Rose, their marriage was rocky at best, and Glory was talking separation." She glanced at Quincy. "But Susan got pregnant again, and you were born."

"So she trapped Glory by having us," Rose said.

Meaning that Quincy truly *was* the proverbial straw that broke the backbone of Susan and Glory's marriage. No wonder her mother had fought with her nearly every day. All that resentment, directed at her. It still hurt. She lifted the hair off her neck and let it fall again. "Gee, I feel so loved."

"You were right, Fiona," Margaret said in a somber voice. "This isn't a pretty story."

"No." Rose blew out a heavy breath. "But I still want to hear the rest of it. Please go on."

"Glory started stopping by the Blue Lagoon after work and staying there until closing time. Tiffani waitressed there—that's how they met. She was an attractive, earthy woman a few years older than Glory. A good listener, with no interest in marriage. She shared his thirst for travel. She also had a savings account she'd been adding to for ages, to finance her wanderlust. The day he walked out on you, they hopped a bus for

Seattle, headed for the airport, and flew off to South America with all that money. Or so the rumor mill said. Nobody's heard from either of them since."

Quincy had barely digested this information before Rose piped up with a question.

"Should we try to find him and let him know about Susan?"

"I don't know how you'd locate him," Fiona said. "His parents are long dead, and who knows what happened to Tiffani's mother. I suppose you could do an Internet search or hire a detective."

"It's not worth the trouble or the money," Quincy said, meaning it. She had no desire to see the man who had traded his family for the chance to travel. "Would he even care? I don't think so."

"If he doesn't need us, we don't need him." Margaret waved her hand breezily through the air.

But the longing on her face told another story.

Fiona glanced at her watch. Her eyes widened. "Land, look at the time. I have a meeting with a client soon." She set down her cup and stood, an uncertain frown pulling her mouth. "Are you girls sorry I told you about your parents?"

"Not at all," Quincy said. "It's good to finally know the truth." Depressing as it was. "Does your client want to look at this place? Because we're willing."

The sooner it sold, the better. She needed the money.

Fiona shook her head. "This particular client wants a town house. Anyway, I'd rather wait to show this house until it's empty."

"What do you think we can get for it?" Rose asked as they walked Fiona to the door.

"I'll pull some comparables and check what they sold for, but frankly, you'll get more if you spend a little on the cosmetics. I'm thinking a fresh coat of paint and new flooring and drapes."

"That sounds like a good idea," Rose said. "Unfortunately, I can't spare the time."

"Me neither." Money troubles aside, Quincy refused to stay in this one-trough town one second longer than necessary.

"We'll be selling this house as is," Margaret added.

"If that's what you want. I'll work up a market appraisal with and without cosmetic repairs. Why don't I stop by with it on Thursday, say three-ish?"

Margaret shook her head. "That's when we meet with the attorney. Can you make it earlier?"

"I have appointments in the morning. It'll have to be early evening. I know, I'll stop in around dinnertime with take-out. Should I bring a bottle or two of wine?"

The way they were plowing through the casseroles, they'd probably need take-out by then. "We'll take care of the wine," Quincy said. "Thursday dinner it is."

"Lovely." Fiona settled her hat on her head, then gave them a caring but mournful smile. "I'll see you girls tomorrow at the funeral."

As the afternoon wore on Rose and her sisters kept to themselves, each tackling a different part of the house. Rose worked on the kitchen, Margaret cleaned out the upstairs bathroom, and Quincy took on the pink bedroom. They'd decided they could work faster this way, but Rose was so preoccupied with the enlightening and painful story of her parents that she often caught herself boxing things for the garage sale that should have been tossed into the garbage and vice versa. She wondered if her sisters were also distracted.

Deep in thought, she took the two-step ladder from the utility and carried it to the stove. Until today, she hadn't realized that Susan and Glory were equally at fault for their failed marriage. She'd always blamed Glory.

At least now she understood why she'd felt invisible growing up. Neither Glory nor Susan had wanted her. They hadn't wanted her sisters, either. Susan had tricked Glory into marrying her and trapped him into staying far longer than he wanted, and his painstakingly carved wood gifts didn't change that.

None of it was Rose's fault, but that didn't stop

the ache in her heart. With a sigh she shook open a trash bag and set it beside the box she'd placed on the stove for garage sale items.

She couldn't help but draw comparisons with her and Danny. She opened the ladder and stepped onto the second rung so that she could reach the double cabinets over the stove. Instead of opening them, she stared at the scuffed but clean beige backsplash behind the stove and thought about her unhappy childhood. No child should suffer the emotional abandonment she had, neglect borne out of parents who were self-absorbed and alienated from each other.

Wasn't that exactly where she and Danny were right now—two separate people, more wrapped up in their own problems than with each other? Not much of a recipe for good parenting.

Yet they both wanted children. Desperately. The question was, did they want them with each other? Rose was beginning to think not. No doubt Danny was, too. Maybe separation, something she hadn't considered until she'd mentioned it last night, was best.

A sick, empty feeling filled her chest. Grief for her mother and the father she barely remembered mingled with devastation over her dissolving marriage. Unable to stand her own thoughts, she jerked open both cabinet doors. Dust and the faint odors of spices long past their prime tickled her nose. Rose sniffed. Then she sniffled.

And cried for the umpteenth time. After a while she dug into the pocket of her shorts for a tissue and blew her nose. Then got busy.

In contrast to the spotless, snow-white stove, the spice tins hidden inside the cabinet were grimy and greasy, some of them as old as she was. Rose figured Quincy would want them for eBay. She didn't know for certain, but she suspected that once again, her little sister was in some dire financial bind. Quincy always spent more money than she earned, and the drifters and freeloaders she attracted didn't help. Margaret was the polar opposite. She never bought herself anything, and as far as Rose knew, never had been involved seriously with a man.

Both roads led to loneliness and pain, but so did marrying a good, decent man you were afraid to share your secrets with. Because if you did . . . Blubbering like a fool, Rose blindly pulled tins from the cabinet.

The doorbell rang. *Danny*. Her mouth went dry and she wiped her eyes with shaky fingers.

Given that the walls in the house were paper thin, Margaret and Quincy had also heard the doorbell. Neither of them rushed downstairs to answer it. They knew who it was. Rose supposed they were giving her and Danny privacy. It was the last thing she wanted.

Heart pounding and hands suddenly ice cold, she hopped off the stepladder. She quickly rinsed her dirty hands, grabbed a towel, and dried them on the way to the door, her legs as heavy as if her feet were made of cement. Sucking in a breath, she unlocked the deadbolt and opened the door.

Gripping an overnight bag, Danny stood on the front step. "How are you, Rose?" he asked, peering anxiously at her through the screen door.

"I'm okay." She couldn't quite meet his eye.

With the afternoon sun at his back and his face hopeful, he looked dear and sweet, the Danny she'd fallen in love with. Her heart responded, expanding with warmth. She wanted to reach up and brush the hair from his forehead. Instead she fiddled with the dish towel and nudged open the screen door with her hip.

As he walked through it and reached for her, she recoiled.

His eyes shuttered. "So that's how it is." Jaw tense, he dropped his bag beside the door. "Where are your sisters?" he asked, as if he, too, needed others around.

"Upstairs, clearing out the junk. It's a mess in here."

"Look at all this stuff." He glanced around, clearly impressed by boxes and trash bags spread over the floor and furniture. "You've been working hard."

"Day and night." Rose closed and relocked the door. "If it's okay, we'd like you to take the garbage bags to the dump tomorrow. You'll probably have to make several trips. We're hoping you'll have it done before the funeral, since afterward, people will be stopping by."

"No problem."

"Thank you." Unable to think of another thing to say, Rose shook out the dish towel, then refolded it.

Danny shoved his hands into his pockets and stared at his shifting feet. He felt like a stranger to her, the tension between them an invisible wall.

Rose turned to the only thing she felt certain of—playing hostess. "I've been working in the kitchen and was about to put a casserole in the oven. Why don't you follow me there and have a glass of iced tea?"

While he sat at the table and nursed his tea she turned on the oven. She moved the box of spices and the trash bag from the top of the stove. Next, she pulled a spaghetti and hamburger casserole from the refrigerator.

"How was your trip?" she asked as she poked holes in the foil covering the casserole.

"Not bad." Danny sat back in his chair. Thumbs hanging from his belt loops, he eyed her. "Are you sure you're all right?"

"I said I was."

Turning away she pulled two hot pads from the drawer and thought about telling him what she'd learned about her parents' shotgun wedding that turned out to be a false alarm. But the subject of pregnancy was dangerous, and the tears were so close to the surface. She was afraid that once she started to cry in front of him she wouldn't stop. She was also afraid of what she might blurt out.

Pulling down spices had sprinkled dust over the stove top, and she grabbed a sponge and wet it. "How was the conference?"

"Why don't you stop fidgeting, sit down, and *look* at me, and I'll tell you about it."

As unstable as she was, she couldn't do that. "I'm not fidgety." She finished cleaning off the stove, then tossed the sponge into the sink and forced her hands still. That lasted for all of two seconds. "I'll make fresh coffee," she said.

"I'm drinking iced tea, remember? I don't want coffee."

Rose didn't either, but she needed something to fill in the nerve-racking quiet. "Margaret or Quincy might."

She sent a silent plea for her sisters to hurry downstairs and rescue her. Of course, they didn't. Rose rinsed out the filter she'd already rinsed after Fiona had left. She scrubbed the clean pot. Added coffee from the tin in the refrigerator and measured and poured in the water. She brushed the spilled grounds from the counter into her hand and then dumped them down the drain. The oven pinged, signaling it had reached the desired temperature. In went the casserole.

With nothing more to do, at last she sat down across from her husband. "Now, tell me about the conference," she repeated, trying to look interested instead of sad and confused.

"I made contact with a potential new customer, a six-restaurant chain in Northwest California. Their headquarters are in Mendocino. I'll be heading there after I leave here for a meeting on Friday. If I close the deal it'll mean a bigger paycheck."

They'd need extra money if they separated. "That's great," she said, forcing a smile.

She felt as if she'd been forcing them all day. Fresh tears filled her eyes and she hastily blinked them back.

"It's okay to cry."

Danny's voice was soft and filled with concern, which only made her feel worse. "It's just fatigue," she lied. "I'm tired." So very tired of secrets and disappointments.

"Me, too. I don't sleep well when you're not in bed beside me. It'll be good to hold you again."

His tender smile hurt unbearably. He still cared. If only she did as well. She swallowed.

Danny sobered, reached out and brushed the bangs out of her face. "Talk to me, honey. Tell me what you're thinking."

His touch burned and so did her secret. Rose averted her head. "Why should I? Every time I try, you pick a fight."

He flinched and she felt horribly guilty. None of this was his fault.

"So you're blaming our fights on *me*." He

jabbed his thumb at his chest. "That's funny, Rose. Ha ha ha."

"It's not funny at all, Danny. It's pathetic." And she was so confused.

"What's pathetic is that you won't talk to me."

His stubborn expression infuriated her. Safer to be mad than afraid. With a glare Rose pushed her chair away from the table and stood. "Why did you even bother to come here?"

He crossed his arms. "I thought you might need me—another big joke."

"Ahem." From the doorway Quincy cleared her throat. "Are we interrupting something?"

Margaret stood beside her, one eyebrow quirked.

Rose hadn't heard them come downstairs. Embarrassed that they'd caught her and Danny going at each other, she shook her head. "Nothing. Nothing at all."

She could almost see the wheels turn in Danny's head. *Nothing*. Their disagreements had come to that.

Quincy broke the taut silence. "Hello, Danny." Her smile didn't quite reach her eyes, but she stood on her toes to kiss his cheek.

Margaret did the same, adding, "Good to see you."

"Sorry about your mother." Danny glanced at his wingtips.

"Thank you," Margaret said.

Quincy nodded. Then she sniffed. "Smells good in here. I'm starved. When do we eat?"

"Dinner's almost ready." Rose opened the dishes cabinet and pulled out four plates. "Oh, and I made more coffee."

"I'd like to wash up and change my shirt." Danny glanced at Rose. "Where are we sleeping?"

Or should I check into a motel? his eyes telegraphed.

Rose wanted him to do exactly that, right now. That she didn't want to sleep with or even talk to her own husband made her feel hollow inside. Yet the words pushed through her lips. "I've been using the hide-a-bed in the living room," she said, knowing Danny couldn't sleep there. The soft mattress hurt his back.

"But now you'll move into Susan's room," Margaret said. "Since it has the queen-size bed."

Rose shook her head. "We already had that discussion." She set her jaw. "I refuse to sleep in that room."

"Come on," Quincy said. "We took out everything but the bed, bedside tables, and dresser. You yourself dropped Suzette at Bushell's. There's nothing left of Susan in there. It's just a room with a bed."

"Maybe so, but to me it'll always be Susan's room." Rose hugged her waist.

"Luckily, you have Danny to cuddle with and chase away the heebie-jeebies. He'll protect you." Quincy flipped her hair, the way she did when she was nervous. "Won't you, Danny?"

"If Rose will let me." He shot her an appealing look. "Rose?"

She felt trapped, but what choice did she have?

She'd just keep busy and stay out of bed until Danny fell asleep. That way he couldn't nag her about what was wrong, or expect sex. "Fine," she said.

Chapter 8

While Rose and Quincy cleaned up after dinner and Danny filled his rental car with swollen trash bags, Margaret crept upstairs to call Bruce.

She felt like a little sneak, but if Quincy and Rose found out they'd tease her. When all she wanted was a research update.

The walls in the house were thin, so using an old trick of Quincy's she opened the window, popped the screen, and crawled onto the roof where no one downstairs would hear her. After being stuck inside all day, even the hot, dry air felt good. The sun was about to set, and the cloudless sky was twilight pale. Due to the extreme dryness of the region, there were no mosquitoes or pesky gnats.

Margaret watched someone down the street where the Murchisons lived, watering the yard. This was a stranger. No one she recognized. Mr. and Mrs. Murchison must have moved. On the sidewalk directly below, a couple, also strangers, kept pace with a young girl pedaling a bike with training wheels.

Observing these mundane activities made Margaret wistful. For what, she didn't know. Living in a condo meant she didn't have to bother with watering anything but the flowers on her deck. And though she certainly liked children, she didn't want her own any more than she wanted a man to share her life with. She was better off alone.

Except that oddly, she missed Bruce. Margaret squinted at her watch. It was close to eight. Was he still in the lab, or had he gone home? She punched in his cell phone number, which she knew by heart. She'd always been good at remembering things like that, she told herself, forgetting that she hadn't memorized either of her sisters' numbers.

As the phone rang she caught her breath in anticipation. It rang and rang. Maybe he was out on a date. The very idea bothered Margaret, which was both unsettling and confusing. She was about to hang up when he answered.

"Hello, Margaret."

His brisk deep voice thrummed through her. "Is this a bad time?" *Are you with someone?*

"Not at all. I'm sitting on my deck all by my lonesome, enjoying a beer and the sunset. I almost didn't answer." His voice was deeper, and she imagined him pulling the phone closer. "Glad I did."

Pleasure rushed through her. Smiling, she glanced back at the window she'd crawled through. She could see his bouquet on the dresser, the colors vibrant even in the growing darkness.

"Thank you for the lovely flowers," she said.

"Any time. How are you?"

"It's been hard, but I'll survive. How did the chromatography tests turn out?"

"Pretty well. I had to rerun a few, though."

He updated her on the past few days, answering her many questions along the way. Then there was nothing left to say.

"I should let you go," she said, not looking forward to rejoining her sisters and the added tension now that Danny had arrived.

"I'm in no hurry. Still coming back Sunday?"

"Absolutely." She couldn't wait to get into the lab again. "I'll be glad when this is over."

"I know how rough it is. I went though this same thing five years ago when I lost my dad—heart attack."

"I didn't realize," Margaret said. "I'm sorry."

"It was before we started working together." She could almost see him shrug. "Things may seem pretty dark right now, but trust me, in time you will feel better."

"That's good to know. I'll pass it along to my sisters."

"How are they doing?"

Margaret had mentioned Rose and Quincy a few times, but nothing about the emotional distance between them. She wasn't about to go into that now. "About the same as I am. We laugh, we cry, we remember, and we wish . . . we wish some things had been different."

She hadn't intended to admit something so private and personal to Bruce. But somehow talking on the phone seemed safe.

"I understand completely," he said. "My father and I didn't have the best relationship. If there was a way to go back and change that, I would."

It was almost as if he'd read Margaret's mind. "Me, too, but we can't."

"No, and that leaves two choices—whine about what could have been and live a life of regret, or accept that what was is over and done with, learn from it, and move on."

Sage advice, indeed. "Spoken like a man who knows."

"And then some. I can say from personal experience that the first choice leads to sleepless nights and misery."

Maybe so, but moving on wasn't so easy. Especially when Margaret was partly at fault for driving her father away.

"When is the funeral?" Bruce asked.

"Tomorrow, and I dread it." Facing all those people—including Susan's former lovers—she didn't feel up to that.

"I hear you. But people need the ritual for closure. Somehow the service, whatever it is, helps us accept a loved one's death."

Food for thought. "I'll keep that in mind."

"It'll be an emotional day, for sure. I'll call you tomorrow night around this time and check in."

Because Margaret liked that idea she couldn't let him. "No. I mean, don't bother. I'm sure it'll be fine. We'll talk in the lab Monday when I get back."

"I see. I thought . . . Never mind." His voice was decidedly cooler. "Good night, Margaret."

The click of the phone felt as lonely as the dark night.

Later that night, sitting with her sisters after working for hours, Quincy yawned and stretched. "It's been a long day, and I still have to dye my hair black."

"Black," Rose repeated without her usual disapproval. "That'll be an interesting change."

She'd been tense and subdued since Danny had arrived—even now, a good thirty minutes after he'd turned in. That she was still up worried Quincy and was why she hadn't headed upstairs just yet.

"I think it's appropriate for the funeral." She pulled a strand of red hair through her fingers and studied it. "This color is too wild and sexy."

"Because of your long, wavy hairstyle," Margaret said, "you could pull it back in a ponytail and be done with it."

"That's what *you* do," Quincy said. Margaret

never styled or fixed her straight, dull-brown hair. She just anchored it limply behind her ears. "I like this hairstyle, so it stays. I'm coloring it tonight." She studied Margaret with a critical eye. "You know, there are some great products on the market, including rinses that add shine and body. Something like that would do wonders for your hair."

Margaret hesitated, then shook her head. "Not interested."

Quincy shrugged. "Suit yourself." She eyed Rose. "You can get rinses for dishwater blondes, too. I happen to have some upstairs, if you want to try it."

"No thanks." Rose yawned.

She looked exhausted and sad clear to her bones. "You ought to go to bed," Quincy said. "I'm sure Danny's wondering why you haven't."

"I'm not sleepy."

"Right, and I'm a college professor. You can't hide from him forever," Quincy said.

"Thank you, Dr. Phil. I can't deal with Danny right now." Rose studied her plain nails, then sighed. "I'm too stressed about tomorrow. Boy, am I dreading the funeral."

"Bru—a friend told me that the ritual of the service will make it easier to accept Susan's death," Margaret said.

"Talked to Bruce, did you?" Quincy smirked. She couldn't help herself. "I hope you thanked him for the flowers and asked him out."

Looking as if she wanted to say something but knew she shouldn't, Margaret scrunched her lips tight. It would be so easy to goad her into commenting and liven up the evening. But Quincy was too darned worn out.

"I'm with Rose," she said. "I dread tomorrow something awful. Susan in a casket." She grimaced. "Plus, it'll be weird to meet her lovers. I haven't seen any of those men in ages. What are we supposed to talk about, anyway? Whether Susan was any good?"

Predictably, Margaret put her head in her hands. As for Rose, instead of reacting, she fiddled with the salt-and-pepper shakers in the middle of the table. By her zombie like expression, she wasn't even listening.

Quincy could only guess what was on her mind. "You're going to ask for that separation, aren't you?"

Looking alarmed, Margaret spoke before Rose could. "She shouldn't make any hasty decis—"

Quincy silenced her with a gesture. "Let her answer for herself."

"I don't know." Rose bit her lip, her gaze darting from Quincy to Margaret before it fixed on the table. "I can't talk about it." Her hand fidgeted restlessly in her lap. "Please don't ask me to."

"Fine. Then I give up." Quincy threw up her hands. "We have a long, hard day ahead of us tomorrow, and I'm about to drop. I'm going to color my hair and turn in."

"So am I," Margaret said. "Go to bed, not change my hair."

Quincy and Margaret stood, but Rose stayed in her chair.

"You should get some rest, too, Rose," Margaret advised.

"I want to sit here awhile longer."

"You know best." Standing behind Rose, Margaret touched her shoulder, looked at Quincy, and gave her head a dismal shake.

"I'd wish you sweet dreams, but I don't think any of us will have those tonight," Quincy said. "So I'll just say, I hope we all sleep through our nightmares, because we need the rest."

While Quincy colored her hair she stewed about her sister. Half an hour later, when she was raven-haired—quite attractive with her fair skin and blue eyes, she thought—and sitting in bed, her legs under the covers, she shared her concerns with Margaret. "Rose is as white as these sheets," she murmured. Sound traveled easily through the house and she didn't want Danny or her sister to hear. "And with those circles under her eyes, she looks like crap."

Margaret, who apparently had been doing nothing but staring into space, nodded. "Worse than I've ever seen her," she replied in an equally low voice. "When I touched her shoulder tonight . . ." She gave Quincy a pained look. "Skin and bones. I can't imagine her living without Danny, and I think the idea is eating her alive."

"I agree. They belong together."

"What do you think we should do to help?"

That Margaret was asking Quincy for advice pleased her. "I'd say give them plenty of space, but they have that at home. Whatever's bothering them won't be helped by that. I think we should stay close in case Rose needs us."

"Then we will." Margaret linked her hands together on top of the covers. "Losing Mother isn't helping matters, and after what we learned about her and Glory today . . . Trapping him into marriage. I had no idea."

"Big shock, huh?"

"Huge. It'll take awhile to process. With all that's happened, this is no time to make life decisions. I just hope Rose listened to my advice and takes her time deciding about Danny."

"Hope is a good thing," Quincy said. It certainly kept her going, especially during the tough times. Like now. She *hoped* for a better job, and *hoped* for decent money from the garage sale and the house. "I always thought Glory left because of me."

"You?" Margaret's eyebrows shot halfway up her forehead before she shook her head. "It definitely wasn't you," she said as if she knew for certain.

"Why else would he leave on my birthday? He wanted to make the point that I was one too many. Susan blamed me for that, too."

"Wrong again. She didn't blame you, she— never mind. Time to go to sleep."

Margaret shut off the bedside lamp between them with a firm click. The covers rustled as she lay down.

Blinded by darkness, and not quite ready for sleep, Quincy bunched her pillow under her head and turned on her side toward Margaret. "What were you about to say?" she asked.

"Nothing. What made you think Susan blamed you?"

"For starters, she never said one positive thing, just yelled at me all the time, even when I behaved myself. She never acted like that with you and Rose."

"We didn't stir up trouble the way you did," Margaret said. "Why do you think Susan went head-to-head with you all the time?"

"Because she couldn't stand me."

"If that were true she'd have let you run wild without a word. She cared."

"She had a heck of a way of showing it." Quincy snickered. "An occasional 'I love you' or 'good job on the book report' would have been nice. And a hug or two."

"For all three of us. She wasn't the warm, fuzzy type. Knowing what we do now, I'm amazed she treated us as decently as she did.

Her own childhood—living with that strict, joy-less spinster aunt—must have been awful."

"I suppose." Quincy sniffed, inhaling the smell of her freshly colored hair and the floral scent that came from the bouquet from Bruce.

She heard Margaret yawn and knew she was ready to sleep. But lying in the dark, talking to her sister, was a new and enjoyable experi-ence. Somehow it was easier to be honest in the dark, and Quincy wasn't quite ready to let go of the intimacy. "Margaret?"

"Mmm?"

"Do you ever wonder why Glory never con-tacted or tried to see us after he left?"

"I used to, but I stopped years ago. What's the point, when we'll never know?"

She was right, but Quincy still wondered. "Do you ever think about finding him?"

"No. Do you?"

"I wouldn't mind if he looked me up, but I'm not about to spend the time and money searching for him." Even if she had the re-sources, which she didn't, she wouldn't know where to start. "Wouldn't it be interesting if he showed up at Susan's funeral? She'd roll over in her grave and have a heart attack."

"Very funny. I think we'd all die from the shock."

She could hear the smile in Margaret's voice.

"Her lovers, too. Can you picture Glory con-fronting them?" Beyond the yearbook picture

Quincy couldn't picture her father. Thirty-some years had passed since he'd been the buff, teenage jock captured in the yearbook photo. "Of course by now, he's probably fat and bald, and no threat to any of those men."

"I doubt we'll ever know."

Leaning on her elbow, propping her head on her fist, Quincy tried to make out Margaret's face. No luck. "Do you really think I look like him?"

"You have his eyes and the same dimple in your cheek. Of course, you're prettier."

Quincy grinned. "You have his eyes, too, Margaret."

"I do?"

She could hear her sister's surprise. Even though Margaret couldn't see, she nodded. "They're your best feature."

"I didn't know I had a best feature."

"Everyone does. You could accentuate them with makeup. If you want I'll show you how in the morning. And I really think a brightening rinse would do wonders for your hair."

"I don't know . . . No, I don't think so."

Quincy heard her shift in bed and knew she'd turned away to face the window. Dismissed, over and out. So much for a cozy chat between sisters.

"I guess we should go to sleep now. Night, Margaret."

"Good night, Quincy."

Chapter 9

Wednesday

An hour before their mother's funeral, Rose, Danny and her sisters exited the car in the near-vacant parking lot shared by Bushell's Mortuary and Shadow Falls Church.

The late morning sunlight was blinding and hot as sin, and the katydids were loud. Rose glanced at Danny in his sports coat and tie. "You may as well take off that jacket."

Thin-lipped, he did. They hadn't spoken more than a dozen words since she'd crawled into bed after midnight. Rose knew that was her fault, but at the moment she could barely deal with her own emotions, let alone Danny's.

Quincy stared openly at them. Her hair was black now. Bouncing as it did around her shoulders, it was quite dramatic. The contrast with her fair complexion was stunning. Her black dress, a sleeveless linen thing that while not tight or clingy, nevertheless accented her every curve, was striking. Strappy black heels highlighted her long, perfect legs. Rose was sure she hadn't intended to look sexy today, but all the same, she did. It must be close to a hundred degrees. How did she manage to look cool and unfazed by the heat?

Sweat beaded Rose's brow, and under her suit jacket her armpits grew damp. She'd dressed in a modest, black raw silk suit sewn by her own hand, but next to her sister she felt dowdy. She'd never felt that way until Quincy had pointed out that she dressed as if she were a senior citizen. Well, there was nothing to be done about that now.

"I'm not used to this heat anymore." Beyond caring that sweat ringed the armpits of her off-white shell she pulled off her jacket. "Let's go inside and cool off."

Quincy glanced at the mortuary and paled. "Who wants to skip the last peek at Susan and head into the church instead?"

Rose didn't want to visit the casket, either, but skipping the viewing seemed somehow wrong. "If you don't want to see your own mother one last time, fine. But I'm going in there."

"Me, too," Margaret said, clasping a light-weight shawl. For once even she wore a dress— a black, sleeveless thing as unflattering as a potato sack—and clogs.

She dressed like a clod, yet Quincy never said a word about it. Why did she pick on Rose? Though to be fair, so far this morning she hadn't mentioned anyone's outfits. All the same, Rose felt her censure. She certainly felt it from Danny. Not for her clothes, for her coolness toward him.

He relieved Rose of the jacket and Margaret of her shawl. "I'll go into the church and wait with you, Quincy."

"Um, I think I'd better go with Rose and Margaret."

"Will you come with us, too?" Rose asked, for some reason needing him with her.

"If that's what you want." Stony-faced, he moved to her side.

She saw that he didn't want to do this with her, that he was angry. She'd been the one giving him the cold shoulder since yesterday, so his bad mood wasn't unexpected. But it upset her. *My mother is dead and I need you and you don't understand.*

"Forget it." She snatched back her jacket, then dropped her gaze to her sensible black pumps.

"I will." Pivoting away, Danny strode toward the church.

"That was fun," Quincy said.

"Shut up," Rose muttered.

"Why? I didn't say anything wrong."

"Please, don't start with the bickering now." Margaret moved between them. "Let's say our good-byes like good daughters, then head for the church."

Shoes clicking smartly over the concrete entry, they strode through the doors into the hushed, pleasantly cool dimness of the mortuary. Grateful to be out of the sun, Rose again slipped into her jacket. It seemed more respectful.

Balding, pudgy Leonard Bushell greeted them with a sympathetic nod. "Your mother is in the east room, to your left," he said in a soft, funereal voice. "At the moment, there are no other viewers. I'll make sure it stays that way."

Margaret nodded.

With her sisters beside her, feeling tense and slightly sick at her stomach, Rose moved slowly toward the room. Together they stopped in the doorway. Beyond a single vase of lilies, a few chairs along the perimeter of the room, and the polished wood casket lit by dim lights and flickering candles, the windowless, carpeted room was empty.

From where they stood, Rose could see only the back of Suzette's head and the profile of her mother's face. Her unnaturally still, dead mother. She lost her courage. "I don't know if I can do this," she said, gripping the straps of her shoulder bag.

"Me, neither." Quincy recoiled. "I am totally creeped out."

"Why don't both of you go on to the church.

I'll meet you there," Margaret said, her face ashen and tense.

Rose wished Danny were with her. Why hadn't he realized how badly she needed him? She glanced longingly over her shoulder. As if her thoughts had summoned him, there he was. Now she could do this. "Danny's here after all. Excuse me," she said, separating from her sisters.

She thought Quincy muttered, "Thank God," but wasn't certain.

Rose greeted him somberly. "I'm glad you came back."

"You asked me to."

Grabbing his hand she started forward. Danny dug in his heels and nodded at Margaret and Quincy who had hooked arms and were moving in lockstep toward the casket. "Let's give them a moment."

Rose nodded. They seemed to be getting along much better than usual, and she envied them. They broke apart to stand on opposite sides of the casket, Margaret stoic-faced and Quincy tearful. After a moment, whispering, they headed together for the door. Once there they signaled that they'd wait for Rose and Danny.

"Shall we?" Danny squeezed Rose's fingers.

She sucked in a breath and straightened her shoulders. "I'm ready."

Her mother looked as if she were in gentle slumber, and more at peace than she ever had been in life. Someone had styled her hair and applied makeup exactly as she'd always worn it, noticeable but not overly heavy. Seated at her side and facing her, Suzette presumably watched her with freeze-dried devotion.

Maybe it was the dim light, but the dog's eyes no longer glinted eerily. She, too, looked at peace.

This serene woman was nothing like the bitter, self-absorbed mother Rose knew. Filled with unbearable sadness she squeezed her eyes shut, tears leaking out while she said a silent good-bye. *I'm sorry, so sorry.* For what, she couldn't have said.

Trapping his lower lip between his teeth, Danny pulled a handkerchief from his pocket and handed it to her.

Though earlier she'd slipped a full packet of tissues into her purse, she gratefully accepted his gift. "Thanks." She blew her nose and stuffed the hanky into the pocket of her jacket.

Danny reached again for her hand, but she didn't want him to think things between them were okay now. Pretending not to see, she hurried toward her sisters. No one spoke until they were back in the foyer.

"That was unsettling," Margaret said. Her eyes were red and grief-filled.

Quincy sniffled. "I'm glad we did it, though."

"Are we ready for the funeral?" Rose asked.

"No." Clearly struggling to compose herself, Quincy swiped fiercely at the corners of her eyes. "But since the service starts in twenty minutes, we don't have much choice, do we?"

"You'll be okay." Danny gave her an awkward pat on the shoulder.

Rose appreciated his caring gesture. Smiling at her husband through her tears, she felt more confused than ever. She gestured toward the exit. "Let's get this over with."

The funeral was over. Margaret stood at the head of the reception line—as the oldest daughter, she was first—drained but ready to receive the condolences of the sixty or so people who'd attended the service. She'd cried and so had her sisters, but they'd made it through the ordeal.

Now to survive the reception and upcoming burial.

Unfortunately neither the church air-conditioning nor the ceiling fan were any match for the crowd or the sun beating relentlessly through the gauzy white curtains. The crowded social hall was stifling, and no one had started the condolence line.

"Thank God the service finally ended. For a while there, I wondered." Standing beside Rose, Quincy swiped her brow. "I'd kill for a cold beer."

Rose held her finger to her lips and scowled

through puffy eyes. "It only lasted forty-five minutes. And keep your voice down."

"Why? Nobody's listening." Quincy waved a hand toward the clusters of people throughout the room. "They're all too busy gossiping and wondering what to say when they come through the line."

"How do you know they aren't listening? This is a small town and some people have radar ears."

Here we go again. Margaret caught Danny's eye. He was standing at the opposite end of the receiving line, next to Quincy. He raised his shoulder in a shrug.

Wishing she could go home, take a cold shower, lie down, and not see or hear her sisters going at each other for a long, long time, Margaret dabbed the perspiration from her forehead with a tissue, glanced at the worthless fan making lazy circles overhead, and silently urged people to move it.

"Don't look now, but here comes lover boy number one," Quincy said. "Matt Greenwald may be in his fifties, but he's still handsome. I wonder where his wife is?"

Margaret frowned at her little sister, whose impish expression worried her. "Do me a favor and don't ask."

"At least he started the line. But that's a double-edged sword." Rose gnawed a nail. "I don't know what to say to him."

"You mean besides, 'Was Susan any good in bed?'"

"Don't you dare," Margaret warned.

"Too bad only three of her four lovers showed up," Quincy said. Tom Brewster was out of town. "It'd be fun to compare and contrast all four. We should check out their hands and feet because—ow! That hurt, Rose."

Matt stopped in front of Margaret, and there was no time to referee her sisters.

"You probably don't remember me. Matt Greenwald." Making brief but intense eye contact, he shook her hand in a firm grip. "I'm sorry for your loss."

"Thank you," Margaret murmured.

"Your mother was a friend."

"An *intimate* friend," Quincy quipped in a low voice.

As Matt moved from Margaret to Rose to Quincy, Margaret tensed. If her baby sister went over the line now, she'd kill her.

More people lined up. Margaret accepted the expressions of sympathy while she strained to hear Quincy.

"How well did you know Susan?" her sister asked Matt.

"There was a time when we were close," he replied. "Your mother helped me through a rough time. She was a good listener and a valued friend."

"Was she? I'm sorry Mrs. Greenwald couldn't be here."

"Helen wanted to come, but she's home with the summer flu. She and your mother played Bunko together on Thursday nights."

Bunko?! "My mother played Bunko?" Margaret said to Julie and Bud Avery who stood in front of her. When they looked confused, she gestured toward Quincy. "I just heard him say that Mother played Bunko."

"Susan never played games," Quincy said.

Rose shook her head. "Not in our lifetime."

"Yes, she did," Matt said. "Every Thursday night for the past three years or so. She was good at it, too."

Julie nodded. "I sometimes play. Every time I went, your mother was there, laughing and enjoying herself."

Margaret no more could imagine Susan enjoying herself than she could picture her playing a game. She made a mental note to ask Fiona about that later.

Matt Greenwald moved past Quincy to Danny. The line was longer now, and Margaret lost herself in shaking hands, wiping her eyes, and accepting condolences.

Lover number two, Frank Vale, was every bit as attractive as Matt. He offered his sympathy and so did his wife. Both mentioned Susan's warmth, sense of humor, and willingness to lend a hand when needed. Qualities she'd never shared with her daughters.

Margaret spotted Eric DelVaio near the end of the line. Of the three ex-lovers present, he was the handsomest. His wife was with him, but looked as if she'd rather be someplace else.

Once Eric moved past, his wife leaned fractionally closer. "My husband still carries a torch for your late mother," she murmured without warmth.

"But in the end, he married you," Margaret said. "That's what counts."

As the line dwindled and mourners filed toward the snack table, Quincy squeezed in between Margaret and Rose. "Susan sure went for the lookers, didn't she?"

"You do the same thing," Rose said. "Both of your ex-husbands were movie-star handsome."

"Only on the outside."

"Does this mean you've given up good-looking men?" Margaret asked.

"Just because a man is sexy doesn't mean he's a jerk." Quincy glanced at Danny. "Look at Danny. He's cute and sweet, too."

He flushed. "Thanks, Quincy."

Rose narrowed her eyes. "Don't you dare go after my husband," she hissed low enough that he couldn't hear.

Wondering what would happen next, Margaret held her breath.

Quincy looked hurt. "As if I would," she huffed in an equally low voice. "Thanks a lot, Rose. I was only pointing out that Danny is quite a guy—in case you forgot."

"I didn't. I—"

Time to intervene. "Ahem," Margaret said. "Here come a few more people."

"This better be the end of it." Quincy sighed. "My feet are starting to hurt. My behind, too, since Rose is acting like a pain in the ass."

The last person in line, a tall, slender, gentle-faced man in glasses who Margaret didn't recognize stopped in front of her. "Ira Lamm. I'm sorry for your loss."

"Ira Lamm from homeroom?" Quincy slanted her head.

Margaret noted a flash of interest in her youngest sister's eyes and frowned. This was no time for flirtation. Though Ira Lamm wasn't Quincy's type—not muscular or handsome enough. Knowing Quincy, she'd flirt anyway.

"That's me." Lips curling in an almost smile, he moved toward Quincy. "Hello."

"What brings you here?" she asked.

"Your mother did some paralegal work for me."

"Oh?" She tossed her hair.

They chatted a moment, then Ira held up a finger, signaling that he'd be right back. After talking briefly with Danny and Rose he returned to Quincy. They spoke in low voices.

Then Quincy glanced at Margaret. "Since there's no one else in line, Ira and I are going to get something to eat and sit down."

If her sister wanted to spend her time flirting

with a virtual stranger, it was none of Margaret's business. Like it or not.

"Looks like we're done here," she told Rose and Danny. "We leave for the cemetery in roughly thirty minutes, so if either of you wants something to eat or drink, better grab it now."

Chapter 10

"It's been a long time," Quincy said, searching her mind to remember something—anything—about Ira Lamm. He'd been in the honor society, she recalled, and had been quiet and reserved in homeroom. Beyond that, she drew a blank.

He seemed to know everyone in the room. People nodded and shook his hand and smiled as if he were somebody important. He wasn't shy anymore, either. Or the string bean he'd once been. Still on the thin side, but more filled out.

"Wow," she said as they piled plates with finger food and sandwiches. "Everybody knows you."

"They should. Except for six years of college and grad school, I've lived here all my life."

The mention of college jogged her memory. "You went to Harvard, right? Boston is such a great town. Why in the world would you move back to Podunk, USA?"

"This is where my family lives and where my

roots are," Ira said. "Shadow Falls is and always will be my home."

"Ah." She couldn't think of anything more to say, so she relied on the old standards of thrusting out her chest and fluttering her lashes.

Ira didn't seem to notice, or if he did, to care.

"Lemonade or coffee?" he asked.

"Lemonade, please."

From the sweating metal pitcher he filled two glasses. He handed her one and they carried their plates and drinks to a row of empty chairs along the wall.

He waited for Quincy to sit down before he took the chair beside her. "What are you doing these days?"

She'd never been ashamed of her work before, but for some reason now . . . she wanted Ira to think well of her. Then again, she was what she was, and if he looked down at her, he wouldn't be the first. Besides, in a few days she'd leave Shadow Falls forever, never to see him again.

She squared her shoulders. "I work in Vegas, as a cocktail waitress."

No sense telling him that she'd also worked at half a dozen food-related jobs, including hostess at a pancake house and assistant manager at one of the Golden Arches, or that she'd been fired five days ago.

"That's hard work," he said without a smidge

of sarcasm. Behind the tortoiseshell frames of his glasses his eyes were respectful and kind. "The nonstop hustle bustle, the smoke and the drunks. I expect you're always fighting off men."

"You don't know the half of it. Last week this jerk pinched my behind. The first time, I let it go with a dirty look. The second time, I told him to keep his hands to himself. The third time, I slapped him." She almost blurted out the part about losing her job, but only an idiot lost a cocktail waitressing job. That was one particular shame no one in Shadow Falls, her sisters included, would ever know about.

Ira set his plate on his lap and his glass on an empty chair. "I thought that by now you'd be married to some lucky guy with maybe a kid or two and running your own restaurant."

"I tried marriage, twice, but it didn't work out." She sipped her lemonade and realized she hadn't dusted off her restaurant dream in ages. She didn't have the smarts or the money to run a business. "You remember about the restaurant?"

"I remember lots of things about you. You made homeroom fun."

"I did? Seems like all I did was get in trouble for talking instead of studying."

Ira grinned, exposing straight, even teeth. "You were friendly and popular. I was an introverted geek. I lived vicariously through you."

Darned cute for a geek, she thought, especially when he smiled. "Since I always got sent to the principal's office or earned more detention, living vicariously through me couldn't have been much fun."

"Actually it was very instructional. I learned a lot about not getting caught."

The twinkle in his eyes charmed her. For the first time in days, she laughed. "I could use a few tricks, if you feel like sharing."

"If I told you, I'd have to kill you."

"Better not tell me, then. What are you doing job-wise, Ira?" *Are you married? Do you have a girl-friend?* she wanted to ask, but what if there was a special someone? That would be depressing. Then again, after Sunday she'd never see him again, so what did it matter?

"I run a little Internet business called Applied Cryptography," he said with a modest shrug.

"Oh. What's applied crypt-whatever?"

"Cryptography. We solve computer problems, write code, and build computer applications people use every day."

"Uh-huh," Quincy said, but she didn't understand. "What kinds of problems?"

"Among other things, the kind created by hackers. We stop them from stealing or corrupting data. Say a business needs to transfer sensitive data across the Internet where anyone could intercept it. My company creates products that allow the business to easily encrypt the data before they send it. Then if the wrong person intercepts it, he can't read it."

This made sense. "Wow. And you like doing that?"

"Quincy," Rose called out as she and the graying Reverend Hill, who looked hot and tired, headed toward her.

As usual Rose was scowling, her eyes telegraphing irritation. Quincy could think of nothing she'd done to earn her sister's disapproval over the past half hour.

She glanced around. Margaret, Danny, and Fiona stood by the door. Most everyone else was gone. She bit her lip. "I think it's time for the burial."

"I am sorry about your mother."

"Thank you."

They stood. Ira shook Reverend Hill's hand. He turned to Quincy. "It was good talking to you. I wish it could have been under better circumstances." He nodded to Rose, who nodded back.

Quincy felt comfortable with Ira. She didn't want him to leave. "You're welcome to join us at the cemetery," she said.

"Afraid I can't." Ira shook his head. "But I will drop by the house later."

"I'd like that. Bring your wife or girlfriend," she added, because she had to know.

"Never been married, and at the moment I'm unattached."

Quincy smiled to herself. "I'll see you later, then."

* * *

Rose couldn't get over Quincy's behavior, and as she, Danny, her sisters, and Fiona moved toward their cars she let Quincy know it. "Flirting with Ira Lamm on the day of Mother's funeral? For shame."

The angry flash in Quincy's eyes out glared the sun. "I wasn't flirting. Ira and I were talking."

"I'll lay you odds, it wasn't about Susan." Why that infuriated Rose so, she couldn't have said. But seeing her sister animated and happy when she herself was miserable . . . Rose had wanted to throttle her.

"You bet your life it wasn't. It was nice to talk about something else for a change. Ira's an interesting man. He runs a little Internet business."

"Hardly little." Fiona chuckled. "Applied Cryptography is huge. Fortune five hundred companies hire him. He has clients all over the world."

"No kidding?" Quincy looked even happier.

"Applied Cryptography?" Margaret's eyes widened. "Hassell Pharmaceuticals uses them. I had no idea a Shadow Falls boy was behind the company. I'm impressed."

This irked Rose all the more. "Puh-lease," she said. "Discussing Ira's business success is not appropriate right now. It doesn't look right."

Quincy snickered. "You sound like Susan. 'Appearances are everything.'" She made an aha face. "No wonder we don't get along. You're just like her."

Insulted and appalled that she in any way resembled her mother, Rose scoffed. "I am not."

"Yes, you—"

"Stop it!" Margaret cast an apologetic look at Fiona. "I'm sorry you and Danny have to hear my sisters acting like children."

"No need to apologize, Maggie," Fiona said. "I consider myself family."

Rose waited for Margaret to correct her about the nickname, but Margaret didn't.

Their rental car was a dozen feet away. "I've been in this family four years now." Danny glanced at Rose. "My wife is always mad at somebody. I'm glad that for once it's not me."

Was that true? Shouldn't Danny be sticking up for her instead of embarrassing her? *You want mad, Danny, you've got it*. Fuming, Rose raised her chin. When he tried to take her arm, she jerked away.

Near the parking lot exit an officer on a motorcycle waited beside the hearse. Several cars were lined up, but they'd left a space for the family.

Danny unlocked the car and opened all the doors to air it out.

"Where's your car, Fiona?" Rose asked.

"Over there." Fiona gestured at her silver BMW across the lot.

"Would you like me to come with you?" she

asked, thinking she'd rather not be around Danny, Margaret, or Quincy.

She kept her gaze on Fiona, but felt her family's shock.

Now who was worried about appearances?

Fiona shook her head. "You belong with your husband and sisters. I'll see you there."

Some thoughtful soul had set a canvas canopy over the burial plot and beyond, protecting Rose, her family, and the few people who showed up from the sun. But not the harsh heat. Tears mingling with sweat, Rose clasped the shovel handle with her sisters.

The three of them holding it together was awkward. They dropped the first scoop of dirt onto their mother's casket, then set down the shovel. Rose claimed her purse from Fiona. She hadn't let Danny hold it for her because she still was seething over what he'd said. She wasn't always angry. She wasn't! Nor would she forgive him. Ignoring his puzzled gaze she bowed her head for the final prayer.

"May your rest be this day in peace, and your dwelling place in the Paradise of God," Reverend Hill read.

Words that should have comforted. But Rose was too angry for comfort.

"Amen," she murmured with everyone else.

Then it was over.

They thanked Reverend Hill, Margaret

handing him a check for his services. Then they thanked the rest of the people who had come and invited them over later. Finally they took turns hugging Fiona, who promised to drop by, too.

Danny and Rose's sisters turned and headed toward the car, which Danny had parked under a shade tree. One of the few things he'd done right today.

Shading her eyes with her hand, Rose trailed them.

"I'll ride in back with Quincy," she offered, leaving Margaret to sit beside Danny.

The air-conditioning bathed the car in cool air. As Danny drove toward the house, Rose settled against the seat and closed her eyes. "I'm so glad it's over."

"It was rough," Quincy agreed. "I'm completely exhausted."

"So am I." Margaret sighed. "What an ordeal."

"You all did great," Danny said.

Group praise came easily to him. Would it kill him to say something nice about *her*? Just once? Rose opened her eyes and glared at the back of his head. He used to, but lately . . . Fresh anger burned through her and her whole body tightened.

"I'd kill for a nap," Quincy said. "I'd even settle for packing more stuff. Instead we're stuck with visitors the rest of the day."

"Maybe it's for the best, to keep our minds

occupied." Rose knew exactly how to do that—stay busy. "As soon as we get home, I'll brew the coffee, make up a batch of fresh iced tea, and slice up some of the pies and cakes."

"Okay," Quincy said. "I'll push the boxes against the wall so there's space for people to move around. We should've done that earlier, but who had the time?"

"I'll help," Margaret offered.

Danny glanced at Rose in the rearview mirror. "What do you want me to do?"

"Go to hell, for all I care."

The instant the words left her lips she regretted them. Margaret gasped. Quincy's brows shot up. Danny stiffened.

"I apologize, everyone," Rose said. "This day has been harder than I thought."

"Apparently." Quincy pulled a nail file from her purse and buffed a nail.

Margaret swiveled in her seat to look at her. "You don't owe me an apology, you owe Danny." She cut her gaze toward him before turning around again.

Rose chewed her bottom lip. "You're right. You didn't deserve that, Danny."

He shrugged and remained silent, but the car zoomed forward, as if he couldn't wait to get to Susan's and away from Rose.

She felt like a witch. Quincy had been right, she *was* a lot like their mother. Filled with self-loathing, she wrapped her arms around her waist. Tears blurred her vision.

If only she had a baby to love. She'd be happy then.

Please give me a baby, she silently begged the universe. *If you give me a baby, I'll change.* She would. Starting right now.

With her fingers she dried her eyes. "Danny? I truly am sorry."

"I heard you the first time." His shoulders looked as wooden as his voice sounded, and she knew she wasn't forgiven.

Quincy knew it, too. She aimed a pitying look at Rose. Margaret said nothing, but her stiff spine spoke volumes. None of them thought much of her or her apology. Neither did Rose.

It wasn't fair to Danny to be saddled with her. He deserved a woman who loved him and could give him a baby. She swallowed a sob.

It was time to take action. Tonight when they were alone she would ask him for a separation.

Chapter 11

Any minute now, people would start arriving to pay their respects. Her thoughts flitting between straightening up and the hostilities between Rose and Danny, Margaret pushed a box into the coat closet. "Someone has to talk to Rose," she told Quincy in a low voice that Rose, who was bustling around in the kitchen, couldn't hear. "The way she treated Danny today . . . nasty."

"The worst." Quincy stacked a box on top of another along the wall. "I wouldn't treat cow dung that badly. She said she was thinking about a separation. Maybe this is her way of forcing Danny to leave."

Margaret hoped not. "I don't know why she can't *talk* to him instead. I hate that their marriage is falling apart."

"I know." Her sister blew the hair out of her eyes, then grabbed another box. "They were the one couple I always figured would make it."

"Between Mother's death and clearing out the house, she can't be thinking straight." Margaret certainly wasn't. With mood swings and crying jags, she hardly recognized herself. "I wish we didn't have to empty the house or stack these boxes." She wiped her hands on her denim skirt—she and Quincy both had changed—then hefted another box. "I wish Susan hadn't died."

"If wishes were dollars, I'd be a gazillionaire. What I could do with a gazillion dollars . . ."

Light footsteps warned that Rose was headed for the living room. Unlike Margaret and Quincy, she was still in her suit, jacket and all.

"The coffee's brewing, the tea's cooling in the refrigerator, and the cakes and pies are sliced and arranged on serving trays. Where's Danny?"

"We sent him out to buy wine and beer," Margaret said. "People are sure to want it."

"Ah."

With that little word the starch left her spine. Suddenly she seemed small and frail and sad.

It was hard not to feel her pain. Harder still to realize there was nothing Margaret could do to make her feel better. Except sympathize. "Poor you," she said. "I'm so sorry—"

"I don't want your pity." Rose enunciated each word through gritted teeth. "I'll be all right."

"Sure you will," Quincy muttered. "What you

and Danny need is a private, no bullcrap talk. Not when you get back to Sacramento, but here and now."

Margaret agreed. "Once all the guests leave, Quincy and I will go out and give you some privacy."

"I'd appreciate that," Rose said. "For what I'll be saying, we should be alone." Her unhappy gaze dropped to her feet.

"So you *are* going to ask for a separation." Quincy darted an anxious glance at Margaret, and Margaret understood she wanted her to do something.

She cleared her throat. "As I said before, this is no time for big decisions. Wouldn't it be best to let your feelings settle?"

"We all know it's too late for that. You heard what I said in the car. I told my husband to go to hell." Rose made a harsh sound, a cry without tears.

"You were distraught," Margaret said.

Quincy nodded. "And exhausted. Anybody could've blurted out those words."

"That's no excuse." Rose's eyes filled. "Please, can we drop it? Any minute, people will start showing up." Visibly pulling herself together, she blinked and glanced around. "Thanks for moving some of the boxes. This place looks much neater." She nodded at the blank space above the mantel. "And without the knickknacks and Suzette's portrait, a whole lot emptier."

"Everyone knows we're leaving Sunday and getting ready to sell the place," Margaret said. "They'll understand."

"But hey, if it bothers you, Rose, we *could* rehang the portrait." Quincy's mouth quirked, and Margaret figured she was trying to lighten their moods. "Since Danny hasn't taken it to the dump yet. It's propped on the side of the house with the rest of the trash."

"No—"

"Absolutely not—"

Rose and Margaret spoke at the same time.

Quincy grinned. "Just testing." She glanced at her watch. "It's almost two. I wonder when they'll start showing up?"

"Any minute now," Margaret said. "We could pack a box or two while we wait."

"You're a slave driver, you know that?" Quincy crossed her arms. "Hell, no. After the day we've had so far, I say we relax." She perched on the newly cleared coffee table.

Margaret would've chosen the sofa, a chair, or the ottoman. Not Quincy. And those emerald green, low-rider shorts and the skin-tight belly top that left her navel exposed? Inappropriate and shameful. Margaret pursed her lips. She caught herself and realized both the facial expression and the shrill voice in her head were eerily like Susan.

Repelled at the very thought, she silenced the voice and flopped onto the sofa. "It's been an emotional wringer of a day, for sure. All in all, I thought the service and burial went well."

"Susan would've approved." Rose leaned against the wall. "I was amazed to see so many people. They said surprisingly nice things about her, too."

"They had to," Quincy said. "It's bad to speak ill of the dead."

"Still, a sense of humor? Always there to lend a helping hand?" Rose shook her head. "Those are traits I never would have associated with Susan."

"Don't I know it," Quincy said. "For a while there, I wondered whether people were at the wrong funeral. Why didn't she show us her warm, friendly side?"

"Because we were just her daughters. We didn't matter." Margaret knew she sounded whiney and sorry for herself, but painful and wretched as it was, she'd spoken the truth.

"Appearances were what counted with Susan," Quincy said.

The comment set Rose chewing her lower lip. "Do you really think I'm like her?"

"I don't see it," Margaret said.

"Sometimes I do." Quincy shrugged. "But heck, in some ways, we're *all* like her. Rose worries about appearances. My judgment, especially concerning men, is as bad as hers was. I mean, look who she married. Susan hid her feelings from her own family, and so does Margaret."

Insulted, Margaret stiffened. "That's not true. Susan and I are—were—as different as Seattle and Shadow Falls."

Except hadn't she just heard Susan's voice in her head? And didn't she also hide her feelings? That was how she protected herself from getting hurt.

"Well, for flawed people like Rose and me, all we can do is be aware of our faults and work like hell to change. You, being so smart and all, are already perfect," Quincy said, looking innocent and sweet.

Now she'd gone too far. It was obvious, too, that she expected a rise from Margaret. Not about to take the bait, pretending a superiority she didn't feel, Margaret looked down her nose at Quincy.

"I'm a hell of a lot smarter than you, who never even attempted college. Someday that flawless face and body will sag and wrinkle, and then where will you be?"

Quincy's eyes flashed. "At least I have sex on a regular basis." She tossed her head and directed a pitying look at Margaret that infuriated her. "You can't have that with a test tube, can you, Mags? Or wait . . . maybe you can and do. Maybe *that's* why you're so unhappy."

"I'm not unhappy!" Dismissing her plan to stay calm, Margaret curled her hands into fists and glared at her baby sister. "As for your disgusting, despicable—"

"Hush!" Pushing away from the wall, Rose eyed Margaret and Quincy with tight-lipped disapproval. "We have enough to worry about without you two fighting like children."

"At last you know how *I*'ve felt the past few days," Margaret muttered.

Now that Quincy had unleashed her anger she wanted to keep right on yelling, maybe pick a fight with Rose, too. Except, Rose was right. This was no time to explode. Silently she counted to ten, which did nothing at all to calm her.

While Quincy posed on the table like a pinup girl in a 1940s magazine, taunting her with her beauty, Margaret told herself she felt sorry for her. *That* did the trick.

"You know who wasn't at the service?" Rose said in a determined voice Margaret knew was designed to change the subject. "Arthur Tremayne."

"That's right." Margaret frowned. "I wonder where he was."

"Some kind of lawyer emergency?" Quincy said. "We'll find out when we meet with him tomorrow." The doorbell rang and she dropped the pinup pose. "It's showtime, folks. Who wants to answer the door?"

With her emotions so close to the surface Margaret wanted only to disappear. But that wasn't possible. She stood but made no move for the door. "It's unlocked. They'll wander in."

"This isn't the usual 'hello' from neighbors,"

Rose said. "It's a pay-your-respects-after-the-funeral visit. Besides, since the door has been locked the past few days, people might think it still is. If you two will set the food trays on the dining room table, I'll greet our guests."

Visitors arrived in a steady flow, staying long enough to chat and eat and drink something. For a solid hour, every time the door opened Quincy expected to see Ira. She was beginning to think he wasn't coming. Her sharp disappointment surprised her. She barely knew the man. After burying her mother today, how could she even *think* about Ira Lamm? But he was definitely on her mind.

Shortly after the first throng—Dr. McElroy, Mrs. Overman, Fiona, and two neighbors—arrived, Danny had returned with the wine and beer. He and Rose carefully avoided each other. Quincy hated to imagine what would happen when the last of the guests cleared out. It would be tense in here and not pretty. Partly because of Rose and Danny, and partly because Quincy was spitting-nails mad at Margaret.

The things she'd said!

Quincy was so much more than a beautiful face and body. *Name one thing good about you besides your looks,* jeered a mean little voice in her head. Quincy couldn't think of a thing. Which terrified her. What if Margaret was right?

Quincy refused to go there, and she wasn't

wasting one second thinking about what her tight-ass sister had said. She steered clear of Margaret, but just to bug her, played up her assets big time. The men in the house showered her with the looks and attention she craved, and because beauty attracted everyone, some of the women did, too.

She was standing at the dining room table pouring coffee for appreciative, ninety-year-old Sam Mortimer from down the block when Ira at last showed up.

"Hello," she cooed with a sultry, pouty-lipped look guaranteed to stir his masculine blood.

Ira didn't react, didn't check out her cleavage or shoot hot looks at her legs. His gaze stayed on hers as it had at the reception. Quincy wondered if he was gay, but no. With his expression on the warm side of neutral, he was definitely hetero.

Mr. Mortimer glanced from her to Ira and his wizened face brightened in a grin. "Thank you for the coffee, Quincy. Now I'd best sit down before these old legs give out."

"Do you want help?" she asked.

"What I want is to drop sixty years and court you." He glanced at Ira and winked. "Guess I'll leave that to young Ira here." Chuckling soundlessly he clutched his coffee and toddled back to the living room.

"I've heard stories about old Sam," Ira said. "Back in the day, he was quite the ladies' man."

"Now he gets his jollies by waking up in the morning, or so he said. He told me that walking over here under his own steam tickled him."

"I hope I'm that healthy at his age. How're you holding up?"

"All right." Refusing to show him her pain Quincy nodded at the table. "As you can see, there's plenty of food and drink. What would you like—coffee, iced tea, beer, or wine?" Or me? *Please want me so I won't feel so alone.* In full kitten mode, she angled her head and fluttered her lashes.

"Nothing, thanks."

Nope, he wasn't interested. Disappointment stung, so sharp she wanted to cry. Though she was certain her face reflected none of her inner turmoil, Ira's expression turned questioning.

"How are you *really?*" he asked.

He had the softest, gray eyes. The kindness in them undid her. Tears gathered in her eyes. *No.* She wouldn't cry. Not now. "Not so great."

She swiped her eyes and shot a hasty glance at the living room where Margaret, Rose, and Danny stood in separate groups, chatting with visitors. Her sisters didn't appear to have heard or even noticed her. Sam Mortimer, who was seated beside Doc McElroy on the sofa and engaged in conversation, had already forgotten her. Quincy had never felt so empty and alone, so utterly worthless. Her face crumpled. Fighting an embarrassing breakdown, she bit her lip, hard.

"Let's get out of here," Ira said for her ears only.

Blinking furiously, unable to speak, she nodded, letting him clasp her elbow and steer her through the living room.

"We're going to get some air," he announced.

The room quieted. With her gaze fixed on the carpet she could only imagine her sisters' expressions. Shock, surprise, disapproval? Probably all of the above.

Then they were through the door, Ira closing it behind them. The screen door slapped shut. The late afternoon sun was less brutal than earlier in the day, but the air still felt like the inside of a heated oven. Even so, it wasn't hot enough to banish the chill inside her.

"My car is a few blocks away," Ira said. "We're going for a drive."

Quincy wondered where he was taking her, but she was too much an emotional wreck to ask.

He let go of her arm. They covered the distance in silence, Ira matching her stride. Thankfully he didn't try to make conversation. Their footsteps clicked over the sidewalk, accompanied by the sound of a barking dog. Somewhere nearby, children laughed and called to each other. The everyday sounds soothed and calmed Quincy, and by the time they reached Ira's car she'd pulled herself together enough to admire the forest green convertible coupe with admiration.

"Nice wheels."

"It's fun to drive, too."

He opened the passenger side. Quincy slipped into the soft tan leather bucket seat, warm from the sun but not overly so.

An instant later Ira slid into the driver's seat, which was pushed back to accommodate his long legs. "Do you mind the top down? I'll keep the windows up to cut down on the wind."

She thought briefly about her hair, but decided she didn't care if it got whipped and tangled. "Not at all."

"Great. Here's something to protect that pretty hair," he said as if he'd read her mind. He opened a compartment between the seats and pulled out a silk scarf.

It was a lovely silver color and looked new, but Quincy caught the faint scent of expensive perfume. That made her stop and wonder just how many women had ridden in this car. A jealous pang cut through her. For heaven's sake, she hadn't even thought about Ira since high school.

She pulled down the visor and peered into the mirror. Thanks to expensive, waterproof liner and mascara her eye makeup was still in decent shape. Her eyes were red, though, and her lipstick needed freshening. But she'd left her purse and makeup kit behind. Bloodshot eyes and natural lips would have to do. She covered her head, bandanna style, knotting the scarf ends under the back of her hair.

Ira settled a tweed cap with a small bill on his head. He pulled a pair of Gaultier sunglasses from behind the visor. "These are prescription, but I'm not too blind. You could probably see out of them."

The thoughtful offer touched her. Fresh tears gathered behind her eyes. God, she was emotional. Sniffling, she shook her head. "I'll be fine. You go ahead."

"Okay, but don't say I didn't warn you." He traded his regular glasses for the sunglasses. With the green reflective lenses and the cap at a jaunty angle he looked like a wealthy playboy. "Hope you like Miles Davis," he said as he turned on the CD player. "Buckle up."

As a rhythmic song Quincy didn't know filled the car, he shifted and eased away from the curb. At first the ride was smooth and easy. Then he reached the mostly empty freeway. Shifting gears he rode the accelerator until the trees and dried grass blurred.

"Now we're smokin'," he said, flashing his teeth.

Despite the closed windows, wind whipped Quincy's face and stung her eyes. No wonder he'd offered her the sunglasses. She could no longer hear the music, only the wind. She lifted her face and closed her eyes, and her troubles blew away.

"You look like you're feeling better," Ira said over the noise.

She opened her eyes to find him grinning. "Much," she said, smiling. "Where are you taking me?"

"Someplace that always cheers me up."

Ten minutes later he signaled, slowed, and followed the off-ramp. Quincy glanced at him. "That was fun."

"You ain't seen nothin' yet." Mouth twitching, Ira signaled again and pulled into the Dairy Queen.

Never would she have guessed. She raised her brows at him. "This is what cheers you up?"

He nodded. "Every time. What do you want?"

Quincy hadn't been here in ages. She studied the large menu posted on the side of the building. "The mint Oreo blizzard looks good."

"Excellent choice."

At this time of day—the clock on the dash said it was just after five—there were plenty of parking spaces.

Ira pulled into a shady spot under a tree and killed the motor. He tugged off his cap and laid it on the dash, but left on the shades.

"Sit tight. I'll be back."

She watched him enter the squat brick building, his long stride graceful. Dressed in slacks, tassel loafers, and a short sleeve shirt, he looked clean cut and decent. Not at all like the kind of man she usually dated. She unknotted the scarf and did her best to fluff her hair.

Five minutes later he was back with a cardboard tray bearing two mounded ice cream cups, spoons, napkins, and two glasses of water.

Dipping her spoon deep, Quincy tasted the ice cold custard treat. She closed her eyes and sighed. "This is heavenly."

"You have great taste, Quincy Lansing." Ira's grin faded into a curious frown. "Or is the last name different now?"

"Still Lansing. I didn't want to keep either of my ex-husband's names." She wrinkled her nose in distaste.

"That bad, huh?"

She nodded, then asked the question foremost in her mind. "Why are you being so nice to me, Ira?"

"Because I like you. I always have."

Darned if her eyes didn't fill again. "Thanks." She dipped her head. "I like you, too."

"You know, I'm a good listener. If you need a friendly ear, I'm your man."

He shut up and returned to his ice cream, giving her time to compose herself.

Quincy needed to talk to someone safe. When she once again felt in control, she set her ice cream cup in the coffee cup holder between the seats, slipped off her sandals, turned sideways, and hugged her knees. Not easy to do in the small car, but she felt more comfortable this way. "I do need a friendly ear," she said.

Ira nodded. He wiped his mouth, stuffed the crumpled napkin into his cup, and settled it beside hers. "I'm all yours."

Quincy doubted that, but she'd take what she could get. "You know how some people are close to their mothers?" Ira nodded. "That wasn't the way it was between Susan and me. We hardly ever had a civil conversation. Mostly we fought over one thing or another. The last time I saw her was Thanksgiving four years ago. That was the year all of us—Margaret, Rose, Danny, and I—came home. None of us has been back again until now."

Propping her chin on her knees, she slanted a look at Ira. "Are you sure you want to hear about this?"

"If I didn't, I wouldn't have offered to."

She believed him. "That Thanksgiving, for some reason, which we later found out was because Susan and her longtime lover Eric Del-Vaio broke up—did you know about that?—she was horrible to all of us."

"I knew about Eric," Ira said.

"Well, none of us did. We all thought she was celibate and had been since our father left. Anyway, that November Susan was a complete witch. She picked at all three of us girls until I thought I'd lose my mind. Eventually I blew up at her. We all did. Then we started in on each other. Things were so bad that we never did cook the turkey."

Quincy recalled Susan shoving the raw bird into the trash in a fit of anger. Rose had pulled it out again and rinsed it off, but it was no use. "Poor Danny must have wondered what he married into." She considered telling Ira about the troubles between Rose and Danny, but that story wasn't hers to tell. Sighing, she shook her head. "What a disastrous trip."

Ira offered a wry smile. "Sounds like a real fun holiday."

"It was months before any of us spoke to each other again. I hardly ever thought about Susan and when I did, I'd get mad all over again. But now . . ." She swallowed. "I miss her. I wasn't ready for her to die."

"I can't even imagine." Ira touched her bare shoulder, his fingers warm and comforting. "At least you have your sisters."

Quincy let go of her legs, pivoted in her seat, and sat up. "We don't get along so well. They . . . they don't think much of me." She frowned at a tiny mole just above her knee.

"How can that be?" Ira said, sounding so puzzled that she looked up and met his gaze. "Anyone can see you're a good person."

Hiding her melting heart, she scoffed. "I'm not so good. I've done things I'm not proud of."

"Who hasn't?"

"I never even went to college."

"Education has nothing to do with good-ness."

Quincy didn't believe that for a second. Worthwhile people had college degrees. "All I know how to do is waitress. Tell me one good thing about that."

"It's an honorable job. If you like it and you give it your all, there's something to be proud of."

"Proud?" She laughed. "Cocktail waitresses check their pride at the door." She almost told him about getting fired, but because she still had some dignity, held her tongue.

"You can always go back to school. It's never too late."

Quincy shook her head. "My grades weren't the best. I'd never get in."

"From time to time I teach a class at Shadow Falls Community College. I happen to know that they need students. You could get in there without a hitch."

"Really?" That something she'd crossed off the list of possibilities was now available both excited and scared her. "But I don't live here."

"Surely Las Vegas has a community college or two. You could check on the Net and find out."

The idea intrigued her. But she didn't have the money for school. She couldn't even pay next month's rent. Her stomach twinged at the thought. What she needed was a job. "I'll think about that."

The sun was low now, and according to the clock she'd been gone nearly two hours. "There's still a lot to do at the house. I should get back. But thanks for listening, and for the ice cream."

Though nothing had been solved or changed, she felt happier for airing her thoughts.

"Any time." Ira traded his shades for his regular glasses, collected the trash, exited the car, and tossed everything.

When he returned to the car, Quincy again tied the scarf under her hair. "You say I'm a good person. What's good about me?" she asked, unable to stop herself.

"You're friendly, and you have a heart of gold. And you're funny, too. You make me laugh." His warm eyes crinkled at the corners.

He didn't mention her looks. Quincy found that . . . disappointing. But also refreshing. Hadn't she always wanted a man to like her for who she was instead of for her face and body?

"Thank you," she said.

Ira nodded and started the car. Within minutes they were flying down the freeway, passing the other vehicles. This trip was even more exhilarating, probably because her heart felt lighter.

Later, as he pulled onto Mayfair Street, she

glanced at him. "You're a great guy, Ira. Why aren't you married?"

Eyes on the road, he shrugged. "Haven't met the right woman yet."

"She'd have to be pretty special," Quincy agreed.

The car rolled to a stop in front of the house. There were lots of parking spaces now, likely meaning that most of the visitors had gone home. Reluctant to return to the tense household, Quincy tugged off the scarf, unknotted and carefully folded it.

"Thank you, Ira. This was just what I needed."

"Any time."

He returned the scarf to the compartment between the seats. Then opened his door and came around to open hers. She'd never been with a real gentleman before.

As they strolled toward the front door she knew he wasn't likely to kiss her. But if he tried, she'd let him. Though it wasn't quite dark, someone had turned on the porch light. They stood together under its dim glow.

"Fiona Applebee is coming for dinner tomorrow night," she said. "We're having takeout, so it won't be fancy. Would you like to join us?"

"You bet," he answered without hesitation. He glanced at her lips, then leaned down and kissed her cheek.

The sweetness of it warmed her heart.

"Take care, Quincy."

"I will. Good night, and I'll see you tomorrow around six."

Humming, she stood on the porch and watched him drive away.

Chapter 12

Margaret opened the front door to find Quincy standing there with a dreamy look on her face. This was hardly the time to traipse off with a man and do who knew what, and she resented her youngest sister's thoughtlessness. "About time you got back," she snapped, slipping through both the front and screen doors.

Quincy's faraway expression faded into an irritated frown. "It's not even seven thirty. What are you, the curfew patrol?"

"I don't care what you do at home," Margaret said. "But here, now . . . show some respect."

"Screw you." Pushing past her, Quincy clasped the screen door latch.

"You can't go in right now." Margaret laid a staying hand on her forearm. "Danny and Rose are 'talking.'" Worried sick, she gave her head a grave shake.

"Well, I'm sorry, but I have to pee."

"Hold it."

"I have been, for the last half hour." Quincy pressed her thighs together. "I'd drive over to the gas station, only Rose has the car keys. Could I borrow yours?"

Margaret shook her head. "I left everything inside. I was going for a walk. Why don't you come with me?"

"So you can insult me even more? No thanks."

"You haven't exactly been nice to me, either." But Margaret had started it, and she owed her sister an apology. "I'm sorry for what I said this afternoon. I was tired and hungry and stressed. That's no excuse, but there it is."

"What about a few minutes ago?"

"I'm sorry for that, too."

"Apologies accepted," Quincy said. "But I still have to pee."

"Ruth Adele won't mind if you use her bathroom." Margaret gestured toward the neighbor's bungalow a few houses away.

"What'll I tell her? I don't think Rose wants her marriage problems aired in public."

"That we're out walking and don't feel like going back home."

"That'll work."

They started down the block. While Margaret waited, Quincy jogged up Ruth Adele's front step and rang the bell. Seconds later the front door opened. She dashed inside. Within two minutes she backed out the door, waving good-bye.

Margaret watched her hurry across the small porch and down the steps. Her hair was a mess and she seemed far more at ease than she had this afternoon. She'd probably slept with Ira. It wouldn't be the first time she went off with a man she barely knew. Disgusting, but saying so wouldn't get Margaret anywhere.

"Feel better?" she asked, keeping her expression easy.

"Tons. Ruth Adele wanted me to stay awhile, but I told her you were waiting and that we needed this walk."

They headed forward, the waning daylight casting shadows over the dips and cracks of the sidewalk.

"Where did you and Ira go?" Margaret asked in a carefully neutral tone.

"Dairy Queen. He drives this fabulous little convertible Mercedes coupe. With the wind whipping around it felt like we were flying."

This wasn't what Margaret had expected. Quincy seemed so . . . exhilarated. "You went to the Dairy Queen?" she repeated. "Then what?"

"Then nothing." Quincy widened her eyes. "Don't look so surprised. What'd you think, that we went to his place and tangled the sheets?"

Margaret couldn't stop a shrug.

"Thanks a lot, Mags." Quincy lengthened her stride, leaving Margaret behind.

As much as the nickname irritated her, Margaret bit back a retort. She felt too drained for another fight. She hurried to catch up with her sister. "Your hair's tangled and you're in such a good mood, I thought . . . Sorry."

"I realize it needs combing, but with my purse in the house . . . Naturally you wouldn't know that sex-mussed hair looks more like this." Quincy pulled her fingers through her curls, then fluffed it from underneath. "See?"

"For your information, I *have* had sex, and I *do* know about sex hair." It had been awhile, but Margaret remembered. "I said I was sorry."

"So you did. That's three times tonight, an all-time record." Quincy deadpanned a confused frown. "Are you feeling okay?"

"Ha ha." They reached the end of the block and turned left. "Tell me about Ira."

"You're right about one thing. Thanks to him I *am* in a better mood. It's funny. We never hung out in high school or anything, but I can tell we'll be good friends."

"*You* with a male friend?" Margaret couldn't hide her skepticism.

"Why not? Ira likes me for myself. He says I have a heart of gold." Quincy twirled a lock of hair around her finger, then did it again. "He doesn't even think I'm sexy."

"Then he's blind."

"Maybe, or maybe I'm not his type. Either

way it's nice for once to be liked for *me* instead of sex. Though it'd be nice if he liked me for that, too. You know?"

Not exactly. The men in Margaret's life cared mostly about her expertise and knowledge. As far as she knew she'd never been sought out for her sexual attractiveness. Her thoughts darted to Bruce, who maybe found her attractive. But probably not.

They turned another corner. One more turn and they'd be back on Mayfair. A sprinkler spattered drops onto the sidewalk, barely missing Margaret. She was too busy thinking to notice. She'd certainly never been told by anyone that she was a good person. Of that she actually felt jealous. She shoved her hands into the pockets of her skirt.

"Earth to Margaret? Where'd you go?"

"Nowhere." She forced a smile. "Of course I know what you mean. Do you think he's gay?"

"Ira's one hundred percent straight." Quincy aimed a warning look at Margaret. "You stay away."

"I wasn't asking for that reason." If she were going to be interested in any man, which she wasn't, it would be Bruce.

"Good." Quincy fiddled with her hair again, working her fingers through the snarls.

Neither spoke again until they were nearly at the end of the last block before home.

"Before I forget," Quincy said, "I invited Ira over for dinner tomorrow night."

"Hmm," Margaret said. "Sounds like a budding romance to me. With you leaving in a few days, are you sure that's wise?"

Quincy shot her an exasperated look. "I told you, we're just friends."

Somehow Margaret doubted that. "Right. You did let him know Fiona will be here, and that we're having take-out?"

Quincy nodded. "So, when did everybody leave?"

"About an hour ago. Rose heated up the last casserole for dinner. Unfortunately Mrs. Ingersol's Tuna Sweet Potato Delight wasn't delightful at all. Throw in the tension between Rose and Danny and it was an altogether miserable meal." Remembering, Margaret grimaced. "Be glad you missed it."

"Poor you," Quincy said. "I missed dinner, period. All I've had since the reception is ice cream, and I need to eat something soon." Her stomach rumbled. "Too bad we don't have the keys to one of our cars. We could pick up groceries or burgers. Maybe I should go back to Ruth Adele's after all and beg food. . . ."

As they strolled onto Mayfair Street, Danny stormed out of the house. Head down and stride heavy and angry, he jerked open the door of his car, slid in, and slammed the door. Moments later the engine roared to life. Tires screeching, he tore out.

"Forget about my empty stomach," Quincy said. "Rose needs us."

* * *

Rose had done it, asked for a separation.
Now she sat numbly on a box, her back against
the unyielding wall, while her cruel mind re-
played the whole ugly scene. Danny, tense and
white-faced, his mouth working but soundless.
His eyes glittering with pain and fury and his
big hands clenched into fists.

He was not a violent man, but this had
scared her. Trembling, she'd caught her
breath and braced for whatever might come.
At the very least, she'd expected him to hurl
harsh words at her. But instead of yelling at
her, instead of fighting for their marriage,
Danny had walked away.

Which could mean only one thing—that he,
too, wanted this separation.

Their marriage was over.

It was what Rose wanted. Yet her heart felt as
if it had been ripped in two. Too bereft to cry,
she buried her hot face in her ice cold hands.
Danny, come back.

The door clicked open. She peeked hopefully through her fingers. But it wasn't Danny.
Margaret had returned, and Quincy was with
her. Rose's spirits plummeted further, and she
was sure she would die. She considered slipping into the bedroom and closing the door,
but she didn't have the energy. Besides, with
her heart truly broken, and stripped of dignity

and pride, she no longer cared what her sisters thought.

They moved toward her with hushed steps and distressed expressions. An anguished sound pierced the air. Rose realized it had come from her own throat.

Margaret touched her shoulder and gently squeezed. She sat down on an adjacent box and wrung her hands like a worried mother.

Pinning Rose with an anxious gaze, Quincy, too, sat down. "We saw Danny leave."

"Go away." Rose glowered at them, hoping the unfriendliness would drive them from the room.

Neither seemed daunted or intimidated. They both stayed put, their eyes beacons of love and support.

Deeply touched, she let out a sob. "Danny doesn't care at all. He's g-gone."

Her sisters murmured soothing sounds.

"He'll be back," Quincy said.

Margaret nodded. "Of course he will."

"No, he won't. Our marriage is over. Oh, God." Shaking and empty, Rose hugged herself.

"I didn't see a suitcase in his hand," Quincy said. "Doesn't he have some meeting with a client on Friday? He would've taken his things if he meant to leave here for good."

She was right. Rose dug into the pocket of her suit jacket and found the hanky Danny had loaned her this morning—a lifetime ago. She dabbed her eyes, which was pointless, since the tears continued to roll down her cheeks. "He might come back, but our m-marriage is over."

"No it isn't," Margaret stated with such conviction that Rose stopped crying and gaped at her. "Danny loves you, and you love him. If you didn't, you wouldn't be so upset."

"Maybe, maybe not." Quincy scooted so close, her knees almost touched Rose's. "Even when you hate the guy, breaking up a marriage hurts. Take it from a world-class expert." She rubbed Rose's back soothingly.

Rose's aching chest felt hollow, yet also oddly full with sisterly love. She cried harder.

Quincy's hand stilled. "Look at me, Rose."

"What?"

"I want you to imagine yourself five years from now. Do you want Danny in your life then, or not?"

As upset as Rose was, she knew the answer right away. "Yes, I do. I love him."

"I knew it," Margaret said.

Quincy frowned at their oldest sister. "We don't care, Margaret." She turned back to Rose. "Now that we all know you want him in your life, you'll tell him. Then you'll make up and that's that."

"You don't understand." Rose blew her nose. "I can't tell him."

A line appeared between Quincy's eyes. "Sure you can. Just open you mouth and say, 'I love you, Danny.'"

"Not that, the other thing."

"Huh?"

Rose longed to explain, but she simply couldn't. Covering her lips with her fingers and shook her head. "I can't tell you, either."

Her sisters exchanged puzzled looks.

"Yes, you can. Why don't you practice on us?" Margaret suggested in a soft, cajoling voice.

She made it sound so easy. But Rose had borne her secret alone for so long that sharing it was impossible. "I can't." She squeezed the damp hanky in her fist. "I've never told anyone."

"Maybe it's time you did," Margaret said.

"Because whatever it is, it's eating you alive." Quincy inched back, giving Rose the space she needed, but her eyes never wavered from Rose's face.

Unable to bear her sisters' concerned, curious gazes, Rose looked down and flicked a shred of cardboard from her skirt. Through watery vision she noted a grease stain and frowned. She really should've changed after the service.

"I did something terrible," she at last admitted so softly she barely heard herself.

"Can't be worse than some of the crap I've pulled," Quincy said. "Unless . . . You're not addicted to drugs, are you?"

"Me? Drugs? No way."

"Didn't think so. Did you fool around on Danny?"

"I'd never do that!"

"Charge up his credit cards behind his back?"

"No."

"Empty his wallet when he was passed out and pretend somebody else stole his money? Or call his new girlfriend, who he was seeing on the sly, and tell her he had VD?"

Margaret looked shocked. "You really have pulled some rotten stunts, Quincy."

"I always had my reasons. But I'd bet a year's worth of pedicures Rose hasn't done any of those things." She tilted her head and offered a warm smile. "You don't have it in you to stoop so low."

Quincy's faith in Rose loosened her resolve. "I can't get pregnant," she confessed in a whisper.

"Aha." Quincy looked relieved. "That's not so terrible. Happens all the time. Maybe you can fix it."

"Have you seen a fertility specialist?" Margaret asked.

"No."

Quincy rolled her eyes. "Then make an appointment."

"You sound just like Danny." Rose shoved the hanky into her pocket. "It's not that simple."

"Sure it is," Margaret said. "You pick up the phone and call. Or get Dann—"

Quincy silenced her with a look. "Nothing is

ever as simple as it seems. Is it money? I don't have any, but once I find a new job . . ."

Forgetting her own problems for a moment, Rose gaped at her in surprise. So did Margaret. "You don't have a job?"

Quincy ducked her head. "I left it the same day Susan died."

"I *knew* it was something like that," Margaret muttered. "What's the big secret? Why didn't you tell us?"

With a scowl Quincy tossed her head. "Will you for once be quiet? Now is no time to dig into my screwed-up life. Tonight is about Rose."

"I have some money saved up," Margaret said. "I could lend you—"

"It isn't the money." Rose locked her hands together in her lap. "I-I'm afraid to go."

"Danny'll be with you," Quincy said. "All you have to do is ask him."

Margaret leaned forward. "I have a friend who went through a year at a fertility clinic. You get a physical, a little poking and prodding, one or two blood draws, and some solid medical counseling. Nothing to it, really."

"We have friends who did the same thing," Rose said. "That isn't the problem."

The urge to share her secret was stronger now, but once she told them, there was no recalling the words. She bit back her confession, and it clogged thickly in her throat.

"Do you have a needle phobia or something?" Quincy asked.

"A good therapist can help," Margaret said. "Preferably one skilled in hypnotherapy."

"I once dated a hypnotherapist." Quincy tapped her finger to her lips. "He seemed like a nice guy until I found out he was married. Maybe Rose should let them put her to sleep first—"

"That's silly," Margaret said. "Rose wouldn't want to put herself in—"

"Hello, I'm still here. I don't have needle or any other kind of phobia, and I don't need hypnotherapy." Fully intending to hold on to her secret forever she blurted it out. "The truth is, I had an abortion when I was nineteen. Danny doesn't know."

There, it was done. She held her breath and waited for the ceiling to collapse.

"Huh." Quincy shrugged. "I never knew."

"That must've been hard." Margaret's expression was neither disapproving nor scornful.

Neither of them said anything more. Was this as far as it would go? Rose couldn't believe it. Nor could she believe how much better she felt now that she'd told her sisters.

She decided to tell them the rest. "He was the first man I ever slept with. We weren't in love, and at the time, neither of us wanted children. He paid for the abortion and we went our separate ways."

"That could happen to anyone," Margaret said. "Lots of women have abortions."

Quincy nodded. "Two of my friends have

had several. Not my preferred method of birth control, but hey, as you well know, sometimes unwanted pregnancy happens."

"What you did when you were nineteen should have nothing to do with your fertility now," Margaret added.

"Unless you went to some back-alley hack?" Quincy said.

"I didn't. I was only six weeks along, and the doctor did it legally and safely."

"Well then." Margaret brushed her hands together. "That's not the reason for your fertility problem."

"Doesn't sound like it," Quincy said.

Afraid to believe them, Rose frowned. "How do you know? What if God is punishing me for what I did?"

Quincy snorted. "You don't honestly think that, do you?"

In the wake of her reaction, Rose felt silly for the belief she'd carried for what seemed forever. Sheepish, she nodded.

"If there's a fertility problem, it's purely medical, so you push that God punishment business right out of your head," Margaret ordered with a dismissive wave. "Besides, you've punished yourself more than God ever would. For your own peace of mind, you need to see a fertility specialist."

"But if I do, I'll have to tell Danny about the abortion." The very thought scared Rose. Her nervous fingers caught a button on her sleeve and twisted it.

"Your medical history is between you and your doctor," Quincy said. "They won't tell Danny if you don't want them to."

"Are you sure?"

Margaret nodded. "It's the law. Medical history is confidential unless you decide to share it."

Rose felt stupid for not knowing what her sisters obviously did. "But what if he somehow finds out anyway? I'm afraid."

"What's he gonna do, walk out?" Quincy's mouth quirked. "He just did that."

Margaret scowled at her before turning to Rose and softening her mouth. "Danny's a good man who loves you. He won't hold your past against you, I know it."

"But if for some reason he does," Quincy said, "good riddance. At least give him the chance to stand by you."

For the first time in a long while, hope stirred in Rose's chest. Followed by terror. Her fingers twisted the button so hard, it fell off, landing on the carpet. Absently she leaned down and picked it up. "What if he doesn't come back except to grab his things and leave?"

"You won't let him do that, not without telling him everything." Leaning forward Quincy grasped Rose's chin. "Everything. All right?"

With her sister holding her head and staring into her eyes she couldn't very well shake her head. She blew out a breath. "Okay, I'll talk to him as soon as he comes back."

"Atta girl." Quincy released her.

Margaret gave a thumbs-up.

"Now that we've settled that, I'm gonna eat." Quincy stood. "Do either of you want a snack?"

Deal with a problem and dismiss it. That was Quincy. Rose almost smiled. She felt better, but not good enough to eat. She did want Quincy's company, though. "I'll sit with you."

"Me, too," Margaret said. "Then we'd best get back to work."

Quincy groaned. "There you go again, pushing us. Can't that wait till tomorrow? I'm totally drained."

"We can't spare the time," Margaret said. "Besides, Rose should keep busy. Tonight is a good time to look through Mother's desk and file cabinets for documents Arthur Tremayne might want."

Rose had forgotten about that. Fresh anxiety clawed at her stomach. "What if Danny comes back tomorrow instead of tonight and we're at the lawyer's?"

"Will you relax?" Quincy said. "Our appointment isn't until three, remember? By then, Danny will be on his way to the Seattle airport. Don't worry, he'll come back here tonight." She glanced at Margaret. "If we're not meeting Arthur until mid-afternoon, we'll have the whole morning to sort through Susan's office. I say we open a bottle of wine and relax."

Rose needed to be stone cold sober when she told Danny the truth. "I don't want to drink," she said. "And Margaret's right. I need to do something to keep my mind off Danny. We may as well start on Susan's office."

"That's two against one." Margaret looked triumphant. "Don't forget, we also have a garage sale to get ready for."

Quincy opened her mouth but Margaret cut her off. "And don't say we'll do it when we get back from Arthur Tremayne's. Fiona and Ira are coming for dinner, and who knows when they'll leave?"

Now that Rose was calmer, she was also curious. "You invited Ira tomorrow night?" She waited until Quincy nodded to ask the next question. "Speaking of Ira, where did you two go earlier?"

"Dairy Queen. We're friends," Quincy insisted, flushing.

Rose found that most interesting.

Chapter 13

Two hours later, after emptying their mother's small office closet, one desk drawer, and a file cabinet labeled FINANCIAL INFORMATION, Rose stood and stretched her back. What a day it had been.

Combing through financial documents forced her to focus, and for long moments she managed to push her problems from her mind. Trouble was, they always flooded back—especially when she took a break. Like now. Facing Danny and telling him everything . . . The very thought was so daunting, she felt sick with fear.

The only way to stay sane was keep busy. Determined to do exactly that, she glanced at the fat trash bags piled across the floor. "We haven't found much for Arthur."

"What about the house documents and the safe deposit box key?" Margaret said. "Those are important."

She was sitting on the floor in front of the

bookcase sorting through the books, which were mostly law volumes. "I wonder whether Arthur will want any of these?"

"He probably has his own," Quincy said from the chair in front of the desk. "We should bring him the bank statements—at least the last few years' worth." She picked up the most recent statement and frowned. "There sure isn't much in Susan's bank account. Six hundred in savings and three fifty in checking. She was poor—about as bad off as me."

"Speaking of money," Rose said, "I changed my mind about that speeding ticket. If you can't afford to pay it, I will."

Her little sister's surprised expression was priceless.

"I'm writing the check tonight. But I appreciate the offer." Quincy thumbed through more of the statements. "I know Susan paid off the house, but how the bejeezus did she take care of the maintenance and repairs *and* feed and clothe us without falling into a black hole? Do you think her boyfriends gave her more than sex?"

"Are you implying that our mother slept with those men for money?" The idea shocked Rose.

"Sometimes I wonder about you, Quincy," Margaret said with obvious disapproval. "Susan was far from perfect, but she'd never stoop to that."

"Talk about jumping to the wrong conclusion." The dimple in Quincy's cheek flashed. "I only meant that maybe now and then Susan's lovers helped out with groceries or bills. To be nice and express their appreciation for her company. God knows, there's nothing wrong with a monetary gift now and then."

Something Quincy would know firsthand. Men always had showered her with presents. Rose couldn't help wondering if Danny would ever again buy her a gift. *Please, please let him understand when I—*

"Rose?" Margaret said, and she realized she'd drifted away.

She gave a jerky nod. "Right. Quincy makes a good point."

Judging by her little sister's baffled look the conversation had moved on.

Margaret unfolded her legs, stood, and gently pushed Rose toward the office door. "Why don't you go downstairs and relax."

Knowing Danny could walk in at any time, relaxing was impossible. "I'd rather keep busy," Rose said. "What else should I do?"

"Turn on the computer and check for other documents," Margaret suggested. "Or compose a letter to Susan's clients, in case they haven't heard about her death."

"The only way that would happen is if they lived on Mars," Quincy said.

"Still, it needs to be done."

In no mood to write a letter, Rose turned on the computer, which stood on a small table adjacent to the desk. "I'll search for documents."

While it blinked and hummed to life, she

gestured Quincy out of the chair, then sat down and rolled it toward the computer.

"Once we finish in here, the rest should be easy," Quincy said, dropping to the floor. "I sure am glad of that."

"You haven't finished the pink bedroom," Margaret said. "And don't forget the dishes, silverware, and pots and pans."

"And the junk in the basement," Rose added. "I—" Downstairs, the front door opened. Her mind blanked, her stomach clenched, and her words died. "He's here." She laid her hand over her pounding heart.

"Rose?" Danny called out.

She shut off the computer. Stood. And tried to smile. "Wish me luck."

"Just be yourself," Margaret said. "We'll be up here if you need us."

Quincy blew her a kiss. "Let your love shine through, and you'll do fine."

Rose hoped they were right. Saving her marriage depended on it. Swallowing, she squared her shoulders and headed downstairs to tell her husband everything.

As soon as Rose disappeared down the stairs, Quincy glanced at Margaret. "I don't know about you, but I'm fresh out of concentration. Let's finish the office later."

For once dropping the don't-stop-even-if-you're-about-to-drop attitude, Margaret nodded. They headed for the pink bedroom.

"I sure hope they straighten things out," she said, sounding doubtful.

Quincy felt more optimistic. "Have faith. They love each other."

"That may not be enough."

"This whole mess came about because of Rose's secret. Once she tells Danny about the abortion and asks him for a second chance, they'll patch up their differences and return to the land of the happy people. Then maybe you and I will become aunties. Wouldn't that be fun?"

Not that Quincy would ever *see* the kid. She and Rose didn't exactly visit each other.

"It would be, but first they should work out their problems. Otherwise it'll be too hard on the children."

As they both knew all too well. "They will," Quincy said. At the sound of Danny and Rose's raised voices, she crossed her fingers. "I hope."

"I hate when people fight, and I really don't want to be here right now." As they entered the bedroom, Margaret cast a wishful look toward the window. "We should leave."

"You told Rose we'd be here if she needed us," Quincy reminded her. "Besides, we can't very well flounce downstairs, now can we? And I'm way past crawling onto the roof, grabbing the nearest tree limb, and working my way down. Even if that old maple was still alive, and it's not." She yawned and stretched. "I'm so tired, I could sleep through an earthquake. I'm going to bed."

"I'm not ready yet, but I suppose I could catch up on my reading." Margaret glanced at the latest issue of *The Lichenologist* on her side of the shared bedside table.

The very name of the thing bored Quincy. She figured Margaret would be asleep before she finished one page, but she bit back the comment. *Not tonight, honey.*

By the time Quincy washed her face and changed into an extra large T-shirt, Rose and Danny were out and out shouting. Anybody with halfway decent hearing could make out every word.

"You asked for a separation, Rose, and dammit, you're getting one."

"I told you, I made a mistake! Please, Danny—"

"Go to hell! That's what you told me earlier. Was that a mistake, too?"

The harsh voices, the nasty words were unbearable. Quincy plugged her ears and padded quickly into the bedroom. Margaret wasn't reading—the open magazine had been tossed to the foot of her bed. She wasn't in the room at all. The gaping window and popped screen told Quincy where she'd gone. She was sitting on the roof. Probably quieter out there.

Determined to sleep, Quincy climbed into

bed and pulled the pillow over her ears. Not even the thick foam muffled the angry voices.

Wincing, she squeezed her eyes shut, curled into a ball, and cursed herself for leaving her iPod at home. Seconds later she gave up on sleep, flipped on the reading light so that she could see, and joined Margaret on the roof. Even hours after the sun had gone down, the shingles were still warm.

"I thought you could sleep through anything."

Light from the lamp allowed Quincy to see Margaret's wry smile. She shook her head. "Not this. The screaming reminds me too much of my own fights." She shuddered. "I just hope Danny's sober, and that he doesn't take a fist to Rose."

"He's not that kind of man." Sitting cross-legged, Margaret stared as if she'd never seen Quincy before. "Some man hit you."

"Tommy, but just once." She'd gotten a black eye and a badly bruised cheek, and her self-respect had been shattered. "One of the many reasons I kicked him out and divorced him."

"Glad you did. You never said anything."

"It's not something I like to talk about. Can you imagine Susan's reaction if she'd known? I'd still be hearing about my stupidity, even from the grave. 'Stupid little tramp, you'll run off with any man who looks at you. Why can't you be more like Margaret or Rose?'" she mimicked.

Despite the cruel things she'd said, Quincy missed her mother. "What I wouldn't give for Susan to be standing here, right now, cutting me down. . . ."

Blinking back unexpected tears she waited for Margaret to lace into her.

Instead she heard her swallow. "Me, too."

Once Quincy pulled herself together, she went on. "What I told you? You're the first and last Lansing, and the only person in Shadow Falls to know."

"Your secret is safe with me. You've been involved with some really rotten guys, haven't you?"

This was far milder criticism than Quincy expected. "Just call me the queen of bad taste in men," she said.

Downstairs, Danny's voice boomed. Rose shrieked right back.

"I can't stand it!" Quincy stuck her fingers in her ears and locked eyes with Margaret.

Who did the same thing. When the noise stopped, she lowered her hands. "Once, a few months before Glory left, he and Susan had a huge fight. It was a summer night just like this. We three girls climbed out here, huddled together, and shook."

Quincy squinted into the darkness, trying without luck to summon up the memory. "I don't remember that. What were they fighting about?"

"I don't know, but it seemed to last forever.

Finally they stopped, and everything was quiet except the katydids and us, breathing. I still recall the feeling of relief. When we crawled back into the bedroom, we heard a few squeaks from the bedsprings and a whimper now and then, but other than that, nothing."

"Make-up sex. The best sex in the world. Let's hope Rose and Danny get there tonight."

For once, Margaret didn't look disgusted. She placed her palms together and under her chin as if offering a prayer.

Quincy leaned back on her arms and studied the star-studded sky. "Beautiful night, isn't it?"

"Lovely. I was out here last night, too, but not this late." Looking as if she'd said something she shouldn't, Margaret closed her mouth.

Now that was interesting. Quincy eyed her. "Oh? I don't remember that. Where was I?"

"Washing the dishes with Rose. I needed some alone time, so I crawled out here."

Nothing exciting after all. "It isn't a crime to sit on the roof, Margaret."

"Who said it was?"

"You're acting like you were sneaking out or doing something wrong."

"And you're imagining things. Everybody needs alone time."

If that wasn't a great line to run with . . . Several quips popped into Quincy's head that would irritate the heck out of Margaret. But at the moment, she was too shook up over Rose and Danny to go there.

"And privacy," she said. "Before there were cordless or cell phones, I used to stretch our cord to breaking so I could bring the phone out here. That way Susan couldn't eavesdrop on my calls."

"I've done that myself. See those three stars? That's Orion's belt."

"Doesn't look like a belt to me."

"Well, it is. Follow those stars up and you'll find Sirius, the brightest star in the constellation of Canis Major, also known as the Greater Dog."

Amazed at her sister's vast stores of knowledge, Quincy shook her head. "You know about everything."

"Not really." Margaret's soft chuckle floated between them. "I know a little about stars because I took an astronomy course in college. My real expertise is botany."

"Lichens. I know." The air was cooler now, and Quincy pulled up her knees and hugged her legs. "What exactly do you do with that stuff?"

Her sister shot her a wary look, as if she suspected sarcasm. "I'm dead-serious," Quincy said. "I really want to know."

Margaret's face relaxed. "Right now we're using thin layer chromatography to look for antibacterial properties in lichen extracts."

"Say that in English."

"Lichens are made up of chemical compounds. Bruce and I are analyzing some of the compounds in certain lichen species, trying to figure out which ones have antibacterial properties. We hope our findings will lead to the development of new antibiotics."

"It all sounds so complicated." And so lonely. "You don't have much human contact. Don't you miss that?"

"I'm better with science than I am with people. And I'm not completely alone. Don't forget, Bruce works with me."

Ah yes, the man who'd sent the flowers, and who Quincy was pretty sure her sister liked. But now was no time to tease her. "So you two could discover some new drug, like penicillin?"

"That's what Hassell Pharmaceuticals hopes. They've given us a deadline of September, which is why now was such a tough time to get away."

So it *wasn't* Bruce that had her so eager to get home. "Wow," Quincy said. "I never knew."

"You never asked."

A comfortable quiet fell over them, broken only by the sounds of katydids and Danny and Rose's loud voices. Which didn't sound quite as hostile as before.

"What happened at your last job?" Margaret asked at last.

Despite the warmth between them, Quincy couldn't share the humiliation. "I quit," she lied. "I never have been able to stay at one place for long."

"Why is that, I wonder?" Margaret asked as if she genuinely wanted to know.

Because inevitably Quincy argued with her boss or did things her own way or otherwise butted heads. "I get bored easily." Which was the truth.

"Because you haven't found your life's calling. Once you do, you'll stick with the job."

Quincy aimed a skeptical look at her sister. "You're saying you never get bored?"

"Now and then; everyone does. Mostly I love my work. That makes the routine parts bearable."

"Plus you have someone who understands how you feel about the job—Bruce." Envious, Quincy sighed. "I've really never had that." Most people she worked with drifted from job to job, just as she did.

"It is nice," Margaret conceded, looking thoughtful and a little dreamy.

She definitely liked Bruce every bit as much as her work. Quincy smiled to herself. "You don't have a boss breathing down your back, watching your every move either."

"True, but I'm still working to please the company that hired me. So you don't like having a boss."

"Not if he treats me like a child he can't trust."

"I wouldn't like that either." Margaret, too,

leaned back on her arms. "If you could do anything in the world, what would it be?"

Run my own restaurant. The idea had stayed in Quincy's mind since Ira had brought it up. She stopped short of telling Margaret, though. They weren't *that* close, and she couldn't handle her sister making fun of her, the one with the lowest IQ, for her dream.

That she could share her secret desire with Ira, whom she hardly knew, but not Margaret, said a lot about their relationship and made Quincy sad.

Margaret was waiting for an answer.

"Um, something in the food business," Quincy said, "but not cocktail waitressing."

"You could do that anywhere. Do you think you'll stay in Las Vegas?"

She'd never considered leaving, but there was nothing holding her to the city. "Probably, because it's so easy to find work there." She hoped. "What about you? Are you planning to stay in Seattle?"

"That's where my work is."

And Bruce.

Quincy realized the yelling had stopped. She cupped her ear. "Hear that? The sweet sound of silence. Now we can get some sleep."

She scooted across the composition tiles, then lowered herself through the window. Margaret followed. By the time Margaret used the facilities and changed into her pajamas,

Quincy was near sleep. Margaret shut off the light.

A feminine moan floated up the stairs, followed by a male growl. Followed by the thump-thump of the mattress pounding against the springs.

Quincy smiled in the dark. "Make-up sex."

Margaret sighed. "Thank goodness."

Chapter 14

Thursday

Margaret was up, dressed, and halfway through her first cup of coffee when Quincy padded into the kitchen, yawning.

"Morning. Did I hear the phone?" She tightened the sash, grabbed a mug, and headed for the coffeepot.

Still warm from last night's conversation on the roof, Margaret smiled. "You did. Josie Jessup from Arthur Tremayne's office called to postpone our meeting. Yesterday Arthur's father had emergency bypass surgery in Seattle, and Arthur won't be back until Sunday night."

"That explains why he wasn't at the funeral." Quincy filled her mug. Without asking, she topped off Margaret's. "This is the first time I can remember that either of us beat Rose awake. Any signs of her and Danny?"

"Not a peep. Thanks for the refill."

Choosing the chair directly opposite her, Quincy sat down. "Small wonder, after all that sex last night. They can't have slept much."

She would start the day talking about sex. "Ssh," Margaret cautioned, finger over her lips. "They can hear us."

"Tit for tat," Quincy replied, but in a softer voice. "We certainly heard *them*. How many times did they do it? Three? Four?" Grinning, she shook her head. "It's a wonder Susan's old bed didn't collapse under all that activity."

Margaret was thrilled her sister and Danny had made up, but a little embarrassed about their loud, amorous activities. Quincy seemed eager to wax poetic about it. With the slightest encouragement she'd go on and on about positions and who knew what else. So Margaret kept quiet.

Undaunted by her silence, Quincy continued glibly on. "Danny has great stamina." Her brows rose and lowered twice. "No wonder Rose loves him."

A remark Margaret couldn't ignore. "You know darned well there are other reasons why she loves him."

"I'm just saying." Quincy's mouth quirked. "Maybe they made a baby."

"I hope not," Margaret said. "Not yet, anyway."

"I know, I know, they should wait until they work out their differences. But with all that screwing it might've happened. . . ."

As if to punctuate the comment, the sounds of water rushing through the pipes and male and female groans floated toward them.

"There they go again." Quincy gave a coy smile. "Sex in the morning in the shower . . . Certainly one of my favorite times and places to do it. Lots less messy than the bathtub. There's something about wrapping your thighs around a man's hips while standing under a pounding showerhead. . . . Umm." She tilted her head back, closed her eyes, and licked her lips.

Having never made love except in a bed, Margaret didn't know. She didn't much like sex, though she knew most people did.

Unwilling to confess so personal a thing and ready to steer the conversation to more comfortable ground, she nodded at the phone. "Back to that call. According to Josie, Arthur wants to reschedule our meeting to Monday. I explained that we're all leaving Sunday, but she said, and I quote, 'This is important. There's a will,' and something about Arthur wanting to meet personally with the three of us at the same time."

"A will?" Quincy said. "Susan was only fifty-one. What was she doing with a will? It's not as if she had a million dollars. What's she got besides the house and the worthless stuff inside it?" A horrified look crossed her face, and she covered her mouth with her hand.

"Unless she wants one of us to keep Suzette. What if we have to dig her up?"

Margaret cringed at the thought. "We won't. That disgusting freeze-dried monstrosity belongs in the ground with our mother, and that's where she'll stay."

Without a clue as to what might be in the will, Margaret, too, was puzzled. "I trust Arthur. If he wants to meet us in person and all at the same time, we should do it. But that means we'll have to stay here until Tuesday. I told Josie I'd talk to you and Rose and call back."

The shower stopped and all was quiet in the bathroom.

"So instead of leaving Sunday we'd be here two more days?" Quincy frowned. "I don't know. I'd rather do e-mail or a four-way call or something." Looking troubled, she nibbled her lip and twirled a lock of hair around her finger. "And you have to get back to your lab."

"I should. I'll have to check with Bruce and make sure he's okay without me for a few more days. He'll probably say he's fine, but it's not fair to him, and I don't feel good about it."

Margaret didn't mind telling Quincy this because now her sister understood about her work. She understood that Bruce was a colleague and nothing more. Yet at the thought of hearing his voice and talking to him, anticipation bubbled up and she couldn't tamp it down. Unnerved, she gulped more coffee. "Do you think you can stay longer, Quincy?"

Quincy lowered her gaze as if ashamed. "To tell you the truth, paying that parking ticket about wiped out my bank account. I really need to get back and find work." She sighed. "Then again, what's another two days? If you stay, I will, too."

"I could lend you something to tide you over," Margaret said. Her own suggestion surprised her, since loaning Quincy money likely meant kissing it good-bye.

Quincy shook her head. "I appreciate the offer, but I couldn't. Don't worry about me. I'll be okay. I always am." Her shoulders straightened with determination. "I'll contact the airline about changing my ticket."

"Wait till we check with Rose."

"Check with me about what?"

This morning Rose, who always dressed before making an appearance, wore a knee-length robe and little else. Her hair was wet. Eyes shining, skin radiant, and expression joyous, she was the picture of a woman thoroughly satisfied and loved. At her side, Danny, dressed to leave, looked equally fulfilled. Margaret envied them. She wondered what great sex felt like.

"Good morning, lovebirds," Quincy cooed.

"Morning."

Rose and Danny shared lazy grins and an intimate look that put a sharp pang in Margaret's chest. "Yesterday Arthur Tremayne's father had emergency heart surgery in Seattle," she explained. "That's why he wasn't at the funeral."

Quincy cupped her mug between her hands. "He won't be back until Sunday night and wants to see us Monday."

"Monday?" Rose frowned. "But my plane ticket is for Sunday. Summer school starts Monday, and I have to be back for it."

"I know, but Tremayne wants all three of us to meet with him," Quincy said. "Something about a will, if you can believe that. Who knows what's in it, but if we show up, we'll find out. Can you please stay a few more days?"

"I don't know." Rose absently scratched her head. "I'd have to find a sub, and I hate to do that." Expression warm, she tenderly touched Danny's cheek. "Plus I don't want to be away from Danny that long."

"It's only two more days," Margaret muttered, stifling the urge to roll her eyes.

Danny kissed the inside of Rose's wrist. Her eyelids fluttered and her lips parted.

Feeling as if she were witnessing a private act not meant for her eyes, Margaret lowered her gaze to the table. "I don't want to stay either, but I'm going to."

Rose pulled out of Danny's grasp and glanced at Quincy. "You're staying, too?"

She nodded.

"Is it okay, Danny?"

"Stay as long as you need to, babe."

"Well . . ." Tiny puckers wrinkled Rose's

brow and she screwed up her mouth as if deep in thought. "Sarah Abbott owes me a favor. I'll call and ask her to sub."

"That'd be great. I'll let Arthur's office know." Margaret stood and moved toward the phone.

"Try to get the appointment first thing in the morning," Quincy said. "That way, if he needs us to run errands or whatever, we'll have the afternoon to take care of it."

Margaret had been thinking along the same lines. "Will do." Danny yawned, and she remembered her manners. "There's coffee if you want it."

"Thanks, but I'm out of time. I'll pick up some on the road." Danny slipped his arm around Rose's waist, pulled her to his side, and kissed the top of her head. "Gonna walk me to the door, babe?"

Placing her arm around Danny's waist, Rose did just that.

"Did you see them?" Quincy whispered as they left the kitchen. "They're just like honeymooners."

"I'm so glad," Margaret whispered back. She and Quincy swapped sappy grins.

Seconds later, Rose ambled into the kitchen, her face lit with joy.

"My, oh my, the air between you and Danny actually sizzled," Quincy said. "There's nothing like good make-up sex."

Flushing, Rose poured herself a mug. Then she laughed. "I'd have to agree."

She and Quincy swapped knowing grins. Margaret felt left out, but a person couldn't have make-up sex unless she argued with her boyfriend, and she never let her relationships get that far.

Quincy gestured to an empty chair. "We're dying to know what happened." She winked. "Even the sex parts, if you care to share."

To Margaret's chagrin her face warmed. "I'd rather you skip that. But we would like to know about the rest." No sense mentioning that she and Quincy already had heard quite a bit of both the fighting and making up.

"You would, would you?" Rose stopped at the refrigerator for milk. After lightening her coffee, she carried her mug to the table and sat down, a pensive look on her face. "Since you asked . . ."

Rose sipped her coffee and gathered her thoughts. At the moment she felt as if the sun were shining from her heart. She hated to dim the warmth by recounting last night's fight with Danny. But Margaret and Quincy had pushed her to be honest with him. Without their encouragement and support she'd never have unburdened herself and her marriage would be over.

Rose owed them hugely. They deserved to know what had happened.

She set down her mug. "When Danny came back last night, he was mad and hurt and thinking divorce." That they'd come so close to losing each other shook her and she rubbed her arms. "After the way I treated him and the things I said, who could blame him? I apologized and begged his forgiveness, but he was too angry to listen."

"So we heard," Quincy said.

By her somber expression, Rose knew she wasn't joking. Heaven above. All the horrible accusations she and Danny had hurled at each other . . . Mortified and unable to look at either of her sisters, she fiddled with the sash of her robe. "I know how thin these walls are in this house, but last night . . . I guess there were other things on my mind. I'm so embarrassed."

Rose glanced up in time to see her sisters exchange looks.

"Quincy's kidding," Margaret said. "We didn't hear all that much."

"That's me—Miss Tease. We climbed out the window and sat on the roof for quite awhile. Out there you can't hear anything."

That was a big relief. "I finally got Danny to listen," Rose went on. "I told him everything— about the abortion and my fears that I might not be able to get pregnant because of it."

"Was he upset?" Margaret asked.

"Yes, but not because of what I did. Because

I hid my past from him all these years." Rose still marveled over that. Why on earth had she held on to her secret for so long? "When I explained that I was afraid to tell him, he was even more hurt."

Rose felt terrible about that. Needing to do something with her hands, she took a paper napkin from the stack someone had set out and worried it between her fingers. "I asked him to pretend he was me and stand in my shoes. How would he feel? That helped, and he finally understood."

"That was smart of you," Margaret said.

Quincy nodded. "I wish I'd thought of it myself."

"Feel free to use it any time. I crossed my heart and swore I'd never, ever again hide anything from him. That's when things really calmed down." That Danny trusted Rose after what she'd pulled awed her. "We're going to schedule an appointment at the fertility clinic right away. So there you have it. I only wish I'd told him sooner. We could have avoided this whole mess."

"You did what you did," Quincy said. "Mega congratulations on working out your problems. That's one thing I don't do so well."

"You would if you had a great guy like Danny."

Chapter 15

On hold with Josie Jessup and still at the kitchen table, Margaret idly listened to Quincy and Rose discuss an *O* magazine article by Maya Angelou. They did this without squabbling or uttering a single sarcastic comment, a true miracle.

Neither Margaret nor her sisters had moved in ages. They were too busy talking about life and occasionally shedding tears over Susan. Margaret couldn't remember a time when she'd felt so comfortable with her sisters. Yet pleased as she was about this newfound harmony, she didn't quite trust it. Habits were hard to break, and any second they could slide back into tension and hostility.

At last the phone clicked and Josie came on the line with an appointment time. As soon as Margaret hung up, she shared what she'd learned. "Our new appointment is set for eight Monday morning."

Quincy grimaced. "That's early, all right. So, what'll we do this morning?"

"First on my agenda is to get dressed," Rose said. "Sitting around in my robe feels decadent." Her chair scraped as she pushed it back. "Then I'll change my plane ticket."

"I happen to love lounging around in my robe." Quincy stretched. "But in this town you never know who might drop in. I'd better shower and get dressed, too." She glanced at Rose. "Let me know your new flight info and I'll try to coordinate the departure times."

Had Quincy ever sounded so agreeable? Margaret could hardly believe her ears. "Don't forget, we have a garage sale to get ready for," she said. "So after you two lazybones get dressed, we should work on it. We also need to finish Susan's office and the rest of the pink bedroom. Remember, we're having company tonight and they may not leave until late."

"You think?" Quincy's eyes lit up before she dipped her head in an uncharacteristic show of shyness.

Obviously she liked Ira, but she always had been quick to fall in love without a thought for the consequences. That she was leaving town in five days wouldn't stop her. A broken heart was inevitable, and Margaret felt bad for her sister. She also thanked her lucky stars that she'd never let herself fall in love.

"While you dress I'll call Bruce," she said in her best nonchalant voice.

Not casual enough, given Rose's curious look.

"She has a lot riding on her research and a tight timeline," Quincy explained.

Rose gaped at her as if she'd lost her mind, and Margaret laughed.

"She's exactly right. It's only fair that I let Bruce know I'll be a few days late."

"You probably should steer clear of the roof," Quincy said with a wink. "This time of day it's too hot up there. But no worries. With the shower running I won't hear a thing."

"Me, either." Rose stood, collected the empty mugs, and carried them to the sink. "Since I'll be in the bedroom, getting dressed."

It seemed that despite last night's conversation with Quincy, despite repeatedly explaining to both sisters that Bruce was nothing more than a respected peer, neither was convinced.

Once again Margaret set them straight. "I don't care if you do eavesdrop, since we'll be discussing work. Time's a wastin' and the garden's dry as a bone. I think I'll wander outside and water while I make that call."

"You don't want to get those expensive Birkenstocks wet." Quincy slipped out of her purple-and-chartreuse-striped flip-flops. "Wear these."

Five minutes later, wearing sunglasses and the ridiculously loud flip-flops, hose in one hand and cell clamped between her ear and shoulder, Margaret waited for Bruce to pick up.

He answered on the third ring. "Hello, Margaret," he said, sounding as if he were smiling. "This is a pleasant surprise."

The already sunny day brightened further, and for one instant Margaret glimpsed what her life might be like if Bruce were more than the man she worked with. But letting him into her heart was risky and scary, so she shut the door on the very thought. "Not so pleasant," she said. "I'm afraid I have bad news. Our attorney was called out of town for a family emergency and can't meet with us until Monday. We're stuck here until Tuesday, which means I won't be in the lab until Wednesday."

She didn't mind the extra time with her sisters—as long as the warmth between them lasted. But she hated to let Bruce down.

"No problem," he said. "I hear water running. Don't tell me you're about to step into the shower."

His tone was suggestive and she couldn't help but recall Quincy's comments about sex under the pulsing water. Margaret swallowed. Told herself she didn't want a sexual relationship with Bruce.

"I happen to be watering the flowers," she replied, hiding her confusion behind a cool voice. "It's hot and very dry here, and we've sadly neglected the garden." The drooping dahlias, sagging snapdragons, and sad-looking roses—everything was parched.

"You've had more important things to deal with," Bruce said. "How'd it go yesterday?"

He meant the funeral. "It was hard." The grief that was always there flooded her. She still seemed to be riding an emotional roller coaster, racing from happy to sad to pleased to confused to upset within moments. "I'm awfully glad it's over. You were right, though, the formal ritual helped me say good-bye. But it still hurts."

"I know."

He didn't, not really. He knew nothing about Susan or Glory or Margaret's role in driving her father away. But in the silence that followed, she felt his concern, and it warmed her.

"Thank you," she said.

"For what?"

"Caring." She aimed the nozzle at the soil around the rose bushes. Water pooled on the hard earth before slowly seeping into the ground, and she turned the subject to work. "So, what are you doing right now?"

"Don't you mean, what am I wearing?"

They were back to that. Margaret frowned, then realized he was teasing. He probably had been earlier, too. Feeling foolish, she joined in the game. "I know the answer to that. Jeans, a Polo shirt, and sneakers."

"Right you are. Your turn. What are *you* wearing?"

The low, intimate timbre of his voice thrummed through her. This was no lighthearted tease. Afraid of where the conversation was headed, she sprayed her own feet. The water was shockingly cold. She jerked the nozzle up. "Shorts, a T-shirt. and Quincy's flip-flops. Seriously, what's happening at the lab this morning?"

"At the moment I'm repeating the same tests I ran yesterday." He went over the details. "If I get the same results, I'll write up the findings. Once you review them I'll forward them to Hassell."

They always worked that way, reviewing each other's work. Margaret lifted the nozzle and sprayed a row of dusty dahlias. Water misted over the flowers, making a faint rainbow. "That sounds exciting."

"It is, but it'd be a lot more fun if you were here."

"I know, and again, I apologize—"

"No need. Sure, I get pretty sick of hearing my own voice, but I am a great listener."

She laughed at this joke. "How many hours have you been at the lab this week?"

"I'm averaging twelve to fourteen per day."

Taking up her slack. "I thought so. I owe you, and I promise to make it up to you. When I get back, why don't you take off a few days and *I'll* put in the extra long hours."

"Not necessary. But if you really want to pay me back, have dinner with me."

Because she wanted to, she frowned. "We've

been through this before, Bruce." She watered the snapdragons. "You know how I feel about that."

"I'm not asking you to fall in love with me, Margaret. All I want is one meal together, away from the lab."

She could hear his disappointment and pictured his brows drawn close together, his blue eyes wounded.

Given that she'd dropped their entire workload on his shoulders, dinner was the least she could do.

"All right," she said. "Dinner. But only as friends, and it's on me."

As the mid-afternoon sunlight streamed through the living room window, Quincy swiped her brow with the back of her hand. "I never realized getting ready for a garage sale was so much work."

She and Margaret were sorting items into piles by category. Clothing, gardening tools, kitchen gadgets, lamps, and more filled every surface. Wielding a felt-tip pen and a wheel of green stickers, Rose followed them to price and sticker each item. They'd made significant progress, but weren't nearly ready.

"I don't see how we'll finish this and the office and pink bedroom before dinner, plus move this stuff so Ira and Fiona can sit someplace," she added.

"We'll have to tackle what's left upstairs tomorrow night," Margaret said. "We'll just tell the Friday shoppers to come back Saturday for more."

"Okay by me." Quincy wanted to slip away now and soak in the tub, repaint her toenails, change her hair color, and otherwise make herself pretty for Ira. In the light of day she had to admit that while she liked that he saw inside to her heart, it surely wasn't enough to hold his interest. She wasn't half as smart or educated as Ira. No, beauty and sex appeal were her finest assets. She related best to men in a sexual way, and everyone knew it. Despite what she'd told Margaret, and herself, last night—that she wanted to be Ira's friend— what she really wanted was to sleep with him.

Tonight she'd make him notice her attributes or die trying. Eager to get to work on herself, she frowned. "I don't see why we should sticker everything. Can't we just make up prices as we go?"

"If you want to get the highest price possible for everything, labeled prices will help." Margaret brought Rose a large, flat box filled with knickknacks and junk.

Since this morning's call to Bruce she'd been in an especially cheerful mood. Quincy hoped something more than work was brewing between them. She was dying to ask, but with her and Margaret getting along so well, she wasn't about to.

Thanks to plenty of hot sex, Rose was happy, too, but lack of sleep kept her yawning. She did it again as she reached for a fresh roll of stickers. "I thought we didn't care what this stuff sold for, as long as we got rid of it."

"Quincy doesn't have a job right now, remember?" Margaret said. "She really needs the money."

Rose looked contrite. "Sorry, I wasn't thinking."

"That's okay," Quincy said. "I don't like to think about getting fired, either."

"Fired?" Margaret's eyes narrowed. "You said you quit."

"Which is it?" Rose asked.

Nothing to do now but come clean. Quincy picked up a large glass ashtray she'd found in the attic. Who knew where it had come from or why Susan had kept it. "I was fired for slapping a customer who pinched my behind one too many times."

"Honestly, Quincy. You could've just said so."

Margaret looked hurt. And pissed. So much for warm fuzzies between them.

With a sigh, Quincy pushed her hair behind her ears. "I couldn't. It was my fault for losing my temper." She cringed. "And I was ashamed."

"Your fault?" Margaret scoffed, hurt replaced by indignation. "Sounds to me as if the *customer* was at fault. You were sexually harassed and you shouldn't have been fired. Isn't that illegal?"

"If it isn't, it should be." Rose tsked.

"You could sue your boss and be rehired."

"I'd rather not," Quincy said. "I hated that job."

"I don't blame you one bit." Rose began pulling stickers from the goods she'd just spent hours labeling.

Margaret frowned. "What are you doing?"

"Marking up these prices. For Quincy."

While the aroma of Italian take-out filled the air—they'd put the dinner Fiona had brought in the oven to keep warm—Quincy, her sisters, and Fiona chitchatted. Quincy in the armchair nearest the door, Margaret in the other, and Rose sharing the sofa with Fiona. Ira hadn't yet shown up, and Quincy felt as excited and nervous as a teenage girl.

Fiona eyed the mountains of garage sale items everywhere. "How ever did you manage to do all this in just a few short days?"

"By working like dogs," Quincy said.

"I have an idea. Since it's been a long few days and you girls are here a few extra days, why don't we postpone listing the house until Sunday? That way we all can relax tonight and enjoy ourselves."

Seeing no reason why they couldn't wait, Quincy glanced with a shrug at her sisters. Rose nodded.

"Fine," Margaret said.

"Excellent. Now that I'm not working tonight, I believe I'll try a little wine." Fiona plucked a wineglass from the newly cleared coffee table and handed it to Rose. "Would you, dear?"

Rose filled it and Fiona took a lengthy sip. Quincy wondered how much their dinner guest would drink tonight. She intended to limit her own consumption. This evening was all about Ira. Despite her full day she'd managed an hour to herself and had changed her hair color, repainted her toe- and fingernails, and made up her face. She was now a platinum blonde with sooty lashes, red, glossy lips, and what the nail polish bottle called Love-Me-Forever Red nails.

She hoped Ira liked the look, along with her spaghetti strap, red and white sun dress and the sexiest red summer heels ever. Making herself comfortable she crossed her freshly shaved legs and felt the slender silver ankle bracelet kiss her ankle. If Ira's eyes didn't pop out of his head, she'd be surprised.

For that to happen though, he had to show up. It was almost six thirty and she was sure she'd told him six. Had he changed his mind, or had her instincts failed her again, leading her to trust one more male she shouldn't? Hiding a frown she tilted her wineglass to her lips.

"Was it difficult?" Fiona asked. "Setting prices on your mother's belongings?"

Margaret shook her head. "Not really."

"There's nothing in that pile that means anything to me," Rose said.

"Or me. The hardest part will be taking it all outside at dawn." Quincy's stomach growled. She offered a sheepish smile. "It's been awhile since lunch."

"It certainly has," Rose said. "I could eat a buffalo."

She'd been snacking all afternoon. No doubt this morning's shower sex had revved up her metabolism.

"We can't eat without Ira. I wonder where he is," Margaret said, voicing Quincy's very thoughts. Twin worry lines appeared between her eyebrows as she darted a glance at Quincy.

That alone was enough to bring on a bad case of the butterflies. Quincy feigning indifference. "I don't know, but if he doesn't show up soon, screw him." She glanced at Fiona. "Pardon my French."

"If he said he'd be here, he will be." For the first time Fiona really looked at Quincy. "You look lovely tonight. That dress showcases your beautiful figure. I only wish your mother could see you."

Quincy could just imagine that. Susan would stand there, the unhappy slant of her mouth, crossed arms and narrowed eyes conveying her disapproval. *You look like a stupid little tramp. What will people think? I'm so embarrassed.*

Put in her place, Quincy hung her head. Susan may be gone but her voice lived on. It was almost funny. Only instead of laughing, she teared up. "I wish she could, too."

They all exchanged watery smiles.

"I like this hair color much better than black," Rose said, wiping her eyes.

Margaret nodded. "Ira will love it."

That was the plan. Used to compliments, Quincy smiled. "Thank you, all. The truth is, this is one of the few clean dresses I have left. That's why I wore it. Not for Ira." *Liar.* She drained the last of her wine and decided one more couldn't hurt. "While we're waiting, I could use a refill. Anyone else?"

Her sisters declined, but Fiona held out her glass.

Quincy was headed for the kitchen and a fresh bottle when the doorbell rang. Her heart seemed to stall in her chest, but her legs carried her forward.

"Aren't you going to answer the door?" Margaret said.

"I'm busy. You go ahead."

A few seconds later she heard Ira's deep voice.

"Ira's here," Margaret called out. "And he brought you something."

A gift. This was a good sign, even if he *was* forty minutes late. Quincy's temper simmered. "I'll be right out."

She took her sweet time uncorking the bottle. By the time she sashayed into the living room, the front door was closed against the heat. Standing in the entry, one hand behind his back, Ira nodded at her.

Quincy handed Fiona the bottle before she let herself look at him. Dressed in jeans and a green, short sleeve Oxford shirt that was open at the collar and rope sandals, he looked comfortable and casual, not at all like a wealthy businessman.

"Hello," she said as if she didn't care at all that he'd shown up.

"Sorry I'm late," he said, looking genuinely apologetic. "Something came up at the office."

Tossing her head and flashing a phony smile, Quincy acknowledged his excuse. He couldn't call?

"I tried calling," he said as if he'd read her thoughts, "but the phone seems to be off the hook. And I don't have your cell number."

"Oh." Quincy didn't have a cell—too expensive.

"Off the hook? How did that happen?" Rose muttered. "I'll get a glass for your wine, Ira. Excuse me." She headed for the kitchen.

"I should check on the food." Fiona followed her.

"And I need to use the powder room," Margaret said, hurrying away.

Leaving Quincy and Ira alone.

Not about to speak first, she curled her lips into a smile and angled her chin.

"This is for you." Eyes bright behind his glasses, he brought his arm forward and held out not the bouquet of flowers she expected, but a bag from the bookstore.

She frowned. "What's this?"

"Open it."

Quincy pulled out the manual-size paperback book. *Starting Your Own Business.* That he'd taken her dream seriously nearly knocked her to her knees. She forgot that she was mad at him for being late. "Thank you," she murmured, her heart full and warm.

"You're welcome."

His gentle eyes connected with hers, and she knew he could see into her soul—far too intimate. Scary. She retreated to safer, more familiar ground. Lowering her lashes, thrusting out her breasts, and moistening her lips, she waited for Ira's attention to dip to her bare shoulders, her cleavage, hips, and legs. Sure enough, his gaze flicked appreciatively over her.

Now we're cookin' with gas. Pleased that the care she'd taken to highlight her attributes had paid off, she exhaled with relief.

Margaret returned from the bathroom, and Fiona and Rose emerged from the kitchen. Not wanting to show them the book, not certain she wanted to read it herself, Quincy slipped it back into the sack.

"The phone is now on the hook and the food is more than hot," Rose announced as she handed Ira his wine. "Shall we head into the dining room?"

Chapter 16

"More food, anyone? There's plenty." Rose gestured at the half-empty take-out containers grouped on the dining room table.

Seated in Susan's old seat at one end Margaret patted her stomach. "I'm fine, thanks."

"None for me, either," Fiona said from the opposite end, in the seat first offered to Ira.

Most men would've expected to preside over the table. Ira had declined so that he could sit next to Quincy. As successful as he was, he didn't feel the need to assert his maleness, and Rose found that both sweet and interesting. She liked Ira Lamm, who seemed a far sight better than the men Quincy usually chose.

"But I will have more wine," Fiona said. "Join me, Quincy?"

"I'll pass." Quincy, who had stopped at two glasses of wine and a small helping of everything, handed the bottle to Fiona with a telling look.

The older woman had drunk a great deal.

How she managed to function was beyond Rose. She'd never be able to drive herself home.

"I'll take seconds." Ira handed over his plate. He ate like a starving man, yet he didn't have an ounce of extra fat on his body.

After Fiona poured and sipped her wine, she propped her head woozily on her hand and smiled at Ira. "I'm sure the girls would love to hear how you came to hire Susan."

While Ira chewed his mouthful, Quincy canted toward him with avid attention, the pose calling attention to her creamy shoulders and cleavage. Only clean dress, my foot.

Rose wondered what book Ira had given her and why she had all but ignored it, leaving it in the bag and later stashing it upstairs. She also wondered whether Ira would sleep with her sister tonight or later. Clearly it was what Quincy wanted.

What Rose wanted was to shake some common sense into her little sister. No wonder she couldn't stay in long-term relationships. You didn't keep a man by jumping into bed with him. That she was leaving in a few days was probably for the best.

Ira swallowed his food, then wiped his mouth with his napkin. "When I started the company I couldn't afford an expensive lawyer. Eric DelVaio, who was one of my first customers, recommended your mother."

"She was screwing him," Quincy said, leaning closer. "Did you know that?"

Fiona choked on her wine and Margaret's eyes widened.

"Don't, Quincy," Rose warned.

"Well, she was." She fluffed her hair.

Ira seemed fascinated by the way it caressed her shoulders, Rose noted. His gaze darted to her breasts before he raised it to her face.

Quincy's mouth hooked in an impish quirk that highlighted her dimple. "Eric might have recommended her because he was getting his jollies."

Some men would've run with the subject, flirting and adding their own sexual nuances to the conversation. Ira shrugged and gave an "aw shucks" smile that made Rose like him even more.

"I wouldn't know," he said. "What I *do* know is that Susan really knew her legal stuff. She may not have gone to law school but she was awesome. A super lady."

Quincy muttered under her breath. Rose couldn't make out the words, but it sounded like, "Tell me you didn't sleep with my mother."

By the press of Margaret's lips, she also heard it. Too liquored up to notice much, Fiona simply stared at Ira with unfocused eyes.

Whatever Quincy had said, Ira didn't appear to have heard. Just as Rose let out a relieved breath, Quincy opened her mouth.

It was time to move on, and Rose did. "Are . . . Were you still working with her when she . . ." She couldn't finish without breaking down. She shook her head and gestured helplessly.

Looking sympathetic and kind, Ira shook his head. "I have my own in-house legal department now. But over the years I referred many people her way. Her passing is a real loss to Shadow Falls."

"Don't I know it." Fiona smiled fondly, then wiped a tear from her eye. "Already I miss her terribly."

Rose did, too. But having never experienced Susan's warmth she also felt left out. She glanced at her sisters, knowing they did, too.

Silenced at last, Quincy lowered her gaze to her plate. Margaret studied Ira with the usual unreadable expression that meant she was hiding her feelings.

"What did you like most about her?" Rose asked.

"That's easy. Her ability to see the funny side of life and her laughter." Ira smiled at Quincy. "You have the same wonderful sense of humor."

"I do?" Quincy looked stricken. "Oh, God."

"I meant that as a compliment."

"Well, I take it as an insult."

Clearly puzzled, Ira pushed his empty plate away. Worried about what Quincy might say next and not wanting to air the family's dirty laundry, Rose exchanged a *help!* look with Margaret.

It was Fiona who changed the subject.

"Tell us about your work, Ira."

"I don't want to bore anyone."

Quincy's eyes went soft and warm, this time without the flirtatious gleam. "His company stops hackers," she said with pride.

Now Rose understood. For all her sexual posturing, Quincy wanted more than sex with Ira. She'd fallen for him. How she could give her heart to a man she barely knew when she was about to leave town . . . No wonder her baby sister bounced from man to man. She had no common sense.

Rose felt sorry for her. And counted herself fortunate to have both good sense and a man who loved her as much as she loved him. A man who wasn't going away, no matter what.

Even though she was the middle sister, the one most often left out, at the moment she felt like the luckiest woman alive.

Helping Rose clear the table later, Margaret yawned and tossed a stack of empty take-out cartons into the trash. "I thought Fiona would never leave."

"She'd probably still be here if the wine hadn't run out." Rose set plates and glasses in the sink, then turned on the tap.

"I told you she had a drinking problem," Margaret said over the hiss of the water. She felt bad for Fiona and also worried. "She ought to join AA."

"Except that only works when a person admits

she has a problem." Rose rinsed away the remnants of their meal. "I suspect Fiona drinks partly to blunt the loneliness. Now that Susan is gone she has no one except her son, and I don't think they're close."

The words hit Margaret like a fist to the chest. When she was Fiona's age would she be alone and equally lonely? The thought chilled her. Pushing it away, she opened the dishwasher and loaded the rinsed dishes—one last load before they sold everything. "I'm just glad Ira drove her home so one of us didn't have to. It was sweet of Quincy to follow them in another car and drive him back, wasn't it?"

"Sweet? I'd call it calculating. It's obvious that she really cares for him, yet her behavior is . . . well, the most blatant appeal for sex I've ever seen. Why does she sabotage herself that way?"

"Why do any of us act the way we do?" Margaret posed. Not that she approved of Quincy's behavior. She didn't. But since their conversation on the roof her perspective had changed. "She made a comment last night—something about Susan calling her a stupid little tramp— that made me stop and think. I'm sure that's how she sees herself."

"Stupid little tramp," Rose echoed, looking thoughtful as she turned off the tap and dried her hands. "I remember that. I should, since I heard it every time Quincy left the house in tight, skimpy clothes. Which was almost every day. You may be on to something, Margaret."

"Remember what she used to call me?" Margaret asked, adding soap to the dishwasher.

"Plainy brainy," Rose replied without an instant of hesitation. "She said it with a smile on her face, like she was teasing."

Teasing or not, the label had stung—and stuck. Yet Margaret had absorbed and accepted it without question, just as Quincy had. Only in Margaret's case the phrase suited her perfectly. A week ago she wouldn't have admitted that to anyone. But Rose had confided *her* deepest fears, and Margaret now trusted her enough to share this one thing about herself.

"She was right about me. I *am* smart and unattractive." Unable to look at the confirmation she knew she'd find on Rose's face, she latched the dishwasher and started it.

She straightened to find Rose shaking her head. "Susan was wrong. Not about the brains. You have plenty. But you're pretty, too. Your hair is lovely and thick, and you have Glory's incredible eyes."

Quincy had said the same thing about her eyes. Margaret wanted to believe her sisters, but they were wrong. "You need to have your vision checked. I have the brains, Quincy has the looks, and you're the one with the homemaker genes—" Hearing herself, she broke off. And frowned. "I sound just like Susan, don't I?"

"Afraid so," Rose said. "Do you remember what she called *me*?"

Glancing upward, Margaret tried to remember.

A bulb had burned out in the recessed light, she noticed. As for Susan's name for Rose, she drew a blank. "Whatever it was, it's gone from my memory."

"Because she didn't have a nickname for me. She never noticed me enough even for that. I just realized something. The reason I spent so much of my time cooking delicious meals was to win her approval and love. Fat lot of good that did. Yet here I am, still doing it for the same reasons. To make people love me." As the dishwasher rumbled and swished, Rose gave a disparaging snort. "I can't believe I never figured that out."

"Be thankful you did. It's not true, you know. People like you for yourself."

"I'm not so sure of that," Rose said, sounding uncertain.

Oh, the damage Susan had caused. The more Margaret thought about that, the angrier she grew. "Damn her for what she did to us!" She slapped the counter with a satisfying whack.

"Double, triple damn!" Rose said, joining in with a smack of her own. "Ouch." She rubbed her hand, eyes darkening with grief. "How can losing a mother like ours hurt so much?"

"Because flaws and all, she was still our mother and we loved her. That doesn't mean we're obligated to be what she labeled us. It's time to take action."

"How?"

"Watch and learn." Margaret raised her chin. "I am my own person and starting this minute, I am changing my beliefs about myself." What she was about to add felt scary but awesome, and she paused to take in a deep breath. "I am smart *and also attractive.*"

She didn't quite believe the attractive part, but at least she'd said it. "I think I'll take Quincy up on those makeup tips."

"Hooray for you!" Rose clapped. "If you can change, so can I. My value lies in who I am, not what I do for others." She exhaled loudly. "That feels good." An instant later she hugged herself. "Also terrifying."

"I'm absolutely petrified."

In the silence that fell, Margaret and Rose beamed at each other.

"Wow," Rose said. "This is as good as therapy."

"A lot cheaper, too."

They both laughed.

"Wait'll Quincy hears about this," Rose said. "I hope she doesn't see herself as a stupid little tramp. Do you really think she does?"

Margaret did, and nodded. "And I'll bet my job that Susan's ugly nickname is a big reason why she dresses and acts the way she does. But I don't want to hurt her feelings or upset her. So when we share our insights let's tread carefully and speak with love."

"With love," Rose repeated solemnly. "Do you realize the three of us have never said the

L word to each other? Let's change that right now." She smiled warmly at Margaret. "I love you, big sister."

Margaret's throat grew thick with feeling. She swallowed. "I love you, too, middle sister."

They embraced. Pulled back, both with suspiciously bright eyes.

Embarrassed at this unusual show of emotion, Margaret grabbed the dish rag. "I should wipe down the dining room table."

"I'll dry it."

While they worked, the conversation continued.

"Funny, but now that Susan isn't around, there's less tension between the three of us," Rose said as she dried Margaret's efforts with a towel. "Have you noticed that?"

"Didn't I say as much the other day—that Susan drove us apart?"

"Yeah, but I didn't really get it until now."

Full with everything she and Rose had shared and eager to tell Quincy, Margaret glanced at her watch. "Quincy and Ira have been gone over an hour. I wish she'd hurry back."

"Maybe she went home with him."

"Wouldn't be surprised."

If she had, the talk would have to wait.

Parked in Fiona's driveway, serenaded by katydids, Quincy slid her hands over the leather-gloved steering wheel. "You're letting me drive home?"

The tiny lights lining the long driveway bathed Ira's answering smile in a soft glow. "Why not? You followed me here, so I know you can handle her."

"But that was because you were driving Fiona's car." She'd watched him ease the sedan into the garage, then cup the unsteady woman's arm and walk her inside. "By the way, have I thanked you for driving her instead of making me do it?" Quincy pursed her lips seductively and glanced at him through lowered lashes, actions that seemed to turn on the men. "You're a sweetheart, Ira."

"Once I got her into the car she wasn't that bad," he said without a speck of awareness.

Dropping the flirty face, she turned in her seat. "If you don't mind slobbering drunks."

"She definitely was drunk. I wonder what Mason thinks about that."

Her son. "He lives in Spokane, so I doubt he knows."

"Maybe I'll give him a call."

Ira was such a good person. Quincy's heart swelled with warmth. "You're the most thoughtful man I've ever met."

She swore he flushed, but the dim light kept her from knowing for sure.

"It's no big deal. If it was my mother I'd want someone to tell me." He angled his chin. "Are we going to sit here all night, or are you going to start the car?"

Quincy wouldn't have minded sitting, at least for a while. Fiona had turned off the lights inside, meaning she'd gone to bed. At this hour none of the neighbors were out, and even if they were, the trees lining the driveway gave them plenty of privacy. She longed for Ira to kiss her, then take her to his place for a night of lovemaking.

Unfortunately, so far he hadn't put a single move on her. Having noted his interest earlier, Quincy wasn't worried. Some men preferred to show their affection behind closed doors. Maybe Ira was like that. She'd drive to his house and find out. Excitement spiked her blood.

"Buckle up." She turned the key and the motor hummed to life. "This baby purrs like a kitten."

"I'm not sure I want my car compared to a kitten." The corner of Ira's mouth lifted charmingly. "How about a tiger."

Quincy laughed and tossed her head, but the scarf she'd tied under her hair ruined the effect. "Does a tiger purr?"

"Beats me."

She backed into the turn around and aimed the car forward. "Where exactly do you live, Ira?"

Of course she already knew. She'd looked up the address in the phone book.

"Out in the country."

"Ah," she said, inching down the driveway. "Tell me about your place."

"I don't have much yard. Mostly woods, for the privacy."

"That sounds nice. I'd love to see it." She glanced at him.

"Would you."

His brow lifted a fraction and she knew he understood her meaning. They were at the end of the driveway now. She set the brake, then reached over to touch his cheek. "Men have such one-track minds." She smiled and slid her hand down his chest. His very solid chest. As her hand moved lower Ira shifted in his seat and sucked in a breath. Oh, yeah.

Her body began to thrum, and she licked her lips. "That's okay, so do women."

Before she reached his belt, he circled her wrist and removed her hand. "What are you doing, Quincy?"

She saw in his eyes that she'd made a mistake, that he wasn't interested in flirtation or anything beyond it. He didn't want sex, not with her.

"I'm sorry." She dipped her head, noted his hard-on, and felt her cheeks heat. She'd aroused him as she'd hoped, yet he'd rejected her. Confused and hurt, she frowned. "I thought . . . Never mind."

"Quit trying so damned hard to seduce me." His jaw was taut with irritation.

"I said I was sorry."

Feeling foolish and stupid she pivoted in her seat so that she faced forward. She released the brake. The tires squealed as she floored the accelerator and roared down the sleepy street.

Ira gripped the passenger handle. "Slow down," he ordered through clenched teeth.

Angry but not sure why, Quincy jerked the emergency brake. The car bucked and stopped in the middle of the street. "You drive."

Wordless, she exited the car. Marching to the passenger side, she crossed her arms and waited for Ira to get out.

He opened his door. She could feel his questioning gaze but refused to look at him. They traded seats.

"Listen, Quincy—"

Afraid of what he might say, she stopped him with the wave of her hand. "Save it for someone who cares." Turning her head, she stared out her window and pretended that the dark houses fascinated her.

Ira blew out a heavy breath. He drove toward Mayfair Street, not as fast as she had, but fast. Neither of them spoke.

Quincy tried not to think, tried to lose herself in the noisy wind flooding the silence, but her racing mind refused to stop. Ira probably thought she was a slut. Well she was, wasn't she? Hating herself, mortified and miserable that she'd ruined their friendship, she tugged off the scarf. Her hair whipped her cheeks and eyes with sharp little slaps that stung. It was going to be a bitch to get a comb through.

Ira pulled up to the well-lit house. Shoot, her sisters still must be up. She pushed the tangles and snarls out of her face and bit her lip. "I'm sorry, Ira. I shouldn't have acted that way."

"That's the third time you've apologized. Stop it, okay?" He tucked her hair behind her ears, his fingers warm and gentle, but not seductive.

For some reason tears gathered behind her eyes. She would not cry in front of him. She wouldn't. Averting her gaze she jerked away.

"I like you, Quincy."

Then why hadn't he kissed her? Most men would have had her naked by now.

He cupped her chin and turned her head. She had no choice but to meet his gaze.

"You don't have to flirt or play games with me," he said, looking deeply into her eyes. "You're fine the way you are."

Oh, but she wasn't. Without sex, she simply had nothing to offer.

"Okay." She pulled out of his grasp to open her own door. "You don't have to walk me inside, Ira." Her mouth formed a smile. "Good night."

Without a backward glance, she hurried into the house.

Chapter 17

Since Rose and Danny had spent most of the previous night talking and making love instead of sleeping, she was tired. But she was getting along so well with Margaret that she put off going to bed. Plus she still hoped Quincy would come home tonight and that the three of them could talk.

Now, sitting cross-legged and across from Margaret on the small patch of living room floor that was free of garage sale items, she frowned at the arrow she'd drawn beneath her hand lettered GARAGE SALE sign. "I never was much of an artist. This looks like it was drawn by a ten-year-old. I wish I'd found printed signs at Wal-Mart."

"Mine isn't any better. Good thing I chose a career in scientific research and not art."

They smiled, and Rose felt wonderful.

"Quincy's the one with the artistic flair. Too bad she isn't here to help."

"Don't worry, she'll make up for it tomorrow."

Hearing a noise, Rose cocked her head. "Does that sound like a car?" She jumped up, leaned over the sofa, and peered through a crack between the drapes. "It is. Quincy's home. Uh-oh, she's coming up the steps alone, and she doesn't look happy."

Margaret touched her fingers to her mouth. "I wonder what happened? I was sure she and Ira—"

The door opened and Margaret went silent. Rose dropped onto the sofa and froze, her attention on Quincy. Her sister's hair was a wild mess. Her mouth worked soundlessly and tears trickled down her pink cheeks.

Her startled gaze darted from Rose to Margaret. She swiped at the tears and gulped. "I thought you two would be upstairs working."

Alarmed, Rose stood. "What's wrong?"

"Are you okay?" Margaret asked, also pushing to her feet.

"Why wouldn't I be?" Quincy straightened her shoulders and formed her lips into a smile, but nothing could hide the wretchedness in her eyes.

Something awful must have happened. Ira didn't seem like the kind of man to have sex with a woman and dump her at the door, but if he had, if he'd hurt Quincy in any way . . . Rose's fingers curled into fists. "Are you sure you're okay?"

"Why does everybody keep asking?" Quincy

said in voice edging toward hysteria. "I'm
fine." She sniffled. "Terrific." An instant later
her shoulders slumped. "No, I'm not. Ira rejected me, and I f-feel rotten."

Not at all what Rose had expected to hear.
Relief that Ira hadn't used Quincy faded under
her sister's sobs. She'd never seen her little
sister so upset, not even at the funeral. Having
no clue what to do, she looked to Margaret.

Who seemed equally lost. At the same instant, they moved into action.

"Come and sit down." Rose guided Quincy
to the sofa and hastily pushed aside a pile of
Susan's clothes.

Margaret grabbed a roll of toilet paper from
the bathroom—they were out of facial tissue—
and offered it to Quincy.

"Toilet paper—how fitting." Quincy sank
onto the sofa. She kicked off her heels, unrav-
eled a wad of paper, and blew her nose.

Rose and Margaret sat on either side of her,
close enough to touch but not so close as to
smother. Quincy hiccupped, chafed her arms,
and sat back.

"Do you want to talk about it?" Margaret
asked, brushing the hair off Quincy's forehead.

She regarded them both with a suspicious
frown. "When did you two become the love
and comfort brigade?"

"You listened to me the other night, and it

really helped," Rose said, speaking from the heart. "Now I'm here for you."

"Both of us are," Margaret said. "I don't understand why Ira rejected you. At dinner he seemed very interested."

"He did, didn't he?" Quincy sniffled. "I did everything I could to turn him on. I'm wearing clothes that show off my body and the musky perfume men like. I colored my hair and fixed my makeup and nails. I flirted and acted like he was the most important man alive. But none of it worked. Ira doesn't want me." Her eyes filled again, and she bowed her head as if she couldn't bear the shame of it. "I've never been rejected before. What's wrong with me?" In a low voice she added, "Maybe I'm already past my prime."

Rose hated the defeated sound in her younger sister's voice. "No, you're not," she said firmly.

"You're barely thirty. You won't hit your prime for years to come," Margaret added. "With my own ears I heard Ira praise your sense of humor. Didn't you tell me that he thinks you have a heart of gold?"

Quincy nodded miserably.

"He's right," Rose said. "You're also one of the most beautiful women I've ever seen, bar none. If Ira doesn't think so, he's either blind or not as sharp as people say."

Quincy's chin jerked up. "He may be a little

nearsighted, but overall, his eyes are fine, thank you very much. And he's *super* intelligent."

Her quick defense of the man who had hurt her meant that she cared a great deal for Ira Lamm. Feeling her sister's pain, Rose pulled her into a one-arm hug. "Not if he rejected you."

"You don't understand." Quincy pulled away and released an impatient sigh. "He says I'm fine the way I am and that I don't need to flirt or play games."

"In that case, I take it all back," Rose said. "He *is* smart."

"That doesn't sound bad at all." Margaret looked confused. "Am I missing something?"

"He doesn't really know me. You two don't, either."

"Maybe not as well as we once did, but some things don't change," Rose said. "We grew up in the same house. This house. I know that you're sensitive and easily hurt."

"And that you're intelligent and no tramp," Margaret added.

"Yes, I am." Quincy scoffed. "I've slept with so many men—"

"That doesn't mean you're a tramp."

"Oh yeah? Then what does it mean?"

"That you're confused about what you want," Margaret said.

"Oh, I know what I want." Quincy worked a tangle from her hair. "To be loved," she said in a small voice.

Didn't they all. In the long silence that followed

that honest and profound statement, Rose wiped her suddenly wet eyes and thanked God for Danny. Margaret stared at her hands.

"Men don't love me except when they have sex with me," Quincy added matter-of-factly.

She was sadly misguided, and Rose silently raged at their mother for fueling those faulty beliefs. "Have you ever given a man a chance to love you for who you are?"

"Of course I have! I've been married twice, and I've lived with—"

"Without sex, I mean."

Quincy let out a harsh, humorless laugh. "Without sex, they don't stay."

"But Ira's different," Margaret said.

A bitter smile twisted Quincy's lips. "He didn't stay, either, did he?"

The stark expression in her eyes made Rose's heart ache. "Well, I love you." She peered into Quincy's watery eyes. "Not for your beautiful face and perfect body, but for who you are."

"Exactly who am I?" Quincy asked, returning the look.

"My sister. A woman who makes me smile. Sometimes you make me furious, too. But I know I can always count on you when I need you."

Quincy bit her lip. "Really?"

Rose nodded. "Remember that time my period started early and leaked through to my white pants, right before my tenth-grade field trip to the Moyer Cattle Farm? You took off your skirt so I could wear it. You were stuck wearing your ugly blue gym shorts home. And my senior year of high school, when Susan caught me sneaking out with Billy Jackson and I was supposed to be on my way to the library? I knew she'd ground me for a month. You said you were grounded anyway, so what more could Mother do to you, and convinced her that Billy was your date instead. And later, when he dumped me and broke our date to the prom, you talked Sam Perkins into taking me. Sam Perkins! The coolest boy in my class. Every senior girl was green with envy, including the girl Billy dumped me for. Even Susan approved of him." Rose smiled. "Those are just a few things you did for me."

"I'd forgotten about the skirt thing," Quincy said. Her mouth quirked. "That *was* pretty nice of me."

"And all the boyfriend problems you helped us with." Margaret shook her head. "I may be three years older than you, but you always were the wiser one. I'm still in awe of your observations and creative solutions to problems."

Blushing, Quincy threw up her hands. "Enough already." She glanced at the ceiling. "Just tell me what you want and give me back my normal sisters."

Rose and Margaret laughed.

"We *are* normal." Margaret glanced at Rose

and she knew that now was the perfect time to share their insights about Susan.

"What was that look I just saw between you two?"

"We figured out something earlier, something we want to share," Rose said.

"Oh?" Quincy sounded wary. "What's that?"

"On the roof last night you mentioned how Susan used to call you a stupid little tramp," Margaret said.

"Every day of my teenage life."

"That got me thinking about what she called me."

"You mean plainy brainy?"

Margaret lifted her head, the determined glint in her eyes making Rose proud. "Well, I'm not plain."

"Didn't I say that very thing last night?" Quincy scoffed. "And you blew me off."

"For that I apologize. You were right and I was wrong. And by the way, I changed my mind. I *do* want those eye makeup tips."

Quincy's eyebrows raised to comical heights. "Oookay. But what does that have to do with me being a stupid little tramp?"

"Plenty," Margaret said. "Like me, you took those words into your heart and did your best to live up, or should I say down, to them. I'm better than that, and so are you."

Now it was Rose's turn. "I always felt invisible, but I'm not. I realized tonight that I don't have to fuss over people or take care of them to be loved." She still didn't quite believe that, but at least she was going to work on it.

"I'm thrilled for you both." Quincy splayed her hands in her lap and glanced at her dress. "But look at me. Tight, short dress, dyed platinum hair, fuck-me shoes. I look and dress like a tramp, and I flirt like one, too."

"There's nothing wrong with calling attention to your assets," Rose said, and she meant that. "If I had your body, I would."

Margaret nodded. "Just think, you have a good brain to go with your beauty."

Quincy looked skeptical. "I barely graduated from high school."

"Doesn't mean you're not smart. You could've made good grades and gone to college, but you chose not to, that's all. Heck, you could still get a degree if you wanted."

Rose could almost see the wheels turning in Quincy's mind, but she said nothing. Her sister needed time to absorb what she'd heard. "That's all we wanted to say," she finished. "Except that we're sorry about Ira."

"You and me both." Quincy gave a forlorn smile. "But since I'm leaving in a few days, it's probably better this way."

"That's another great thing about you," Margaret said. "You always look on the positive side."

"It's either do that, or sink into a never ending pity party." Quincy seemed to notice the hand lettered signs for the first time. "Who made those?"

"We did," Rose said. "Pretty bad, huh?"

"Afraid so." For the first time Quincy really smiled. "I know we should go to bed because we have to get up early for the garage sale, but I'm not ready. What do you think about moving all this stuff outside now? That way we can sleep an extra hour in the morning."

"I've been mulling over that same thing." Margaret grinned at Quincy. "Great brains think alike."

"You aren't worried that people will steal stuff in the night?" Rose asked.

"Susan never locked her door, and neither does anybody else in this town," Quincy said. "I'd say we're safe. Let me change into cutoffs first."

As soon as she disappeared up the stairs, Rose glanced at Margaret. "Do you think she heard us?" she murmured in a low voice. "Understood, I mean?"

"I don't know. It'll take time before it sinks in—for all of us."

"I wish there was something more we could do." Rose stood, stretched, and headed for a box of kitchen gadgets. "If only Ira had given her half a chance . . ."

"That would've been great." Margaret, too, stood to lend a hand. "But I'm not worried about Quincy. She's a Lansing. She'll be fine."

Chapter 18

Friday

Once Margaret had showered and dressed the next morning, there was barely time for coffee before the garage sale started—let alone time for Quincy to show her eye makeup tricks. Besides, after a good night's sleep her plan to wear makeup seemed silly. Especially for the garage sale people. Who cared what they thought? Leaning over the sink, she frowned at her reflection in the vanity mirror. She really *was* plain, so why bother?

"Maybe you can show me what to do tonight instead," she said to Quincy who stood behind her in the small bathroom, ready to instruct.

Quincy shook her head. "You said you wanted to look pretty, Maggie, and there's no time like the present." Catching herself, she shot a guilty look at Margaret's reflection. "Margaret. I meant to call you Margaret."

Since their conversation last night she'd been friendly and sweet, with none of her trademark sarcasm or embarrassing sexual comments. Margaret liked the new Quincy and hoped she stayed this way. She also hoped her baby sister had truly listened to her and Rose last night.

"I don't mind if you call me Maggie," she said, surprising herself yet again. She, too, was changing, and it was both exciting and somewhat daunting. "And thanks for the reminder— I *do* want to look pretty."

"All right, then." Quincy laid an open makeup case on the lid of the closed toilet. There were pencils, assorted brushes, eye shadows, mascaras, blushes, and powders in every color imaginable.

"That's quite an assortment you have," Margaret commented. "I don't mean that in a negative way," she hastened to add. "Just . . . wow."

"Impressive, isn't it?" Quincy selected a dark brown pencil. "A girl can't have too much makeup, especially when she changes her hair color as often as I do. Different hair color means different makeup needs." She handed Margaret the pencil. "I suspect you want to keep that natural look, right? Draw a line along your upper lid. Do the same on the lower lid, then smudge with this little brush, but not too much."

Feeling clumsy, Margaret followed the instructions as best she could. Per her sister, she added mascara and shadow. When she finished, she set down the tools and pivoted toward Quincy. "What do you think?"

Her sister studied her critically. "Not bad. Do you like it?"

Margaret turned again toward the mirror. She stared at her reflection. She'd never come close to Quincy's flawless beauty, but her eyes definitely looked bigger and bluer without being overly made-up. She met Quincy's gaze in the mirror. "You're right, I have great eyes. Now, what about my skin and lips?"

"You don't need to do much there. Maybe a little blush on your cheeks and a hint of pink on your lips. Hmmm . . . You're fairer skinned than I am, but this will work for now."

Quincy selected colors, then showed Margaret how to apply blush so it looked natural and highlighted her cheekbones. Since her lipsticks were brighter than what Margaret wanted, she settled for pink lip gloss.

"Now for my hair." Margaret pulled at a lock of her limp, shoulder-length hair. "What should I do with it?"

"We don't have time this morning, but if I were you I'd get it cut and styled by an expert," Quincy said. "For now, let's give ourselves garage sale 'do's." She pulled her hair into a ponytail. Margaret did the same.

With her hair pulled back, her eyes looked even bigger. She smiled at her reflection. "I never thought I'd say this about myself, but I look hot." She wondered what Bruce would think, or if she'd have the nerve to fix herself up like this before she walked into the lab.

"Damn straight." Quincy winked. "Look out, single men everywhere. My turn."

Elbowing Margaret aside she leaned into the mirror and deftly highlighted her own eyes, skin, and face. "There."

"I can hardly tell you're wearing makeup." Margaret frowned. "Isn't that look a little too natural for you?"

"It's a garage sale in broad daylight, Maggie. I don't need to be dramatic for that."

She always made herself up to look dramatic, but Margaret kept the thought to herself. Was this change, too, the result of last night? Time would tell.

"Hey, you slow pokes," Rose called from downstairs. "A carload of people just drove up. Get your coffee and meet me outside."

"There goes breakfast," Quincy muttered. "Be right there!"

She quickly applied lipstick, the same color as her toenails, which made her look more like the Quincy Margaret was used to. On the way downstairs, she pulled a pink baseball cap from the hip pocket of her lowriders, slapped it on her head, and pulled her ponytail through the opening in the back.

The main floor was empty of everything except for the furniture that was too big to move outside. Without the furnishings, the living and dining rooms looked worn and shabby. How depressing.

Apparently unaffected, Quincy rubbed her hands together and winked at Margaret. "Let's grab that coffee and go make ourselves some money."

Feeling self-conscious, and fighting the urge to wash her face, Margaret followed her sister into the kitchen.

After a quick cup of coffee from a Styrofoam cup—the dishes and stainless flatwear were outside, ready for the garage sale—and half a piece of toast made under the broiler, Margaret slathered sunblock on her bare shoulders and legs, donned sunglasses, and hurried outside. Though it was only eight o'clock, the rising sun hung bright in the sky and the temperature already hovered on the far side of warm. She hoped the heat wouldn't deter people from coming.

She saw Quincy, who'd skipped breakfast and brought her coffee outside, leading total strangers past assorted items spread over the lawn and into the house to look at the furniture. It was all for sale, though they would keep the beds, kitchen table, and coffee maker until Tuesday morning. If people wanted to buy them now, though, great.

On the far side of the yard, where they'd put the odds and ends, Rose was collecting money for the iron and ironing board from a skinny girl who looked barely out of high school.

Never comfortable with strangers, Margaret doubted she could sell a thing. At a loss for what to do, she surveyed the yard and the various people picking up items, checking out prices, and rubbing their chins. Her gaze lit on Jake and Janelle Gibson. Young and new to the neighborhood, they'd stopped by after the funeral to introduce themselves and pay their respects. They waved her over to the rocking chair that Susan had banished to the attic. The chair Susan and Glory had rocked Margaret and her sisters in when they were babies.

A vivid image of Glory holding her on his lap in that very chair filled her mind. She had no idea where the memory came from, or why it popped into her head now, and she certainly didn't want to feel the wrenching ache in her heart or the guilt for her part in driving him away. Banishing her feelings, she strode toward the Gibsons.

After they exchanged greetings and made small talk, Jake, who was stocky but sturdy, pulled his wife close and grinned. "We got some good news yesterday. Janelle's expecting. Come February, I'll be a daddy."

Freckle-face Janelle beamed. "That's why we want the rocking chair."

Margaret fervently hoped Jake wouldn't do what Glory had done and walk out, never to see his child again. Wondering at herself—why was she thinking about her father today, and why now?—she forced a smile. "Congratulations." Of its own volition her hand stroked one scarred but sturdy oak arm rest. "It's a little scratched up."

"But the price is right. I'll be sanding and refinishing it."

"He loves to do that kind of stuff, and he's great at it," Janelle said, shooting her husband a proud look.

Jake opened his wallet and paid Margaret. "Thanks. We'll take good care of this rocker."

"I'm sure you will."

She pocketed the money, which later would go into the green lockbox they had found in Susan's office. Jake hefted the chair and he and Janelle headed off.

"Good morning, Maggie." Wearing sunglasses and a large hat, Ruth Adele Johanssen fluttered her fingers in greeting and strolled toward her. "Looks like another scorcher." With a somber expression, she glanced around. "Gosh, this is something to see. All your mother's belongings out here like nothing important."

Prickling at the criticism, Margaret removed her own sunglasses and looked Ruth Adele square in the eye. "There's nothing wrong with selling Susan's things. If you find something you want, you're welcome to buy it."

"I've always coveted her good dishes. Will you bargain?"

"I might."

"All right." The sixty-something woman stuck out her beaky nose and cocked her gray-streaked head in a way that reminded Margaret of a chicken. "You look different this morning. Real pretty. I like what you did to your eyes."

Having forgotten about the makeup, Margaret was both pleased and taken aback. Did she really want to call attention to her looks when her brain was what mattered? *You're darned right, you do,* chimed a voice in her head. *You have the right to be pretty AND smart.* She smiled. "Thank you."

As Ruth Adele ambled away toward a box of Susan's clothes, an overweight woman clutching a picture that had hung on the dining room wall headed toward Margaret.

"This is a lovely frame, but I don't want the picture. Can I get a twenty percent discount?"

In the bright sunlight, the landscape print looked faded and worthless. "I have no problem with that."

"Will you take the picture out?"

Across the lawn, Quincy caught Margaret's eye and threw her a thumbs-up before turning to a neatly dressed silver-haired couple.

"I don't want it," Margaret said. "Take the whole thing with you and throw it away at home. You'll still get the discount."

"Oh, but I couldn't take the picture, not without paying for it. It wouldn't feel right.

Please remove it for me. You're welcome to use my Swiss army knife."

Margaret stifled an impatient sigh. "All right."

"Just let me find it."

While the woman dug through a tiny purse that was crammed to bursting, Margaret glanced at the people milling around. Rose was talking with a woman who looked vaguely familiar and was holding a young blonde boy's hand. Someone from high school, she guessed.

"Here you go." The woman handed over the knife.

Margaret knelt on grass so brittle it scratched to work the back of the frame loose. A few moments later, she was able to lift it off.

To her surprise, hidden between the back of the frame and the faded print was a large, black and white photo of Glory. The photographer had captured the mischievous quirk of his mouth and the warmth and humor glinting in his eyes. His gaze seemed to bore straight into Margaret.

"My, that's a handsome man," the woman said.

"Yes, he is." She sounded remarkably calm and detached, but inside, her heart bled. *Daddy.* Slipping the photo underneath the landscape print she stumbled to her feet.

"Are you all right?" the woman asked with concern. "You look as if you've seen a ghost."

In a sense, she had. "It's nothing."

Margaret collected the woman's money. Then, clasping both pictures to her chest—she would hide the one of Glory someplace—she turned away.

As the day wore on, despite the heat and glaring sun, shoppers and browsers peppered the yard in a steady stream. Most were strangers to Quincy, but she enjoyed meeting people and had no trouble striking up a conversation and bargaining when the need arose. As she and her sisters took turns grabbing lunch and snatching quick breaks, the items heaped on the lawn slowly disappeared. So did the living room furniture, the dining room set, and the TV. A man who owned several rentals wanted the washer and dryer. He paid a fair price and promised to pick them up over the weekend.

The lovely green bills that filled the lockbox pleased Quincy no end. Even split three ways, she could pay a few bills.

The energizing interactions with people and the warmth and support from her sisters kept her spirits high. But much as she enjoyed herself, by late afternoon she needed a breather. Sitting alone on a bath towel under a tree in the tiny backyard, she kicked off her flip-flops, tossed the baseball cap aside, pulled the scrunchie from her ponytail, and shook her hair free. Ah, that felt good. The grass was brown and prickly, so using the rough trunk as a back rest, she kept her knees bent and her feet flat on the towel. Sipping from a frosty glass of last night's iced tea she listened absently to the voices floating through the air.

All in all, today had been a big success. Though not much fun for Margaret, who was more introverted than Quincy and Rose. She'd started out in a decent enough mood, but within a short time had turned grouchy and touchy. She simply wasn't used to dealing with people for extended periods. And it was so bloody hot.

Quincy lifted her hair and pressed the cold glass to the back of her neck, her thoughts drifting aimlessly. Susan's office wasn't half cleaned out. Four remaining file cabinet drawers, a good part of the desk, and the files on the computer—could anything be more boring? As tired as Quincy was, finishing the job tonight would be a real pain.

She pulled her hair into a ponytail again and thought about taking Margaret to buy the right shade of lipstick on Sunday afternoon.

Which reminded her that she hadn't freshened hers since lunch. She frowned at her red toenails, carefully painted last night. Already some of the polish had chipped off. Her fingernails were no better, but there was no point repairing them until the garage sale ended tomorrow night.

Given the heat and long day there was a good chance all her makeup had rubbed off. She probably looked like hell and ought to go inside and freshen up. But at the moment she was too darned hot and worn out to care.

Lucky thing Ira couldn't see her now. Not that he'd even notice if she painted herself purple. He wasn't interested. What a fool she'd been to throw herself at him. Cheeks burning, she smacked her forehead twice with the heel of her hand.

The worst of it was, despite having only seen him a few times since high school, despite his not wanting her, she'd fallen for him. Hard. Hunched over, she stared gloomily at the parched earth beneath the dying grass.

She'd always been like that, giving away her heart much too quickly. For her rashness she inevitably ended up on the losing end.

It wasn't that Ira didn't like her. He did, or so he claimed. But that didn't mean a lot. Margaret and Rose might think she was a worthwhile person, but Quincy knew she didn't have much to offer besides her body. If Ira didn't want her sexually, there was no chance for them.

Quincy glanced at her legs, which some men fought to stroke and wrap around their hips. A blissful experience Ira never would have the pleasure of enjoying.

She flipped her hair, absently noting the way

it tickled her shoulder. *Eat your heart out, Ira Lamm.*

For about one second she felt better. Then she huffed out a heavy sigh. A broken heart was no fun at all. Well, she'd been here before. The only thing to do was hold her head high, pretend she didn't care, and move on.

Then never again let herself fall for a guy so quickly. From now on she'd wait for what she wanted—the love of a smart, kind man who wouldn't saddle her with his debts or borrow money and never pay her back.

Except for the love part, the description fit Ira Lamm like a Lycra body suit.

As if her thoughts had conjured him up, she heard his voice from the front of the house. "Where's Quincy?"

"Not here," Rose replied in icy tones.

"When will she be back?"

"We don't know," Margaret said as aloof as Susan used to sound when some boy phoned the house.

Ira didn't deserve that. Forgetting her broken heart, Quincy stood, toed into her flip-flops, and hurried toward the front of the house.

At close to six, many of the garage sale shoppers were gone. Standing at the edge of the yard a few feet from Ira's car, Margaret and Rose faced him with crossed arms and hostile expressions, a protective, sisterly barrier between him and Quincy.

Dressed in a short sleeve striped shirt and faded jeans, Ira shifted his weight with an uncertainty she'd never seen.

Quincy appreciated her sisters' concern, but she was a grown woman who'd been here before. Ignoring the curious looks of the few remaining female shoppers and the worried looks of her sisters, she ambled forward as unconcerned as you please, while inside she was a mess of nerves and hurt. "Are you looking for me?"

Relief lightened Ira's face. He seemed pleased to see her, almost looked as if he cared. Hope stirred in Quincy's chest. But she wasn't that naive.

As he reached for her arm, she shook him off. Shooting her sisters an "it's okay" look, she turned on her heel and led him into the backyard, away from prying eyes. Aware that he probably was looking at her backside, she was careful to omit her usual sexy wiggle. Why bother?

In the backyard she leaned against the sun-warm siding of the house, tugged her tank top over her hips, shoved her hands into the pockets of her cutoffs, and eyed him warily. "What do you want?"

"We need to talk." He raked his hand through his already wind-ruffled hair, which messed it up even more and charmed Quincy.

Annoyed with herself, she frowned. "It's all been said," she stated, proud of her indifferent tone.

"Has it? You were hurt and angry last night,

and I don't think you understood me at all. When you walked away without a backward glance . . ." Gloom darkened his face and he gave a helpless shrug. "I can't handle that."

Quincy couldn't tear her gaze from his. The noise, the heat, everything faded, along with her anger and her resolve. Her foolish heart opened, and she forgave him.

"It wasn't your fault, Ira. I was out of line." Fresh shame swept through her, and suddenly she couldn't bear for him to look at her. "Are we done now? Because I should get back to helping Margaret and Rose." She pushed away from the wall and brushed past him.

"Quincy, wait," he said in a voice so low and pleading, she stopped.

"What?" she asked without turning around.

"Look at me. Please."

Slowly she pivoted toward him.

"I meant what I said last night." Standing several yards from her, Ira met her gaze squarely, his gray eyes penetrating behind his glasses.

"The part about not wanting me?" Hurt flooded her. "I got the message."

He scrubbed the back of his neck. "I never said that, Quincy. What I said was, I like you." He moved toward her, stopping before he got too close. "A lot."

Though she bit back her thoughts, they tumbled out. "If that's true, why didn't you kiss me?"

"What's the rush? We have time."

This puzzled her. She'd never met a man so laid back about getting laid. Pun intended. "In case you forgot, I'm leaving Tuesday morning. After that there's no reason for me to come back here."

"If we start a relationship, I'll be your reason."

"Long-distance relationships don't work so well." Not with a stupid little tramp. *I'm not stupid and not a tramp,* she silently countered. *I'm a good person and I'm smart.* She still didn't quite believe that but at least she'd thought it.

"I have plenty of money. I can fly down to see you whenever I want, or fly you up here to be with me. Between visits we'll talk and e-mail every day."

No one had ever offered her this. Uncertain whether to trust him, she frowned. "There must be scads of women interested in you." Females far classier than she. "Why me, Ira?"

"Because I haven't felt this way since . . . never. I'm comfortable with you and I think you feel the same around me."

He was right.

"I believe we have a chance for something great together, but we won't know till we try. What do you say, Quincy?"

"I'll think about it," she said, intending to do just that. "Yes," she blurted out, making her usual snap decision.

Ira flashed a brilliant grin. "Really?"

His eyes turned tender and warm. Reaching

out he brushed a tiny, dead leaf from her hair.
With that simple, gentle touch she was lost.
And so head over heels. If he'd asked her to
strip naked and make love right here in the backyard where anyone could see, she would have.

But that wasn't Ira. He dropped his hand,
but not his gaze. "You have the prettiest smile."

"Don't lie to me, Ira. All my makeup has
worn off. I'm dirty and sweaty and I know I
look awful."

"Not to me, you don't."

His appreciative look reassured her. Feeling
uncharacteristically shy she glanced down at
her feet and watched him from under her lowered lashes. "You're pretty cute yourself."

"Cute, huh?" He flushed endearingly.

God help her, she wanted to swoon like they
did in the old movies. "I should get back to the
garage sale," she said.

"In a minute." He reached into the hip
pocket of his jeans and handed her a small,
tissue-wrapped packet. "I brought you something."

It was the second gift he'd given her in as
many days. Quincy was used to presents from
men, usually after she slept with them. Ira
didn't fall into that category. She frowned.
"Were you that certain I'd make up with you?"

This time his smile was sheepish. "You can't
blame a guy for hoping and being prepared."

His honesty disarmed and awed her. He was

such a good, straightforward man. "I don't deserve this," she murmured.

"Sure you do. Open it and it'll make perfect
sense."

Quincy turned the feather-light package
over in her hands so that the elegant black and
gold foil sticker holding the paper together
faced her. For some reason, her fingers shook.
She peeled off the sticker. The tissue rustled as
she unfolded it to reveal something soft and
robin's egg blue. She pulled out a long, rectan-
gular, silk scarf so delicate and fine, it fluttered
in the still air.

"It's gorgeous," she breathed.

"You like it." The grin returned, wide
enough to crinkle the corners of his eyes.

He was charming and utterly irresistible.
She, too, smiled.

"The color matches your eyes perfectly," he
said. "When I saw it I had to buy it for you.
Now you have your own special scarf for riding
in my car."

Why this touched her so was anyone's guess.
"Thank you," Quincy said, holding tight to the
scarf when what she wanted was to throw her
arms around Ira and kiss him. He didn't want
that, not yet. In time.

"I thought we could test it out tonight. Are
you free for dinner?"

Wishing she was, she shook her head. "I'd
love to, only I promised to help Rose and Margaret empty out the rest of Susan's office. We

hope to sell the furniture and whatever else we find in there at tomorrow's garage sale." Ira's disappointment was gratifying. "But I am available tomorrow night after seven," she said.

Instantly he brightened. "That'll work. I'll pick you up at seven fifteen. Office furniture is heavy. Why don't I stop by first thing tomorrow and carry it out here for you?"

The plan was to bring people inside to see the office set, but if Ira wanted to stop by . . . "That'd be great," she said, already looking forward to seeing him in the morning. "What should I wear tomorrow night?"

"Nothing fancy. What you have on now is fine."

No way was she wearing an old tank top and faded cutoffs to dinner with Ira. "Exactly where are we going?"

A teasing gleam lit his eyes. "You'll find out."

Quincy wanted to know. "Tell me, Ira. Please, please, please?"

Chuckling, he shook his head. "That'd ruin the surprise."

He kissed the tip of her nose, and she no longer cared where they went. She caught a whiff of his spicy aftershave and knew it would forever be a favorite of hers.

He laced his fingers with hers. "Walk me to my car?"

In a daze she let him pull her along, not caring that the two remaining female shoppers stared curiously. After Ira drove away, she caught Rose's eye and grinned.

"Look what he brought me." She showed off the scarf.

Rose oohed and aahed, and so did the other women. Margaret barely said a word, but her unhappy expression spoke volumes.

"I see she's still in a crappy mood," Quincy murmured. "What's wrong with her?"

Rose shrugged. "I'm starting to get grouchy myself. Once she eats, she's bound to feel better. Let's shoo these ladies out, close up for the night, and grab ourselves some dinner."

Chapter 19

Half an hour after the garage sale ended, Margaret and her sisters sat at a laminated table in a fast food place on the outskirts of town. Being a Friday night and way past the dinner hour, they had the place to themselves.

Not that Margaret cared. Regardless of the surroundings she was in a rotten mood. Selling the rocking chair and then finding the large photo of Glory had stirred up memories and the guilt that had been with her since he'd abandoned the family. Like acid, it was eating holes in her heart and ruining her appetite. She picked up her chicken burger and took a small bite. For all she tasted of it she could have been eating dirt.

"You're pecking at your food like a little bird," Quincy observed between bites of her rapidly disappearing double cheeseburger.

"This isn't like you." Rose popped two French fries into her mouth and devoured them.

Their good humor only made Margaret feel worse. She wished she'd stayed alone at the house. "I'm not hungry, that's all."

"I hope you're not coming down with something," Rose said with a motherly frown.

"Get off my case," Margaret snapped, pushing aside her plate.

Her sisters looked startled. She pretended not to notice.

If only the woman who bought the picture frame hadn't asked her to take out the print. Then she wouldn't have seen that photo and had her whole day ruined. At the moment it was hidden on the shelf in the now-empty closet of the pink bedroom. Out of sight, out of mind.

Unfortunately, in this case the old adage didn't seem to hold.

Margaret sipped soda through her straw, her melancholy gaze on the water ring left by her cup. No matter how hard she tried, and she'd worked at it all day, she couldn't push Glory's image out of her mind. Those eyes and that smile . . .

A howl of pain formed in her chest and pushed to her throat. Only through sheer will did she hold it back. She hadn't mentioned the picture or shown it to Rose or Quincy. Couldn't, not without breaking down. Questions would surely follow, and as emotional as Margaret was, she feared she'd betray herself and let out what had *really* happened that fateful morning Glory had walked out. No good could come from that. If anything, the truth would destroy the new warmth and closeness between her and her sisters. She didn't think she could bear losing that precious sense of belonging, of connection.

No, she couldn't tell them what she'd done. She could tell no one. And she wanted desperately to go home and lose herself in her work. Unfortunately, she was stuck here until Tuesday.

How could she possibly hold herself together for that long?

"So, Quincy," Rose said with forced cheeriness, an obvious attempt to lighten the cloud that had fallen over them, "You showed us the beautiful scarf Ira gave you, but you haven't told us what happened in the backyard. Obviously he's still interested."

After sliding a wary look Margaret's way, Quincy nodded. "He wants a relationship. Says he can fly to Vegas or fly me here any time."

Her laugh was pure joy. Jealousy pricked Margaret, which fueled her guilt even more. Quincy deserved happiness. But if she had to listen to any more lighthearted chatter she'd scream.

"Yippee, skippee." Rose clapped her hands in glee. "I'm so, so ha—"

"Excuse me." Margaret scraped her chair across the tile floor. She stood, then fled for the privacy of the ladies' room.

"Either she really is getting sick, or she's an incredibly rude bitch."

Quincy's words floated toward Margaret. She absorbed them without flinching. Bitch didn't begin to describe what she was.

"Let's give her the benefit of the doubt," Rose replied loudly enough that Margaret knew she wanted her to hear. "It's been a long, hot day. She's exhausted."

Oh, she was exhausted, all right, and sick to death of feeling guilty over a past she couldn't change.

The empty bathroom smelled faintly of disinfectant and urine. The paper towel receptacle was full to overflowing and the sinks water stained and dirty.

Alone in the stall, burying her face in her hands, Margaret cried.

An hour later, dinner over and night upon them, Rose leaned toward her mother's computer screen and scanned through the various folders. She'd meant to do this a few nights ago, but problems with Danny had distracted her. Since then, so much had changed. She smiled to herself. She couldn't wait to talk to him later tonight and catch up on his day and tell him about hers. But that had to wait until she finished here. Without Susan's password she couldn't access e-mail, but she could check everything else.

Most of the folders were work related,

including annual spreadsheets detailing income and expenses. Information Arthur Tremayne might want. Rose hit the print button. While waiting for the printer to spit out the pages she glanced at Quincy who was seated on the floor by the desk slowly combing through the contents of the remaining drawers.

"Remember what you said the other night, Quincy, that Susan was poor? According to the spreadsheets I just found, she earned a decent income, especially the past few years."

"She sure didn't save much." Quincy held up the most recent bank statement, the one they'd found the other night. "We'll need every penny of what's in the bank account and more for funeral expenses and bills."

Margaret said nothing. Showing Rose and Quincy her back, she stooped over a drawer in the file cabinet and pulled out manila folders one by one. She'd started two piles on the floor: one "keep" and one "toss."

Tonight she wasn't herself, and her mood had only darkened since she'd come out of the ladies' room with her eyes swollen and her nose as red as it had been after their mother's funeral.

Rose never had seen her so withdrawn and downhearted. Both curious and concerned, she'd tried to coax Margaret to talk about whatever was bothering her. So had Quincy. But Margaret wasn't saying.

"Man, I'm tired." With a loud yawn Quincy

arched the small of her back and stretched her arms upward. "I need a break." She unfolded her legs, wandered to the window, and peered between the slats of the blinds. Not that she could see anything. It was pitch black out there.

After all of two seconds, Margaret turned from the file cabinet with a frown. "If you're going to stand there doing nothing, you may as well call Ira and go out."

Quincy spun from the window with her chin raised in challenge. "I'm only taking a short rest, so lighten up."

Margaret's lips flattened and her eyes narrowed and the room grew heavy with the familiar hostility and tension that had all but disappeared over the past twenty-four hours.

As sick dread knotted her stomach, Rose fervently wished she was at home with Danny, relaxed and safe in his arms.

"What's your problem, anyway?" Quincy asked, crossing her arms and matching Margaret's stony expression.

Please don't fight. "She's hypoglycemic," Rose said. "She should've brought her dinner home instead of throwing it out."

"Quit talking about me as if I weren't here."

Quincy threw up her hands. "You're so damned touchy, we don't have much choice."

"Shall I fix you a plate?" Rose offered, slipping into her nurturing role. "A sandwich? Fried eggs?"

Margaret's scathing look made her feel as if she'd

committed a crime by asking and reminded her of Susan in an especially bad mood. She shuddered.

"Well, excuuuuuse her for being thought-ful," Quincy said, drawing Margaret's ill will onto herself.

"I didn't ask her to, and I didn't ask you for sarcasm." Clutching a manila folder like a shield, Margaret glared at Quincy. "You didn't work the last hour of the garage sale and you're goofing off now. I resent it."

"Is that what put the burr up your behind?" Quincy tossed her head. "Well, I resent you right back. Telling me what to do and treating Rose and me like trailer trash. Who do you think you are, our mother?" She snorted. "In case that brain of yours went AWOL and you forgot, she's dead. That's why we're all having so much fun right now."

Margaret snorted. "I wish you'd grow up."

"And I wish—"

"Both of you stop it!" Rose stamped her foot so hard the floor shook. She sent a placating look Margaret's way. "Why don't you relax for the rest of the evening and let Quincy and me—"

"Relax?" Margaret gave a hysterical-sounding laugh. "Trapped in this house with you two and a ton of work waiting for me at home?" She sailed the folder onto the "toss" pile, then once again showed them her unnaturally stiff back.

She seemed as if she were about to snap in

half. Worried, upset, and feeling helpless to change things, Rose locked her hands at her waist.

Fists on her hips, Quincy eyed Margaret with a mad-as-hell frown. "Working on Susan's office is hard enough without you being in a shitty mood. For God's sake, either cheer up or get the hell out of here."

Margaret jerked as if she'd been struck. "You know what, I'm finished." She slammed the drawer shut and pivoted toward the door.

Unable to bear for her to leave with things so ugly, Rose tried again to reach out. "What Quincy means is, if you'd just tell us what's wrong, maybe we could help . . ."

A few feet short of the door, Margaret halted and wheeled around. Her face contorted with pain as she sliced the air with her hand. "None of your freaking business! Now leave me alone!"

While Quincy and Rose stood open-mouthed, she stalked out.

Shocked, Quincy stared at the space where a scant second ago Margaret had stood and screamed at them. After they'd been getting along so well, too.

She raked her hands through her hair and turned to Rose, who looked equally shaken. "What just happened? Was it my fault?"

Rose shook her head. "Something's tearing Margaret apart. I just wish I knew what."

"Could be the bad vibes in this room, but we'll never know. If she doesn't want to talk, we can't force her."

God knew they'd both tried. Exhaling a heavy breath Quincy again sank onto the floor in front of a half-emptied desk drawer. "We trusted her with our problems, but apparently she doesn't trust us."

That she thought so little of them stung.

"Sad, but true." Rose bowed her head.

"I don't think I've ever seen her this upset." Quincy stared glumly at the drawer. "She might be jealous because you have Danny, and Ira and I are starting a relationship. Since she doesn't have a man of her own." Then again, Margaret could probably start something with Bruce if she wanted. Maybe that wasn't the problem.

"I don't think she's jealous. She was so happy about Danny and me making up."

"You saw her at the restaurant. She didn't exactly seem overjoyed about Ira."

"I know she's thrilled for you. I wonder what stopped her from saying so." With a pensive look, Rose pressed a computer key. The printer whirred to life. "She was in good enough spirits this morning, right?"

Quincy nodded. "We had loads of fun with her makeup. Then we all got so busy, I didn't talk to her again for several hours. Sometime between coffee and lunch her mood nosedived."

"But why?"

Quincy searched her mind and came up empty. "Beats me."

"Do you think we should go after her?"

"And get yelled at again? No, thank you. I say we leave her alone and empty this room so she won't have to. Let's finish what we're doing, then divide up what's left of the file cabinet."

They returned to their tasks, this time in thoughtful silence. For a while Quincy stewed about Margaret, but then a drawer filled with files of Susan's current clients grabbed her full attention. Included were a good dozen established businesses and well-known individuals. Impressive.

"You should see the names of the folks who hired Susan," she said. "I'm guessing they all know she's gone, but someone should still write that letter." It seemed like the right thing to do. "That was Margaret's idea, but I'm not about to remind her."

"I could write it, but I'm not the best at stuff like that." Rose fiddled with the tiny studs in her earlobes. "Let's ask Arthur Tremayne."

"Are you crazy? Attorneys charge for every little thing." Quincy set the folders aside and sighed. "All right, I'll write it myself before I go to bed."

"Thanks," Rose said, looking relieved. "Except for Susan's e-mail, I'm about through with the computer, but I'll leave it on for you." She stood and moved to the printer to collect what she'd printed. "I've been thinking . . . We ought to erase the hard drive before we get rid of this computer. We could ask Ira to do it. Unless you think we shouldn't bother him?"

Even hearing his name warmed Quincy. "Of course we should. If I know Ira, he'll be happy to help. I'm about finished over here. Aside from the current client folders, most of this stuff is junk." She gestured at the towering pile on the floor. "Looks like another trip to the dump."

"There'll be more once we empty the file cabinet. I'll start with the drawer Margaret was working on and do the one below it if you'll tackle the bottom two."

"Sure. I wonder where she went?" Quincy mused as she slid the empty desk drawers into their slots. She wasn't exactly worried. More . . . uneasy. Margaret wasn't the type to stomp off and disappear for hours. "Do you think she's okay?"

"If not, she will be. I just hope that wherever she is, she finds peace." Rose began to paw through the file cabinet.

Moments later, arms full of green hanging folders, Quincy returned to the desk. She set them down and opened one. Inside were copies of invoices and payments from sixteen years back when Susan had first started her own full-time paralegal business. Not worth keeping, but Quincy decided to look through them anyway. Especially the one for Ira, which was somewhere in the pile. Eager to find it, she combed rapidly through the others, noting more familiar names, including Matt Greenwald, Tom Brewster, Frank Vale, and Eric Del-Vaio. *Well, well.* She set aside Ira's file for the moment.

"Did you know Susan did paralegal work for all four of her lovers? I wonder if they hired her so she'd do *them?*"

Rose made a face. "That's a disgusting thought."

"Doesn't mean it didn't happen. Do you recall when she and Matt were doing the nasty?"

"Wasn't he her first lover after Glory?"

"So Fiona said." Quincy opened Matt's file and thumbed through it. "According to the invoices and payment receipts in here, Matt didn't hire Susan until five years ago, a looong time after they split up. Huh."

Quincy leafed through the files of Susan's other ex-lovers. "Tom Brewster hired her around the same time as Matt, which also was after they split up. She didn't start anything with Frank Vale or Eric DelVaio until *after* she worked for them." Very interesting. "So Susan didn't work with any of them while they were sexually involved. I didn't expect that."

"Too ethical to combine work with pleasure, I guess."

"Somehow when I think of our mother, pleasure

doesn't come to mind," Quincy said. "And we don't know a thing about her ethics."

"We know she wouldn't kill or rob anyone and that she paid her bills and went to church."

All true. "You should see the names of some of the businesses, past and present, that hired her. She must've been a good paralegal."

"At the funeral everyone, including Ira, said so."

"I thought they were just being nice." Filled with a grudging, newfound respect for her mother, Quincy held up Ira's file. "This one is Ira's."

Catching her breath she opened it. Nine years earlier, Susan had guided Applied Cryptography through several legal matters, and Ira had paid her well. *Thank you, Ira.* Quincy's heart expanded. She could hardly wait to see him in the morning and again tomorrow night. And as novel and scary as it was, she could hardly wait to get to know him *before* they had sex.

"That's some pleased expression on your face," Rose said. "You must've found something very interesting in Ira's folder."

"Only that Susan worked for him several times when he started his company. I think that's pretty cool. Just about finished here."

"Me, too. That leaves one drawer for each of us."

"It had better not take long, because I'm fading. Scoot over so I can open the bottom one."

The drawer rolled halfway open, then stuck fast. Quincy tried to jerk it the rest of the way but it refused to budge. "Dammit, it's jammed." Frowning, she pulled out the hanging files she could reach. "Something must be stuck in the back."

On her knees she peered into the drawer. Seeing nothing, she frowned and reached deep inside. Her fingers touched what felt like stiff leather. A hidden bank account book? After several grimaces and grunts, she worked it free.

When she saw what it was, she sat down. "An old, beat-up photo album. Who'd have guessed?" She opened the cover. A musty smell tickled her nose, but she was too taken by the old family photos to notice. "You've got to see this, Rose."

Her sister joined her on the floor. Slowly turning the pages, they viewed pictures they'd never seen, taken when they were a family. Each of them tugged at Quincy's heart.

"Look at this one." She pointed to a picture of Glory, Susan, and the three of them. "And that one, with us rubbing Suzette's puppy tummy. We actually look happy."

"Funny the poses people strike for a camera."

"No, seriously. See how Susan's staring at Glory with love in her eyes? And look at Glory's face." Whoever had taken the photo had caught her father balancing Margaret on his shoulders while he clasped Rose's hand and carried Quincy in the crook of his arm. He smiled at Susan as if he meant it. Squeezing her eyes shut, Quincy tried to recall that happy time. She failed. With a sigh she opened her eyes. "I'd give anything to remember that moment or one like it."

"I can't even remember what he smelled like," Rose said, looking as blue and wistful as Quincy felt.

"Or the sound of his laughter."

Rose pointed to a blank space where a picture once had been pasted. "Remember that photo we found when we cleaned out Susan's bedroom? I'll bet it came from here."

"We should glue it back in. Where'd we put it?"

"I'm not sure."

They flipped through the yellowed pages, pausing here and there to comment or ask questions neither could answer.

"Margaret would know some of this stuff," Quincy said. "I wish she were here."

"Wait till she sees these." Clearly awed, Rose touched her heart. "Fiona told us the story of our parents, but looking at these pictures, I can really see it. How Susan truly loved Glory. I can't imagine what she must have felt when he walked out. If it was anywhere near as miserable as I felt when Danny left . . ." She swallowed and shook her head.

"It probably hurt like hell and then some. Too bad she never talked about it with us."

Rose pointed to a picture of Glory pushing the three of them on a playground merry-go-round, everyone laughing. "In this photo, Glory looks as if he loves us, too."

"If that were true, he wouldn't have left. He'd have divorced Susan, but wouldn't have forgotten about us. Or walked out on my fourth birthday."

"That was awful, wasn't it?"

"Yeah." In no mood to take a walk down that painful lane, Quincy closed the book and set it aside. "It's really late. Let's straighten up in here and get to bed."

"Weren't you going to write a letter to Susan's clients?"

"Too tired now. I'll do it in bed, longhand, and type it up first thing tomorrow."

Twenty minutes later they turned off the office light and closed the door behind them.

Not wanting to leave the photo album behind, Quincy took it with her. "Margaret should see this, but I'm not waiting up to show it to her."

"Me, either," Rose said. "I'm going to climb into bed, call Danny, and then go to sleep. Let's leave it someplace where Margaret will find it."

"How about the floor in front of the door? She can't miss it there."

Chapter 20

Margaret wandered into the kitchen dressed but makeup-free. What was the point of wearing makeup when you felt ugly inside?

Quincy and Rose were dressed and already at the table, drinking coffee from jumbo Styrofoam cups in comfortable silence.

Embarrassed by her screaming fit the night before, Margaret couldn't look directly at them. "Morning."

"Good morning," Rose replied warily.

Quincy said nothing, simply arched her brows and tipped her cup in greeting.

As Margaret poured herself coffee she could feel the tension and knew she was the cause. Feeling terrible about that, she offered a smile meant to put them at ease. Who knew whether it worked.

Having eaten little last night, she was famished.

She filled a disposable bowl with dry cereal, then opened the fridge for milk.

"Did you see the photo album we left for you last night?" Rose asked as Margaret sat down.

Margaret wanted neither to think nor talk about those pictures. Too many painful memories. "See it?" She added sugar to the cereal. "I almost tripped over it."

"That's why we put it on the floor, so you'd be sure to find it," Rose said. "Did you look through it?"

Margaret didn't intend to look through it—ever. Dipping a plastic spoon into the bowl, she shook her head. "It was too late and I was too tired. I left it on the mantel and went to bed."

They wanted to ask where she'd been last night—she saw it in their eyes. She'd taken herself to the drive-in, a place she hadn't been since high school, to watch a double feature. Any movie would do, as long as it allowed her mind an escape, even the original *Planet of the Apes.* As dated and silly as the movie was, it had served its purpose. For several hours she'd forgotten her own problems and taken on those of the characters on the screen. When the second feature, *Beneath the Planet of the Apes,* had started, she'd stayed for it, too.

Margaret didn't want to talk about the movies. She didn't want to talk, period. She bent to her breakfast and for a short while her sisters were gratifyingly quiet.

Then Rose broke the silence. "We finished the office."

When Quincy only nodded, Margaret rounded her eyes in mock surprise. "You're not talking much this morning."

"Nothing to say."

"We filled several more garbage bags," Rose said. "One of us should go to the dump."

"I will after breakfast," Margaret offered. "But that means I'll miss the start of the garage sale."

"We managed without you last night," Quincy said. "We'll manage today."

Rose threw her a scared frown, and looking stricken, Quincy sucked in a breath.

Margaret realized they were walking on proverbial eggshells this morning, not unlike the way they'd often tiptoed around Susan. She winced at the thought. But she was trapped in an emotional hell her sisters could never understand.

Nothing like Susan. And yet, her mother had been in emotional pain, too. Could it be that everything—the coldness, bad moods, outbursts of temper—had stemmed from Susan's own unhappiness and dissatisfaction with herself? Stunned at the revelation, Margaret sat back in her chair. It was so obvious, she wondered why she hadn't figured it out before.

The logical question that followed was, why had Susan clung to her pain year after year? Why hadn't she let go of it and moved on?

Why can't I?

Ann Roth

The time had come to do exactly that: release the old pain and move on with life.

Oblivious to Margaret's thoughts, Rose cleared her throat. "Back to the photo album. We found it hidden in a file cabinet drawer. Why it was there is anyone's guess."

"Remember the picture we found in Susan's bedroom, the one with us in a kiddy pool?" Quincy said. "We think it came from the same album. You should see all the family pictures in there. Rose and I were so little then. We thought if you looked through it with us, you could help us remember."

"Maybe I don't want to remember." Tears burned behind Margaret's eyes. Irritated with herself and wondering how did a person let go of the past and move on, she blinked hard, set her jaw, and stood to toss her spoon and bowl into the trash.

"Nothing wrong with crying again," Quincy said. "I've been doing a lot of that myself. We're all suffering. At least we're doing it together."

"And thank heaven for that," Rose said. "We lived in this house our entire childhoods, so we understand each other in ways no one else can. That's why it helped so much to talk to both of you about the abortion and Danny."

"And about my problems with Ira." Quincy stared solemnly at Margaret. "So if there's anything you want to say, we're here."

Rose gave a loving nod. The sisterly support gently prodded Margaret to open up. She longed to do just that. If she didn't, she just might explode. But she was afraid of what they'd think, of losing their respect and even their love.

The need to talk was stronger. With a deep sigh she returned to the table and sank onto her chair. Hands in her lap, head bowed, she sought for a way to frame her words. "I—"

The doorbell rang. "That's Ira. Sorry." Quincy shot her a look of genuine regret before she jumped up to answer the door.

Margaret's relief was almost as strong as her disappointment. She gave her brow a mental swipe. The past was over and done with and letting her sisters in on what really had happened with Glory wouldn't change a thing. Except that they might feel worse.

For their sakes she'd be strong and keep her problems to herself after all. And she *would* put the past out of her mind and move on. She would.

Rose was watching her with an expectant expression.

"There's really nothing to say," Margaret replied, avoiding her gaze by glancing at her watch. "Only forty minutes until the garage sale hordes descend on us. I'd best get to the dump and back."

By the time the last of the bargain hunters drove off early Saturday evening, Rose was glad

to see them go. The garage sale was over, and
the yard was a disaster. Trampled, sprinkled
with litter, and a deathly brown. "Look at this
place," she said, stooping to collect scraps of
paper and other debris. "Let's move what didn't
sell to the curb and try to revive the grass."

"It is in sorry shape," Quincy agreed.

She'd slipped away an hour ago to bathe
and dress for her date with Ira. Now her hair
was light brown, which was close to its natural
shade. She was dressed in a cap sleeve, beige
linen jumpsuit and flat but feminine sandals,
with soft makeup that made her skin glow.
Rose thought she looked especially beautiful.

Margaret, who was still in a dismal mood,
frowned. "Why waste the water when we'll be
leaving soon?"

"But you watered the other day," Quincy
said. "You know, when you called Bruce."

The frown deepened, and Rose braced for a
nasty retort. For the dozenth time she wondered what was bothering her older sister. This
morning at breakfast she'd been on the verge
of opening up. If only the doorbell hadn't
rung. . . .

To her relief Margaret shrugged instead of
snapping. "I only watered the flowers. We
probably should water them again. As for the
lawn, I say we leave that to whoever buys this
place. And the leftover junk"—she gestured at
the unsold odds and ends—"I'm with Rose.
Let's move it to the curb, put up a FREE sign,

and hope people help themselves. Whatever's left, the Salvation Army can pick up Monday. What they don't want we'll leave with the garbage."

"If you want to move this stuff, go right ahead," Quincy said. "But I'm not about to get dirty, so count me out."

Margaret eyed her. "Naturally you're all dressed up and can't help." The instant the words were out, she looked contrite. "That was mean. I'm sorry, Quincy."

At least she'd apologized. That was something. Rose hoped that tonight, with nothing on the agenda, Margaret would relax. Maybe then she'd feel like sharing her troubles.

Ira pulled up and parked, and Quincy's face lit up. "Don't worry about it, Maggie. I'm in such a great mood right now, nothing bothers me. But if you wait till I get back, I promise to help."

"We'll probably be asleep by then. Don't worry about it. There's not that much stuff. Rose and I can handle it."

"Thanks."

Giving her head a saucy shake, with eyes only for Ira, Quincy plucked the scarf he'd given her from her purse and made a beeline for the car. Ira kissed her cheek. After she buckled her seatbelt he winked at Margaret and Rose and blindfolded Quincy with the scarf. He promised to take good care of her, and she laughed. Less than a minute later, they were gone.

In silence Rose and Margaret moved things to the curb. It was a clear, hot evening, but a rare light breeze stirred the air.

"I hope Quincy has a good time tonight," Rose murmured. "She looked gorgeous. When she walked toward Ira his eyes nearly bugged out of his head. Then when he blindfolded her . . ." Filled with visions of love and romance, and missing Danny terribly, she smiled. "He must be taking her someplace special."

She lifted one end of the battered file cabinet no one had wanted. It wasn't heavy, just awkward.

Margaret hefted the other end and they toted it to the curb. "I just hope his actions match his words," she said, slightly winded, "and that he doesn't hurt her."

"There's no guarantee of that, but he seems to really like her. Look at what he bought her—a book, an expensive scarf that matches her eyes. A man doesn't give such thoughtful gifts unless he cares."

"I'd forgotten about that book." Margaret brought over two ancient, maroon-color suitcases. "What was it, anyway?"

"I don't know. She never showed it to me or even mentioned it." Which seemed odd. Rose made a mental note to ask Quincy about it later. "Maybe it's one of those *Dummies* books that explains cryptography or something." She glanced at the empty yard and brushed her hands together. "There, we're done. I'm starved, and we need something for breakfast tomorrow. We should stop at the grocery on our way to dinner. What do you feel like eating?"

"Anything," Margaret said. "Only, I'm beat and don't feel like going out. Let's call someplace that delivers."

If they stayed here Rose doubted she'd coax Margaret into a better mood and sharing her problems. They needed to get out of the house. "The TV and radio are gone and the place is virtually empty. That leaves us the whole night with nothing to do. You can't just sit around till bedtime."

"Sure I can. I'll read." Margaret yawned.

"You're way too tired for that. We should do something. We'll stop at the grocery, have dinner, and then . . . I know, go bowling. Like we used to."

"As I recall we bowled together exactly twice: once for a youth group fundraiser, and once to get out of the house and flirt with boys." Margaret actually cracked a smile. "I think I rolled more gutter balls than anyone else."

"I'm not much better. What do you say?" Rose elbowed her sister. "It'll be a load of laughs, just what we both need."

To her relief, Margaret gave in. "Oh, all right. But if I get foot disease from those nasty rental shoes, I'm sending you the doctor bill."

* * *

"We're here." Ira shut off the engine.

Quincy heard the click of his seatbelt as he un-buckled. Bursting to know where he'd brought her, heart pounding with excitement, she reached behind her head to untie the blindfold.

"Uh-uh." His hand covered hers, stopping her fumbling efforts. "Not yet."

"Please, Ira, can't I take off this thing?" To her own ears she sounded like a breathless ten-year-old. But she couldn't help herself.

His low chuckle tickled her ears. "Soon, Quincy. Sit tight and I'll be right back."

His door slammed shut. He opened the trunk. Then it, too, slammed.

He hadn't said anything about peeking. Quincy raised her head and strained to see out the lower edge of the blindfold. Unfortunately, she saw nothing but a thin sliver of fading light.

"None of that, now," Ira said.

She could hear the smile in his voice. "Spoil-sport."

Restless, anticipation mounting, she unfastened her seatbelt, then cocked her head to listen. Ira's footsteps thudded softly on the ground, meaning earth, not pavement. In the distance a lark called out. Another answered. She thought she heard a squirrel skittering down a tree. The scent of ripe peaches filled the air, and her empty stomach growled.

Time seemed to drag. Quincy shifted in her seat and shifted again. Where was Ira? She never had been a patient person and waiting was killing her. In one second she was about to rip off the blindfold and—

"Ready?"

Startled, she jumped. She hadn't heard him come back. "I can't stand it anymore," she said, again reaching behind her head.

"Not quite yet."

She willed her hands to her lap. Heard her door open. Strong fingers clasped her arm.

"Let's go." Ira guided her out of the car.

Unable to see where she was going, she held tight to his hand. "This is torture." But fun, too. She smiled.

"Why don't you try to guess where we are?"

"Well . . ." Soft grass tickled her ankles. Soft? The drought in Shadow Falls made for dry, brittle grass. "A park?"

"No."

"I smell peaches. A fruit stand?"

"Nope, but it's good to know your nose works. Okay, wait here." He let go of her hand.

She heard a gate creak open. Placing his palms lightly on her shoulders, he urged her forward a dozen steps. "Now I'll untie that blindfold," he said, still behind her.

"Finally."

He worked the knot, standing so close that Quincy felt the heat of his body and the warmth of his breath. She smelled his spicy aftershave.

Her body began to thrum, and it was all she
could do not to lean back against him. Would
he kiss her?

Her pulse raced and she wished she'd
popped a breath mint in the car. The scarf
whispered over her cheeks. Instead of turning
her around to face him, Ira stepped back. No
kiss for now. Disappointed but trusting that
sooner or later he *would* kiss her, she glanced
around. Twilight sky and broad, leafy trees
heavy with peaches filled her view.

"We're in an orchard," she said.

Of all the places to be in Shadow Falls, she'd
never have guessed. A few yards away, between
the rows of trees, a checkered blanket lay
spread on the ground. Beside it sat a large
wicker basket.

"A picnic." Quincy couldn't remember the
last time she'd picnicked.

"You don't mind, do you? If you stay on the
blanket you won't get that pretty outfit dirty."

"Don't worry about this old thing." Not exactly what she'd told Margaret, but this was different. "That's why God invented dry cleaning."

Ira shook his head and laughed. "What'd I
tell you, Quincy? You always make me smile."
As he gazed into her face, his expression
sobered. "We have the whole place to ourselves: just you, me, and the birds."

The naked heat in his eyes was new. Maybe
he'd kiss her when they sat down. Or maybe he
planned on more than kissing. What if tonight

he meant to have sex and be done with her? Her stomach knotted at the thought. But old beliefs died hard and she knew she'd sleep with him, regardless of the consequences, if he wanted that.

"Quincy?" Furrows creased his forehead. "What's wrong?"

"Not a thing." She forced a smile. "Do you own this land?"

Ira shook his head. "My place is right behind it. The orchard belongs to an old family friend."

"Does he know we're here?"

"No, but he won't care. You hungry?"

"Starved."

"Then please make yourself comfortable." With a flourish he gestured at the blanket. "After you."

She sat down, unbuckled her sandals, and slipped out of them. Ira joined her, then set the picnic basket between them. If he meant to seduce her, it would be after dinner.

"Would you prefer red or white wine?"

"Red."

He pulled a bottle, corkscrew, and two glasses from the basket. His fingers were long and deft, and he quickly uncorked the bottle. After he filled both glasses he handed her one.

"To a great evening," he said, raising his glass.

Quincy did the same. They clinked rims, then sipped. The smooth red wine slid easily down her dry throat. Neither of them spoke, but the silence felt natural and comfortable.

Alone with Ira, surrounded by trees and the slowly darkening evening . . . This was heaven. "It's beautiful here, Ira. So peaceful."

"Isn't it? After the rough week you've had I figured you could use some serenity."

He was so thoughtful. Happier than she'd been in a long time, she smiled. "How was your day? After you helped us with Susan's computer and office equipment, I mean."

"Productive. I spent most of it at the office. Got quite a bit done."

This surprised her. "But I thought you were closed weekends."

"We are, but when you own the business, you work seven days a week. Since it's my company, I don't mind. Once you open your restaurant, you'll see."

Quincy imagined owning a restaurant, working every single day and loving it because the business was hers. Of course that wasn't going to happen, but it was fun to dream about.

"Speaking of businesses, have you had a chance to look at that book?" Ira asked.

"Not yet." Feeling as if she'd let him down, she brushed a leaf from the blanket. "It's been too hectic, as you can imagine."

The real reason she hadn't started the book was because she was afraid that if Margaret and Rose caught her reading it, they'd make fun of her. Or worse, hold her accountable to do something more than reading and dreaming. Since she didn't have the education or the money for school, that wasn't going to happen.

Deep down she knew that she was afraid to try. What if she failed?

"Hey," Ira said. "You don't have to read it unless you want to."

She could see in his eyes that he meant that and would like her regardless. The fear drained out of her, at least for now.

Reading couldn't hurt, could it? "I want to," she said.

"That's great." He smiled. "So, how was the garage sale? From what I saw, there wasn't much left."

"We sold everything else, which is a huge relief." She stretched out her legs, stared at her pearl pink toenails, and thought about the day. "Margaret's upset about something and very touchy."

"Your mother just died. On top of that you dismantled her home in record time. You grew up with the things in that house. Selling them off has to hurt."

"Not as much as you might think. Susan wasn't the best mother, and we didn't have the happiest childhoods. But I told you that."

"Even so, this is a huge change for all of you. Getting used to it is bound to take a while."

"Good point, but this goes beyond the house and Susan's death. I think." She frowned. "I don't really know."

"Have you asked her about it?"

"Yes, and she about tore off my head." Quincy cringed, remembering. Yet this morning at breakfast she'd almost opened up.

"Give her time."

Since they had only a few days left before they all went their separate ways, they didn't have time. Suddenly her stomach gurgled.

The corner of Ira's mouth lifted in the quirk that charmed her. "Sounds like dinnertime. I hope you like Greek food."

"Love it." Quincy licked her lips.

As Ira lifted container after container from the basket, her eyes widened. "Did you make all this stuff?"

He laughed. "Nope, and be thankful, because I'm a lousy cook. My housekeeper, Adara, is Greek and a whiz in the kitchen. Taste."

He popped a bite-size, stuffed grape leaf into her mouth. The flavors of ground lamb, lemon, rice, and spices exploded on her tongue.

She closed her eyes and moaned. "This is soooo good."

"What'd I tell you?" Ira ate one, too.

Her mouth watering, she piled a stoneware plate with more stuffed grape leaves, a generous helping of Greek salad, and freshly baked pita bread.

They tucked into their meal. When Quincy was full and their plates were empty, Ira stacked and reloaded them and the empty containers into the basket. "Are you a dessert eater? I am, and I need something sweet."

Wondering if he meant sex, she swallowed. "What do you have in mind?"

He gestured at the trees. "Peaches, of course."

What a relief. Laughing and wondering when she was going to start trusting him, Quincy shook her head. "We can't. Won't we get in trouble?"

"I'm surprised at you, Quincy Lansing. I thought you liked trouble."

The gleam in his eye no longer worried her.

"Not the kind where you take things from your friends without asking."

"I'd never do that," he said, and she thought he might be talking about something besides peaches. "I did ask. It's okay, I swear."

Chapter 21

Relaxed from a pathetic but fun-filled night of bowling, Margaret grinned as she and Rose unloaded their handful of groceries on the kitchen counter. "You were right to drag me out tonight. I needed it."

"Gee, it feels good to be right." Rose shot her a gleeful look. "I'm not at all tired, are you?"

In far too good a mood to go to bed, Margaret shook her head. "What'll we do now?"

"We could take a walk."

"After being on our feet all day and bowling for hours? Thanks, but I've had my exercise."

"I was hoping you'd say that. Why don't we sit?" Rose gestured at the table and chairs, the only furniture besides the beds still in the house.

As Margaret moved to the table she glanced at the empty walls. "No clock, no pictures, no wall calendar, and no sun catcher hanging in the window. The kitchen looks so strange without them."

"*Feels* strange, too." Rose took her usual seat across the table. "But then, the whole house does." She leaned toward Margaret and lowered her voice. "This will sound weird, but I suddenly can't sense Susan's spirit in here."

She looked so unnerved that Margaret laughed. "That does sound weird, but I know exactly what you mean. Without her personal things in here, this little house could belong to anyone."

"A whole lifetime, gone in a poof. That's depressing."

It was, and Margaret nodded. "The saddest part is that we never had the chance to say good-bye or tell her we loved her." Or for Margaret to apologize for her role in driving Glory away.

Guilt and pain hovered menacingly over her, but she wasn't about to let them in. She would move beyond the past, period. She straightened her shoulders. "On the bright side, a new owner will breathe fresh life into this place and hopefully fill it with happier times."

"Amen to that," Rose said. "I wonder what Fiona will list it for."

"We'll find out tomorrow afternoon. Unless we fix it up though, we probably won't—"

They heard the door open.

"Quincy's home," Rose murmured.

Margaret glanced at her watch. "It's only eleven." Worried, she bit her lip. "I hope nothing bad happened."

"Rose? Margaret?" Quincy called out.

"She sounds excited," Rose whispered, crossing her fingers. "We're in here."

Seconds later Quincy appeared in the doorway, eyes sparkling and face glowing. "Thank heavens you're up. I had the most wonderful time. Ira took me to a friend's orchard. We had a picnic there, the best Greek food ever—his housekeeper is Greek—and fresh peaches right off the tree. Then—"

"Slow down." Rose grinned.

"It was just so wonderful, and I'm so darned happy." Hugging herself, Quincy spun around in giddy joy.

Margaret sent a silent thank you to Ira for treating her sister as she deserved. "Then please go on."

"He finally kissed me." Still hugging herself, she leaned against the doorjamb. "Once in the orchard and again at the front door." A sweet smile curled her lips, and her eyes went dark and unfocused.

Pleased for her, Margaret laughed. "By the expression on your face I'd say you enjoyed that."

"And how. The man kisses like a dream."

"What else did you do besides eat and kiss?" Rose asked, a teasing glint in her eye.

"Talked, believe it or not. Ira's so easy to talk

to and such a good listener. We never ran out of things to say. Isn't that amazing?"

"Mmm-hmm." Rose patted the chair adjacent to her.

Quincy danced over and plunked down. "He's taking me out again tomorrow night." She glanced from Rose to Margaret. "If that's okay with you two."

"Why not?" Margaret said. "Rose and I will find something to do. As long as it's not bowling. I don't think I could bear another night of humiliation."

"You two went bowling?"

Rose nodded. "We picked up some groceries and then headed for Miller's Bowl. We ate there, too."

"Oh, those nachos." In high spirits Margaret smacked her lips and rubbed her stomach. "I could eat them every night."

"You'd get fat, but I suppose you could bowl off the calories." Rose's lips twitched. "Margaret's improved quite a bit since high school. Only half her balls went into the gutter."

Rose didn't tease her often. Margaret chuckled and paid her in kind. "You're not much better. We both were embarrassingly bad."

"But we sure had fun."

They glanced at each other and burst into laughter.

"I wish I'd been there," Quincy said, looking envious.

"You do not," Rose said. "Enjoying a romantic

picnic with Ira and kissing him was far more fun
than bowling with us. And you know it."

"You're right."

This time they all laughed, all in good moods
at the same time. A thoroughly enjoyable experience. Tonight, neither lonely nor alone, Margaret felt wonderful.

"Speaking of Ira," Rose said. "You know that
book he brought you the other night? Margaret and I were wondering about it.

"Oh?" Quincy lost her grin.

"Is it a book on cryptography?"

"No."

What kind of book stole the light from someone's eyes? Margaret had to know. "Well, what
is it about?"

"Nothing, really." Quincy smoothed the
collar of her pantsuit.

"Apparently something." Settled against her
seat, Rose crossed her arms. "Something that
bothers you a lot."

Quincy shrugged, the gesture at odds with
her refusal to look at either of them. "It's just
a book about how to start your own business."

"Your own business?" Margaret knew she
sounded surprised.

"Why would Ira give you a book about that?"
Rose asked.

"I don't know."

While Margaret sat back and dissected this,
Quincy frowned and studied her fingernails.

"Oh, all right," she said. "But if I tell you, you have to promise not to make fun of me."

"Promise." Margaret made an X over her heart.

"Girl Scout's honor," Rose said. She'd actually been a Girl Scout for a year, so that counted.

"Ira bought it for me because way back in high school I said I wanted to run my own restaurant."

It wasn't such a far-fetched idea. "You have restaurant experience and the smarts and personality to succeed," Margaret pointed out. "I can see it happening."

"You can?" Flushing, Quincy dipped her head. "Too bad I don't have the education or the money to get started."

"Ever hear of student loans?" Margaret asked. "That's how I financed my education." That and scholarships.

"Me, too," Rose said. "Once you have what you need from school, you can get a business loan."

"My credit isn't the best," Quincy said glumly. "I doubt I could get a loan of any kind."

Thanks to careful budgeting, Margaret's credit was and always had been excellent. She didn't know what happened when your credit was bad and shot Quincy a sympathetic look. "You won't know till you apply."

"Unless you're afraid to try," Rose said.

Quincy's chin jerked up. "I'm not afraid,"

she stated, so loudly that Margaret realized she *was.*

She'd promised not to laugh. She hadn't promised not to help. "My offer to loan you money still stands. You'll pay me back when you can."

"I'll add in some, too," Rose said.

Quincy stiffened and her eyes flashed. "I told you, I won't do that."

Margaret tensed. She didn't want to fight, not tonight. "Take it easy, Quincy. We mean well."

But Quincy's back remained rigid.

"Look, we don't care if you decide to do this on your own or forget the whole idea," Rose said. "What matters most is that you told us about it. That took guts."

To Margaret's relief, Quincy relaxed.

"I guess it did. I was worried you might make fun of me. Thanks for not laughing."

"If you can't trust your sisters, who can you trust?" Rose smiled. "That's the biggest thing I learned this past week."

If you can't trust your sisters, who can you trust? The question thundered in Margaret's brain.

Rose was right. Both she and Quincy had shared their fears and their hopes several times. They trusted Margaret and each other that much.

Maybe it was her turn to trust them. With that, she made up her mind. She'd tell them everything, right this minute. Before she changed her mind again.

The momentous decision scared her, but also felt right. She cleared her throat. "There's something you should know, something I started to tell you at breakfast. I'm ready to share it now."

Quincy and Rose leaned forward and scrutinized Margaret. It was unnerving, and she wanted to push them away with hostility and sarcasm. But she was through hiding behind either one.

"It's about Glory." She folded her hands on the table, noting that they felt cold and clammy. "Do you remember the day he left?"

"How could I forget?" Quincy said. "It was my fourth birthday."

"I know, and you were crushed." Rose reached over and squeezed her hand. "I remember lots of yelling between him and Susan, right here in the kitchen." She frowned at Margaret. "Why are you asking?"

Now Margaret's whole body was cold, inside and out. She hunched her shoulders and pulled her arms close to her torso. "Did you know Glory came into my room after that fight?"

Baffled, her sisters shook their heads.

"He wanted to talk to me."

Rose angled closer still. "What did he say?"

This was the hard part. Margaret's throat went dry. She swallowed, the sound audible in the sudden stillness. "Since I never gave him the chance to talk, I'll never know." The words opened a floodgate and the rest gushed out. "I was making a birthday card for Quincy, and I still had to wrap her present. There wasn't much time and I needed to hurry. So instead of letting Glory say his piece, I told him to go away and leave me alone."

Quincy shrugged. "Nothing new there."

"You always did that when you worked on projects," Rose said.

"Did I?" Margaret hadn't realized this. She couldn't stop to think what that meant, not now that she'd started talking. "Anyway, when I told Glory to go away, he did. Forever."

"And?" Quincy prodded.

She didn't look appalled or shocked. Margaret gaped at her. "Don't you get it? I screwed up. If I'd let him sit down and say what he wanted to say, he might have stayed longer, and we all could've enjoyed your birthday."

There, it was out. She caught her breath and braced for whatever horrible things her sisters might throw at her.

"Man, are you self-centered," Quincy said. "Glory's world did not revolve around you, Margaret Lansing. If it had, he'd have stayed with the family, or at least kept in touch."

"She's right," Rose said.

Margaret's mind began to whir. She rubbed

the space between her eyes. "What if you're wrong? Because I can't seem to shake the feeling that I'm partly responsible for what happened."

"Baloney." Rose scoffed.

Quincy squinted at her. "Did Susan put that idea in your head? Sure sounds like her."

Screwing up her forehead, Margaret tried to remember. "I don't know, but I don't think so. Glory left right after I pushed him away. I imagine that's why I connected the two."

"A seven-year-old's reasoning," Rose said with a pensive nod. "Faulty, but I can see it."

"Well, I can't," Quincy said. "I blame Susan for never letting us talk about what happened. Don't you remember what Fiona said? She got pregnant with each of us to keep Glory. Instead she drove him away. Maybe at the time we wouldn't have understood, but she could've said *something*—for starters, that they grew apart and he no longer loved her."

"In other words," Rose said, "you're about as responsible for Glory walking out as Quincy and I. No more, no less."

In the somber silence that followed, Margaret realized her sisters were right, that nothing she did or could have done would have altered what had happened that day.

It wasn't her fault that Glory had left them.

The seven-year-old child in her heaved an enormous sigh of relief. A weight dropped from her shoulders, and for the first time in twenty-six years, she felt light and carefree. She threw back her head and laughed, earning startled looks from her sisters.

"I can't believe I waited so long to tell you about this!" An instant later, overcome with love and gratitude, she glanced watery eyed from Quincy to Rose. "Thank you both for listening and helping me understand."

"We could've helped you a long time ago." Quincy sniffled. "I'm glad you finally told us."

"That's what sisters are for," Rose murmured with eyes that glistened.

Quincy brushed at her eyes. "I don't know about you two, but I'm sick of crying. This is our second-to-last night in this house and we ought to make the most of it. How about a slumber party?"

"Aren't we a little old for that?" Margaret asked.

"Don't be a party pooper."

"Sounds fun," Rose said. "But we don't have a TV or radio, and I'm too tired to go out again. How do we entertain ourselves?"

"We climb into Susan's bed and talk until we fall asleep."

Loving the idea, Margaret smiled. "Let's go."

Chapter 22

Monday

At the ungodly hour of seven forty-five, riding in the passenger seat of Margaret's car, Quincy shot an envious glance at her oldest sister. "You look disgustingly perky this morning. And thanks to letting me help you buy makeup yesterday, pretty, too."

"I know." Margaret's smile was bright and self-assured. "I *feel* good." She glanced at Quincy and shook her finger like a scolding teacher. "You, on the other hand . . ."

Quincy grinned. She and Ira had stayed up late talking last night. And kissing, lots of it. So far, nothing more. Ira sure was taking his time, but she didn't mind. Kissing him was wonderful fun, and truth be told, it was nice not to worry about sex just yet.

"I'd rather spend my evenings with Ira than

sleeping. Talking," she added in case her sisters thought otherwise.

"Talking." Margaret glanced in the rearview mirror. "Did you hear that, Rose?"

"I certainly did," Rose said, yawning.

Quincy swiveled in her seat to eye her sister. "What'd you do, stay up late talking to Danny?"

"Yeah, but I slept well, too. A whole lot better than the night before. Sharing a queen-size bed with you two is worse than sleeping on rocks."

But a great time, too. Quincy shrugged. "I can't help it if I hogged the blankets. I had to do *something*, since you"—she glanced at Margaret—"stole my pillow. Just reached across poor Rose and snatched it while I was sleeping."

"Well, you kept talking in your sleep. I needed to cover my ears and shut you out."

"And I got stuck in the cross fire," Rose said. "The middle child always does."

Their friendly banter was worlds away from the hostile insults they'd once flung at each other. Quincy smiled to herself. "Even so, it was my best slumber party ever."

They'd talked for hours, laughed and cried together, exclaimed over the photo Margaret had unearthed at the garage sale and leafed through the family picture album. Later, the darkness, physical proximity, and their strong mutual trust had allowed them to share fears and hopes they'd never voiced. Quincy marveled at the new and special bond between them.

Margaret, who'd been in high spirits since she'd unburdened herself, laughed again. "I'll never understand why they call it a 'slumber' party." She flipped on the turn signal. "We're almost at Arthur's office."

"His building, you mean," Rose said. "He owns it and the land, too."

"Paid for by those fat fees he collects. Having been through two divorces, I know all about *that*." Quincy wrinkled her nose. "I still don't get why he wants to meet with us. So what if Susan left a will. She didn't own anything but the house."

"Unless she lived a double life and bought all kinds of complicated investments," Rose said.

"Wouldn't put it past her. After all, she sort of lived a double life with us. Four lovers, a good income, and practically nothing in the bank. Who knows what fabulous hidden treasures she may have squirreled away?"

"Ha ha," Margaret said. "Don't we all wish."

For a few moments her sisters were quiet. Quincy didn't mind staying the few extra days in Shadow Falls. Spending time with her sisters was great, and getting to know Ira was better than wonderful. Things were so good that she hated to jinx them by leaving. With miles separating them they could grow apart again. And Ira could forget her. Both thoughts made her feel sick.

While she nibbled her lip and worried, Margaret and Rose traded warm comments like the best of friends. They *were* best friends, all three of them, and nothing could change that. Quincy's anxiety melted away, and she knew that even if they fought her sisters would always be there for her. And vice versa. That was the most fantastic feeling.

As for Ira . . . She recalled the loving expression in his eyes and the tender way he'd touched her cheek last night. The way he held and kissed her, as if she were precious to him. No, he wouldn't forget her. Secure in the knowledge that she was loved and wanted, she smiled at the beautiful morning.

But her bills didn't care about sisters or love. They wouldn't wait, and even with her share of the proceeds from the garage sale she needed to hurry back to Vegas and find a new job. Just to stave off bankruptcy. True, there would be money from the sale of the house to dig her out of debt, but collecting it might take months. By then she could be out on the street.

She glanced at Margaret and then at Rose. "I repeat, why are we meeting today with Arthur Tremayne?"

"Maybe he needs our signatures and this is the easiest way to get them." Margaret signaled and slowed. "Whatever the reasons, we're about to find out."

She turned into the paved parking lot of a well-maintained, one-story brick building. Posted in the small manicured yard was an elegant brown and tan ARTHUR TREMAYNE ATTORNEY AT LAW sign. Seconds later she parked and they all exited the car.

At this hour the temperature hadn't yet climbed past eighty and birds twittered and bathed in the sprinklers watering the flowerbeds, grass, and trees in front of the building.

With Margaret carrying the box of bank statements, spreadsheets, and house documents, they headed purposefully inside. The warm colors and comfortable-looking furniture made for an inviting reception area, but the temperature was way too cold for Quincy.

The receptionist, auburn-haired, plump Josie Jessup, who'd worked for Arthur forever and surely dyed her hair, greeted them with a smile. "It's been a long time. Good to see you girls, but what a shame it had to be under such sad circumstances. I'm awfully sorry about your mother."

Since Susan's death Quincy's grief had ebbed and flowed unpredictably. Though seconds ago she hadn't felt particularly sad, now . . . She dipped her head.

"Thank you," Rose said, her voice as subdued as Quincy's mood.

Margaret hugged the box to her chest. "We have an eight o'clock with Arthur."

"And he'll be right with you." Josie stood. "I'll take you into the conference room. Coffee, tea, or water, anyone?"

After two cups of coffee, Quincy was well-caffeinated, but at the rates they'd no doubt be charged, she wasn't about to refuse drinks. "Coffee, please, with milk."

"I'd like milk and sugar with mine," Rose said.

Margaret shifted the box. "Make mine black."

"Coming right up."

Josie ushered them into the plush conference room. They sat side by side at the oblong, mahogany table, waiting for their coffee and Arthur Tremayne.

"These chairs are so comfortable," Rose said as she shifted in the plush leather seat.

Quincy smirked. "That's because they cost a fortune."

In her usual efficient, take charge mode, Margaret pulled the checkbook and folders from the box and arranged them on the table. Quincy appreciated that the oldest sister would act as the spokesperson this morning.

On the wall opposite the door, a brass clock ticked off the seconds, each tiny click tightening Quincy's chest. "Suddenly I'm nervous," she admitted, knotting her hands in her lap. Who knew why.

"I am, too." Rose started to fidget with the studs in her earlobes.

"There's nothing to be nervous about," Margaret said. "So relax."

Her calmness and reassurance did nothing to ease Quincy's mind. Wishing she'd brought a sweater and unable to sit still, she squirmed in her chair. Then shivering, rubbed her bare arms. "It's freezing in here. I hope this isn't an omen of what's to come."

Margaret rolled her eyes. "You've watched too many scary movies."

"Maybe," Quincy said.

But she couldn't shake the feeling that Arthur Tremayne was about to drop a bomb.

"It's been years," Arthur Tremayne said.

Silver-haired, tall, and overweight, dressed impeccably in an expensive dove gray summer suit and a blue silk tie, he was elegant, Rose thought.

He seated himself across the table and folded his hands over a thick folder with Susan's name on it. "I'm sorry about your mother and sorry I missed the service," he said, his expression mournful and sincere. "I heard it was nice."

"It was," Margaret said.

Though Rose and Danny had been in a bad place that day, she agreed about the funeral. "Thank you for the lovely flowers."

"How's your father?" Quincy asked, clutching her coffee mug as if that would steady her nerves.

"Progressing as well as a ninety-year-old man can, thanks. As soon as he's well enough, my wife and I will bring him back to Shadow Falls."

"You wouldn't want to buy Susan's house for your dad, would you?" Quincy asked, leaning toward Arthur and exposing a hint of cleavage. "We could offer you a deal." She fluttered her lashes and formed her lips into a sexy pout.

Here we go. Wondering what her little sister was up to, Rose frowned. Margaret cupped her head between her hands and smiled at the table. Why smile, when any moment Quincy could embarrass them no end?

All business, Arthur shook his head. "Thanks for the offer, but he'll be going into a convalescent home."

Quincy's mouth twitched and she settled back in her chair. "Can't blame a girl for trying. Anyway, we've listed it."

It appeared she would behave, but with Quincy you never knew. The thing was, she meant well—was trying to help in her own, unique way. That didn't hurt anyone, did it? Rose relaxed.

"Who's handling the listing?" Arthur asked.

"Fiona Applegate." Margaret pushed a copy of the agreement toward him. "We signed the papers yesterday."

"Ah, Fiona. She's a good realtor and her agency is top-notch." The attorney scanned the form. "May I photocopy this?"

Margaret nodded. "Of course."

"As you can see by the asking price we won't get top dollar," Quincy said. "Fiona thinks we should paint and put up new drapes, redo the floors and fix up the yard, but we're busy women. We don't have the time." She glanced at the clock. "Speaking of time . . . it *is* money."

"Right. The estate." Arthur opened the folder he'd brought into the room. "First we'll read through the will. Then we'll get to the paperwork."

Curious and interested, Rose leaned forward, along with her sisters, while Arthur located the document. "Ah, here it is. We made copies for each of you." He slid the papers across the table and gave them a few moments to scan through the six pages. "On page one you'll see that it was your mother's wish that you all be present for the reading of this will."

So that was the reason for this meeting.

"If you'll look at the bottom of page two you'll see that your mother leaves the house and its contents to the three of you equally to do with as you please."

"Since we sold everything we could at a garage sale, that's a relief," Quincy said. "Once the house sells, how do we collect the money?"

"The proceeds will become part of the estate. Later this morning we'll open an estate checking account that will be used until the estate is settled. Your mother appointed me as executor," Arthur said. "I trust that's all right?"

Rose and her sisters exchanged quick glances and fractional nods.

"Of course," Margaret said.

"Good. I—"

"Wait a sec." Quincy frowned. "I'm confused. What do you mean, the proceeds become part of the estate?"

"The funds in the estate are used to pay for taxes and any other financial matters," Arthur said. "What's left goes to the three of you."

"I get that part. When do we get the money?"

"That could take as long as a year or more."

"That long?" Quincy looked stricken. "But I need it now."

Rose felt bad for her. She wished Quincy would take a loan from her and Margaret, but she was too darned proud.

"The life insurance policy should help." A smile playing at his lips, Arthur rifled through the folder.

Knowing nothing about any life insurance, Rose frowned.

Margaret eyed Arthur. "What life insurance policy?"

"The one your mother bought when you were little. Ah, here it is, paper clipped with Josie's notes. She called the insurance company last week to notify them and get an estimate of the value. As of Friday, the total amount of the policy is three hundred thousand, six hundred and eighty-two dollars."

Stunned, Rose sat back. "Holy moley."

Margaret's jaw dropped. "Would you repeat that, please?"

"Three hundred thousand, six hundred and eighty-two dollars," Quincy said, her eyes huge with surprise. "Are you sure we're talking about the right Susan Lansing?"

The lawyer's chuckle filled the room. "I'm sure. Split three ways, that comes out to roughly one hundred twenty thousand dollars each. Insurance policies are excluded from the estate, so once we supply a letter and a copy of the death certificate, the money goes directly to each of you, tax-free except for any accrued interest. The interest is taxable on your individual tax returns."

Unable to quite believe what she'd just heard, Rose stared at him. "She never . . . We never knew."

Arthur was still smiling. "So I see. She bought this policy a long time ago because she wanted to ensure that you girls were provided for if something happened to her. She didn't want you to grow up in poverty, as she had. It's a term policy, so once she paid for it, it sat and accrued interest."

"She did that for us?" Quincy shook her head slowly, as if she doubted his words.

"That's right." Arthur settled back in his chair. "I remember the day she bought it, not long after your father left. That was back when I rented a small office around the corner. She was a receptionist then—didn't become a paralegal until later. She walked into my office, sat down, and said she needed advice. I helped her choose what I thought was the best insurance plan, given her budget constraints."

"This comes as a complete surprise," Rose said. Wait till she told Danny.

Your mother wanted it that way."

"I'm *verklempt*," Margaret said in wonder.

Quincy frowned. "Whatever that means."

"Too overcome to speak."

"Me, too." Quincy lifted her hair from the back of her neck and let it drop. "Me, too."

Later, after they signed the documents Arthur needed and opened the estate account, they piled into the car and headed for the house. None of them said much.

Quincy was still in shock. Sitting in the back-seat—it was her turn—she repeated the out-standing news. "One hundred twenty thousand dollars. I'm about to have six figures in my bank account."

"I know." Margaret glanced in the rearview mirror. "It hasn't sunk in yet."

"It probably won't for me until I get the check and it clears the bank," Rose said.

Quincy had no trouble believing her good fortune. "Arthur called the insurance company right in front of us. He sent Josie to Bushell's Mortuary to pick up copies of the death certificate. We dropped his letter, signed and nota-rized by each of us, and the certificate into the mail ourselves. It may take a few weeks, but it's happening." She leaned forward. "Unless this is all a dream. Will one of you please pinch me?"

"Oh, you're awake." Rose glanced over her shoulder and smiled. "Susan's last surprise was a wonderful one."

"She really did care about us." Braking for a red light, Margaret sniffled.

Darned if Quincy's eyes didn't fill. "Money isn't the same as hugs and 'I love you,' but it sure helps. Anybody have a tissue?"

"I do." Rose passed around a packet and all three of them blew their noses.

"What'll you do with your share?" Rose asked Margaret as the light turned green.

"I don't know yet, but I'll probably put some of it away for a rainy day. What about you two?"

"Fertility treatments are expensive," Rose said. "I'll use some of the money for that. If I still don't get pregnant, we'll need money to adopt. Anything that's left will go toward the nursery and the baby's college account."

"Planning for the future." Margaret nodded. "That's smart. What about you, Quincy?"

She didn't have to think long about how to spend her share. "I'll pay off my bills, go to school part-time, and invest what's left." Wary of sharing the rest of her plans she closed her mouth. Then changed her mind. Now that she trusted her sisters, there was nothing to hide. "In case I open a restaurant someday."

Rose beamed and threw her a thumbs-up.

Glancing in the rearview mirror, Margaret grinned. "When you do, I'll be there as often as possible to spend big bucks on meals."

Their support felt really good. Quincy felt loved and respected. And happy. "Maybe you'll bring a special someone with you, Maggie."

A week ago Margaret would have tossed her a surly look and chewed her out. Now she shrugged good-naturedly. "Maybe I will. You know, Quincy, now that you have money, there's no need to rush back to Las Vegas. You could stay here, fix up the house, and see what happens with Ira."

In all the excitement Quincy hadn't thought of this. She sat back against the seat and mulled over the idea. The more she thought about it, the better she liked it. Ira would be pleased that she was staying. But this wasn't just for Ira. She wanted to make the house and yard look nice. "I could, couldn't I?"

"Margaret and I will split the cost of the repairs with you," Rose said. "What a shame we sold everything. You can't very well live in the house as it is. I wonder if the people who bought the beds and kitchen table would mind waiting awhile?" They were coming first thing in the morning, along with the Salvation Army.

Quincy shook her head. "I don't want to live there. Too many bad memories, plus it'll be easier to fix up if it's empty. I'll find a cheap apartment nearby, something I can rent month to month. If you two don't mind, I'll call Fiona and ask her to hold off on the listing for a while."

"Fine by us."

"Should we celebrate our good fortune?" Rose asked. "Have lunch someplace nice?"

Margaret glanced at her. "Is Hal's Steakhouse still open? I haven't been there since Susan took us right before I started my senior year of high school."

Quincy loved the idea. "Super. We'll eat steak, drink wine, and salute Susan for giving us a gift we'll never forget."

Tuesday

Sitting on the roof just after midnight, tired but not about to waste the last few hours with her sisters, Margaret hugged her knees and teased Quincy. "I can't believe you cut short your evening with Ira for this."

"Now that I'm staying a few extra weeks, I can see him whenever I want. I won't be able to see you two for a long time."

"That makes me sad," Rose said. "We should make a pact to share every holiday together."

Margaret felt warm just thinking about it. "It's a deal. We'll take turns going to each other's houses."

"In between, I'll be calling you," Quincy said. "A lot. Here's an idea. Once the house sells, we can meet here to sign the closing papers. We could FedEx instead, but why not use the excuse to get together?"

Margaret thought about her work at the lab.

It still mattered a great deal to her, but so did her sisters. They were family, and you didn't take family lightly. "I'll be here."

A shooting star streaked across the velvety black sky.

"Did you see that?" Quincy said, pointing upward. "That's a good sign. Everyone close your eyes and make a wish."

Margaret wished for happiness for her sisters and herself. She hoped Rose and Danny got their baby, that Quincy and Ira ended up together, and that Quincy bought herself that restaurant. For herself, she wished for the love of a good man. If things went the way she hoped, that man would be Bruce.

"When I come back I'd like to visit Susan's grave," Rose said. "I know she was horrid, but she's the only mother I have—had."

"I totally get that," Quincy said. "I'll go with you."

"Count me in, too," Margaret said, marveling at the loveliness of two sisters who completely understood her and each other. "I wonder what Susan would think about us getting along so well."

"She's probably turning over in her grave right now," Rose said with a smile. "I bet you'll be glad to get back to the lab, Margaret."

"I will," she answered. "There's so much to do, and it isn't fair to dump it all on Bruce's shoulders." For an instant she wondered whether she should say more. Why not? She had no secrets from her sisters. "I never told you two this, but Bruce wants to go out with me."

Quincy angled her head, and though it was too dark to see more than the shadows of her face, Margaret knew she was gloating. "I *knew* those flowers meant more than 'I'm sorry your mom died.' And? Do you want to date him?"

"That's what I wished for a moment ago." Admitting it to her sisters wasn't so difficult.

"I'll keep my fingers crossed for you," Rose said.

"And I'll skewer Bruce if he treats you bad." Quincy winked. "But heck, if he's seen you without makeup and still wants to take you out, he must be interested."

Buoyed by their love and trust, and nervous but exhilarated by the prospect of a future with Bruce, Margaret couldn't argue. "That's a good point."

Hours later, having stayed up all night packing and talking, they gathered on the roof one last time with their Styrofoam cups of coffee. The sky was a pale hint of what it would be later, and birds were starting to twitter in the trees.

"Let's make a toast," Margaret said, raising her cup. "To new beginnings."

"Hear, hear." Quincy tilted her coffee toward Margaret and Rose. "To love and happiness."

"To sisters," Rose said. "To us."

Together they welcomed the dawn.

ABOUT THE AUTHOR

Award-winning author Ann Roth lives in the greater Seattle area with her husband. After earning an MBA, she worked as a banker and corporate trainer. She gave up the corporate life to write, and if they awarded PhDs in writing happily ever after stories, she'd surely have one.

To date Ann has sold fifteen novels, both romance and women's fiction, as well as a novella and a serialized online romance. To contact Ann, visit www.annroth.net or e-mail her at ann@annroth.net.

Say Yes! to Sizzling Romance by

Lori Foster

Unwrap a Holiday Romance
by
Janet Dailey

Eve's Christmas

   0-8217-8017-4   **$6.99**US/**$9.99**CAN

Let's Be Jolly

   0-8217-7919-2   **$6.99**US/**$9.99**CAN

Happy Holidays

   0-8217-7749-1   **$6.99**US/**$9.99**CAN

Maybe This Christmas

   0-8217-7611-8   **$6.99**US/**$9.99**CAN

Scrooge Wore Spurs

   0-8217-7225-2 $6.99US/$9.99CAN

A Capital Holiday

   0-8217-7224-4   **$6.99**US/**$8.99**CAN

Available Wherever Books Are Sold!

Check out our website at **www.kensingtonbooks.com**